W9-CNF-427

ASH WEDNESDAY

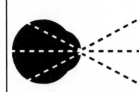

This Large Print Book carries the
Seal of Approval of N.A.V.H.

A FATHER DOWLING MYSTERY

ASH WEDNESDAY

RALPH MCINERNY

THORNDIKE PRESS

A part of Gale, Cengage Learning

GALE
CENGAGE Learning™

Detroit • New York • San Francisco • New Haven, Conn • Waterville, Maine • London

GALE
CENGAGE Learning

LIBRARY OF CONGRESS CATALOGING-IN-PUBLICATION DATA

McInerny, Ralph M.
  Ash Wednesday : a Father Dowling mystery / by Ralph McInerny.
    p. cm. — (Thorndike Press large print basic)
    ISBN-13: 978-1-4104-1106-8 (hardcover : alk. paper)
    ISBN-10: 1-4104-1106-0 (hardcover : alk. paper)
    1. Dowling, Father (Fictitious character)—Fiction. 2. Clergy—Fiction. 3. Catholics—Fiction. 4. Euthanasia—Fiction. 5. Guilt—Religious aspects—Fiction. 6. Large type books. I. Title.
    PS3563.A31166A95 2008b
    813'.54—dc22   2008036826

Published in 2008 by arrangement with St. Martin's Press, LLC.

Printed in the United States of America
1 2 3 4 5 6 7 12 11 10 09 08

For Ruth and Duncan Stroik

■ ■ ■ ■

PART ONE

■ ■ ■ ■

1

"Remember, man, that thou art dust and unto dust thou shalt return."

Father Dowling murmured this formula as he traced a cross on the foreheads of the old people who advanced up the middle aisle of St. Hilary's on this Ash Wednesday. *Remember, man.* No feminist had ever objected to this inclusive term, perhaps wanting to think of it as gender specific. Like *All men are mortal?*

It was the rheumy eye of Monica Garvey staring into his as he applied ashes to her forehead that prompted these irreverent thoughts. Monica was known to complain about the Church's treatment of women, thereby earning the friendly enmity of Marie Murkin, the parish housekeeper. Monica turned and made way for the next penitent. Roger Dowling switched to the Latin formula when Kevin Brown stood before him, eyes closed, head thrust forward.

"Memento homo quia pulvis es et in pulverem reverteris."

Kevin's lips moved as he repeated the words silently. Kevin had given Father Dowling a subscription to the magazine *Latin Mass* at Christmas, and the first issue had arrived some weeks before. Father Dowling said Vatican II's *Novus Ordo* in Latin once a week, on Mondays, and the attendance noticeably rose.

"Why only once a week, Father?" Kevin asked.

"After years of English it takes some getting used to."

"People love it."

It was partly nostalgia, of course. There were few people who, like Kevin Brown, understood Latin. He had studied it as a boy at Quigley when he had thought of becoming a priest. But he had gone on to Loyola and then to law school, prospered, married, had half a dozen disappointing children about whose souls he now fretted. "Thank God, Bridget never saw how they turned out." It seemed that none of them went to Mass anymore. With Kevin there might have been an element of affectation in his championing the return to Latin in the liturgy. A pharisee thanking God he was

10

not like the rest of men? That was unfair. Kevin seemed to think that it was the Church's dropping of Latin that had led to the falling away of his children.

Father Dowling finished distributing ashes and went into the sacristy feeling that his Lent was off on the wrong foot. Unchari-table thoughts, first about Monica and then about Kevin. God knows he had few ag-gravations in his pastoral work. Other pastors had to contend with the uprising of laypeople, women lectors who altered the Scriptures as they read, male clerical wan-nabes hovering about the pastor, a platoon of aids called ministers. Father Dowling re-alized he was in charge at St. Hilary's as others longed to be in charge of their own parishes. A mild feminist and a man who missed the Latin of his youth scarcely added up to a cross. Most of those who had been to the noon Mass and stayed for the distri-bution of ashes would now return to the parish center in the former school.

A man shuffled into the sacristy, a smudge of ashes on his forehead. Father Dowling remembered him; he had been the last in line.

"I hope it was all right, Father." He pointed to his forehead.

"Why wouldn't it be?" The man had not

come to communion. Did he think he must confess before receiving ashes?

"I'm not a Catholic, Father."

"Ah."

"I meant no disrespect."

"It's perfectly all right," Father Dowling said. "It's not a sacrament. Just a reminder of our mortality as Lent begins."

"Quite a turnout."

Father Dowling guessed him to be in his late sixties, maybe more. His complexion was colorless and seemed paler because of his white hair.

"Most of them came over from the parish center. You might want to look into it."

The man seemed puzzled, so Father Dowling explained the use to which he had put the school when there were no longer enough kids in the parish to justify keeping it open.

"What is it exactly?" the man asked.

"Look, come have lunch with me. Mrs. Murkin doesn't like me to be late."

"Mrs.?"

"The housekeeper."

"I don't want to intrude."

Father Dowling said, "She likes it when I ask people to join me." She liked anyone with an appetite greater than his. On the way to the rectory he asked the man his name and so was able to announce it when they passed through the kitchen.

"Mr. Green, Marie. Nathaniel Green. He has agreed to have lunch with me."

Marie harumphed. "On Ash Wednesday? Some treat."

"I'm not Catholic," Green said.

Marie gave him the fish eye. "I made no provisions for that. You'll have to fast and abstain with Father Dowling."

Marie made it sound like bread and water. But it was a broiled white fish and mixed vegetables, peas and corn, that Marie put before them.

"I was telling Mr. Green about the parish center, Marie."

"You retired?" Marie asked their guest.

Green smiled. "Is that a requirement?"

"No," she said, "and you don't have to be Catholic, either. Many of them will be older than you."

Marie's manner with Green was brisk and oddly distant. She swept into the kitchen; the door swung to and fro and then stopped.

"I have been in a rectory before," Nathaniel Green said. "Before I married."

"You married a Catholic?" Father Dowling said.

"I used to be a Catholic myself."

"Did you get tired of it?" A light note

seemed best, given the way Green had introduced the subject.

"After her death, I just let it go."

Father Dowling nodded. Every life had its tragedies, sooner or later.

"I gather that wasn't recently," he said.

"No."

"And now you've come back."

"You make it sound easy."

No need to press it now. If Green had come to church on Ash Wednesday, that might mean something, and then again it might not.

"Why don't you let Marie take you over to the parish center and introduce you around?"

"Oh, I'm sure she's too busy," Green protested.

From the kitchen came a voice. "Give me five minutes and I'll take him over."

2

Madeline Clancy had taught school, fourth grade, until she had had enough. She took early retirement, tried a number of fill-in jobs, but the compensation was hardly worth it, and besides, she could live comfortably enough on her pension. Fifty-seven was young for a retiree, and it seemed even

14

younger when, prompted by her Aunt Helen's unctuous accounts, she came to the St. Hilary senior center.

"You want to volunteer?" Edna Hospers had asked.

Madeline wasn't quite sure why she had come, but the fact that most of the people were at least as old as Aunt Helen explained Edna's assumption. "What would I do?"

"That depends on how much time you could give."

"I'm retired," Madeline said.

Edna stepped back, a look of surprise on her face.

"I took early retirement." She was flattered by Edna's reaction. If she volunteered to help Edna, she could have the advantage of coming to the center without having to explain her relative youth. "What does anyone do here?"

"Oh, the old folks are content enough just being together. Bridge, shuffleboard, gossip."

They were standing in the doorway of what had once been the school gym. There were several tables of bridge; a man and woman were playing shuffleboard against imaginary opponents. One old fellow frowned over a game of solitaire. In the corner three men and a woman were watching a ball game on television. They seemed to be asleep, but then something happened on the screen and they erupted into cheers. Edna led her down the hall and up the stairs to her office.

"This used to be the principal's office," Edna said.

"I taught school."

"Here?"

"Oh, no." Madeline paused. "I did go to school here, though."

Madeline had noticed the class pictures lining the lower hallway, wondering if her own class was there.

"Sometimes we have talks," Edna went on. "Lectures, mini courses."

Madeline shook her head. "No teaching."

"What did you teach?"

"Fourth grade. Last year I taught creative writing for six weeks. Night school."

"Why not try that here?" Edna asked.

As therapy? That's pretty much what the course last winter had amounted to. Everybody seemed to want to tell everybody else all about themselves. Well, the least they could have done was put it into English. But her students had resented what they regarded as tampering with their creativity.

Edna didn't press it. "Once a week we have an excursion, to the mall, to a museum.

Can you drive a minibus, Madeline?"

"I never have."

"It's really not much more than a station wagon."

It was too late now to say that she had come in the expectation that she would just be one of the old people. A little bridge was pretty inviting, and there had been a row of women sitting in chairs against the wall, knitting, talking. Aunt Helen was arguing with a man in a corner. They were the only ones who took notice when Edna and Madeline looked into the gym.

"Helen Burke is my aunt," Madeline said. "It was she who told me about the center. Who's the man?"

"Kevin Brown." Edna smiled. "Probably a theological argument. Ever since the Motu Proprio on Latin in the liturgy came out, they've become defenders of the faith. Usually against one another."

Madeline could believe it. "I'll be whatever help I can."

"Good, good. For now, why don't you just get acquainted. I try to keep organization to a minimum. Older people don't like being treated like kids."

Neither did kids, in Madeline's experience.

"Tea?" Edna asked.

"I'd love some."

So they had tea. Edna made a little ritual of it. No tea bags, a metal tea egg she filled with carefully measured spoonfuls of tea, the water put on to boil. That first time, there had been the careful exchange of trivia as each woman tried to find out about the other.

"How long have you been directing the center?" Madeline asked.

"Since it opened."

During the following weeks, tea in Edna's office had become a daily event. Madeline learned about Edna's husband, Earl, who had spent time in Joliet but was now free at last.

"It was like getting married all over again," Edna said.

Madeline grew uneasy, fearing that Edna was alluding to marital lore and might want to confide. Marriage was a great mystery to Madeline. She found men, except for Jason, and he was her cousin, an almost alien species and got along with them only as long as she thought of them as pupils.

In her creative writing class an overweight woman with braided gray hair and a voluminous dress had turned in stories that verged on the pornographic. There were complaints from the other aspiring writers when Deirdre read her stories to the class.

"With your imagination you should try science fiction," Bailey grumbled. He justified his own formless compositions as Chekhovian.

"Wachovian, you mean."

Bailey had been a financial adviser, and his stories usually stressed the importance of prudent investments. "You should try Esperanto," Deirdre advised.

Not that any of them was really interested in what the others wrote. They suffered through the readings in order to earn an audience for their own efforts.

Helping Edna at the center brought back memories of Madeline's school days at St. Hilary's. She found her class picture in the lower hallway and stood for a long time staring at the mousy little girl in the front row smiling shyly into the sunlight. In sixth grade, she had actually thought of becoming a nun, largely because Sister Rose Alma was such a wonderful teacher and recognized Madeline's gifts. Well, she had become a teacher if not a nun. Now such memories and the convenience of Father Dowling's noon Mass had given her faith a shot in the arm. On Ash Wednesday, she and Edna went over to the church for a well-attended

19

Mass and for ashes afterward. When was the last time she had started Lent with a smudge of ashes on her forehead? When was the last time she had thought of observing Lent seriously?

It was early in the afternoon when Marie Murkin brought Nathaniel Green to the center.

"Oh my God," Aunt Helen said when the two of them entered. "What's he doing here?"

"Who is he?" someone asked.

Helen inhaled deeply before answering. "Nathaniel Green!"

3

After turning Nathaniel Green over to Edna Hospers, Marie Murkin beat it back to the rectory. Father Dowling looked up from his breviary when she burst into his study.

"Do you know who that was?" Marie asked.

He slanted a ribbon across the page and closed the book. "That depends on whom 'who' refers to."

"Nathaniel Green! You did know, didn't you?"

"Help me," Father Dowling said.

Marie dropped into a chair. "The man

who murdered his wife!"

Father Dowling's eyebrows lifted. That was all the encouragement Marie needed. Sometimes of late she got to the supermarket and forgot what she had come for, but her memories of anything connected with St. Hilary's parish during her long tenure as housekeeper were sharp and detailed. She told Father Dowling about Nathaniel Green as if she were reading a script.

It had all happened almost ten years ago. The Greens were parishioners, always at Mass on Sundays, but that was about the extent of their involvement in the parish. Who could blame them, with the flaky friars in charge, flopping around in their open-toed sandals? Oh, lots of parishioners had liked the Franciscans, and why not? They made getting to heaven sound as easy as a trip to the Loop in Chicago. And the sermons! Rambling anecdotal narratives of whatever in the previous week had caught the preacher's fancy, about as religious as a car commercial. A used car commercial. And they treated Marie pretty much the way they treated the janitor. For several years Marie had agonized about staying, losing hope that she could shape up the friars, and then, as if in answer to her novena to

21

St. Anthony of Padua — she had decided to fight friar with friar — a miracle. The Franciscans told the cardinal they could no longer spare men for St. Hilary's, and for the first time in years a priest of the archdiocese was assigned as pastor. Roger Dowling, the best boss Marie had ever had, not that she would tell him that. Ever since, Marie had felt that she and Father Dowling were a team, bringing sanity back to St. Hilary's. Of course, the death of Florence Green had been before his time, but you'd think he would have read about it in the paper or caught it on television news.

Anyway, she told Father Dowling, Florence Green fell ill, cancer. The diagnosis, the prospective treatments, and the likelihood that they would do little but postpone her death had brought on depression and then despair. The friar who was then pastor, Father Hyacinth, was summoned to her hospital room. Florence's refusal of treatment became the favorite lugubrious topic at the dining room table, and Marie had been privy to it all, storing it away in the hard drive of her memory.

"She refuses treatment," Hyacinth announced at table.

"Isn't that her right?" asked Placidus.

"It's like suicide," said Boniface.

"She has cancer," Hyacinth said.

"There's no cure for cancer," Placidus pointed out.

Hyacinth said, "The doctor thinks that with radiation and chemotherapy it could be brought under control."

"But for how long?" Placidus wanted to know. "It would only be a postponement, not a cure."

Eavesdropping, hovering around the table, keeping the kitchen door ajar, Marie had followed it all, trying to decide whose side she was on. She sympathized with Florence. She told herself that Florence was doing what she herself would do in the circumstances. Cancer spelled a death sentence, and Marie had known of parishioners who went through months and months of treatment and died anyway. That view was represented at the dining room table.

"Everyone's going to die sooner or later," Hyacinth said.

"Not everyone has cancer," Placidus observed.

The topic had not diminished the appetite of the friars, and Marie was in and out of the dining room, half tempted to join in the discussion but not sure what tack she would take.

"What would you have said, Father Dowling?" Marie asked.

He tipped his head to one side. "It would just be a general problem for me now. The friars were confronted by a concrete case."

"Oh, come on. Does someone with cancer have a right to refuse treatment?"

"Why don't you just tell me the story, Marie. Did she refuse treatment?"

"Finally she left it up to her husband."

"And?"

"The treatments began," Marie said.

"Would the doctors recommend that if there was no hope?"

Marie dropped her chin and looked at him over her glasses. "How many oncologists do you know?"

"Oncologists?" Father Dowling said.

"Isn't that a weird word? It's scarier than 'cancer specialist.'"

"So Mrs. Green began treatments. What was the effect?"

"Apparently good. Then she had a relapse, and Father Hyacinth gave her the last sacraments."

"She asked for them?"

"Nathaniel did!" Marie leaned forward. "It was part of his plan."

The treatments had seemed to work. Florence's cancer went into remission, and her depression lifted. Shortly before, she had been certain death was imminent, and then she was told she had a future, maybe years of life. Despair gave way to cautious hope. Father Hyacinth became an I-told-you-so at the rectory table, and who could blame him? Then the relapse, and Nathaniel Green asked him to give Florence the last rites.

Marie sat back for dramatic effect. "That day he killed her."

"How?"

"He pulled the plug," Marie said. "She was on a life support system. He was always at her bedside. After the last rites, he pulled the plug. He was still sitting beside the bed when the nurses came in and found Florence was dead. They asked what had happened. He said he had killed her."

"And?"

"Hyacinth was sure it could be hushed up, but Nathaniel wouldn't have that. He went to the police and confessed to murder. They checked it out, and eventually he went to trial."

The judge had insisted that Nathaniel had to have a lawyer, and he had chosen Tuttle.

"Tuttle?" Father Dowling was surprised.

"It was like a death wish, Father. Tuttle's defense was that it was a mercy killing. Nathaniel Green was convicted of manslaughter." Marie made it sound like Al Capone's conviction for income tax evasion.

"And sent to prison."

Marie nodded. "Yes, and now, obviously, he's out."

Marie fell silent, wondering what she expected Father Dowling to say. Serving lunch to a man who had killed his wife had required iron discipline on Marie's part. She had leapt at the suggestion that she take Nathaniel Green over to the senior center and then had hurried back to tell Father Dowling this story.

" 'There are eight million stories in the Naked City,' " Father Dowling murmured. "Do you remember that program?"

"Is that all you have to say?"

"I'm glad I met him."

"Glad?" Marie asked.

"The poor fellow."

Marie just stared at Father Dowling. He sounded like Father Hyacinth.

"What about his wife, Father Dowling?"

"May she rest in peace."

Marie rose, her lips a thin line. She crossed her arms. Then she turned and marched back to her kitchen.

Well, what had she expected Father Dowling to say? Tuttle had argued that Nathaniel was merely carrying out his wife's wishes. The trial had engrossed the friars. Hyacinth had been called as a witness, offering the theological opinion that what Nathaniel had done was not murder.

Boniface was outraged. "So if someone asks me to shoot him it's all right?"

"You'd probably miss," Placidus said.

It was their merry laughter that made the friars hard to take. Of course, priests dealt with death and other tragedies all the time, so who could blame them for getting used to it? "The poor fellow," Father Dowling had said. Marie had to admit that the somber Nathaniel seemed to be carrying his punishment around with him.

"Did you love your wife?" the prosecutor had demanded of him.

"More than myself."

"You didn't kill yourself."

"Oh, yes, I did."

4

Captain Phil Keegan unscrewed the plastic tube and let a cigar slide into his free hand. He moistened it, struck a match, and soon Father Dowling's pipe smoke was joined by the acrid smell of Phil's cigar in the pastor's study. Phil rotated the cigar in his fingers and nodded.

"Sure I remember Nathaniel Green,

27

Roger. The guy couldn't wait to be found guilty and sent off to prison."

"Guilt would have that effect."

"Ha. People with blood on their hands usually claim to be innocent of even original sin."

"Murder was the original sin. Original actual sin," Father Dowling corrected himself, as if a theologian were listening in.

"If it was murder," Phil said.

"Wasn't he found guilty of manslaughter?"

"Labels. Green killed his wife." Phil spoke with the contempt of a widower who still half hoped that his wife would be waiting for him when he went home at night. A sentimentalist with a gruff exterior.

"How?"

"He shut down her life support system. He admitted right away what he had done."

"And went to trial, Phil."

"With Tuttle as his lawyer." Phil's tone required no comment. Tuttle was the bottom-feeder of the local bar.

"How did he plead?"

"Guilty, of course, but everyone goes into court on the assumption of innocence."

"But he confessed?"

"That doesn't count, Roger. Tuttle argued that it was a mercy killing. I suppose that is

28

what prompted them to call it manslaughter."

"That didn't leave you much to do," Father Dowling said.

"Oh, we investigated it. Cy Horvath interviewed everyone at the hospital, friends of the couple, everyone even remotely involved, but all it did was seal Green's fate. Finding out that everyone liked the guy and thought him a devoted husband couldn't trump the nurse's testimony that when the monitors at the nurses' station went haywire and she ran into the room, Green was sitting there with the tubes still in his hand."

"He showed up in the church on Ash Wednesday," Father Dowling said.

"I got mine at St. Hedwig's," Phil said hastily. He meant the blessing with ashes. St Hedwig's was downtown, an old church dwarfed by the buildings around it, not far from the courthouse.

"Marie took him over to the parish center."

"He's old enough," Phil said.

"Well, he paid the price for what he did."

"His wife's still dead."

Phil might have been drawing attention to the paradox of remorse. Not that he would ever call it that. It was a paradox Father Dowling faced in the confessional. A person repented of his sins, confessed them, and received absolution, but even when the penitent was returned to the state of grace, the effects of his sins did not go away. This was dramatically true in such a case as Nathaniel Green's. It was clear that he felt remorse. Had he confessed to a priest? His remark that he was no longer a Catholic seemed the answer to that. Certainly he had paid the civic penalty for what he had done. Nonetheless, as Phil said, his wife was still dead. Nothing he or anyone else did could change that, not prison, not contrition.

Nathaniel Green had continued to come to the noon Mass, staying in his pew at communion time. He had continued to come to the senior center as well, but in church he knelt alone in his pew and afterward went back to the school building alone. Father Dowling, on his way to the rectory after Mass, often saw Nathaniel shuffling slowly down the walkway to the school, a solitary figure carrying his invisible burden.

In the meantime, Father Dowling had been reading up on what Nathaniel had done, puzzling over the distinction between killing and letting die. He was most interested in a distinction Pius XII had made between ordinary and extraordinary means of medical help. The pope had decreed that no one was under an obligation to make use of extraordinary medical means when death was inevitable. It seemed a spoor worth pursuing. Had Florence Green's life support system amounted to extraordinary means to keep her alive? Whom should he call?

Basil Spritzer, a Jesuit at Loyola, was often consulted on medical ethical problems by the local media. No. Spritzer put one in mind of the Jesuits Pascal had caricatured in *The Provincial Letters.* He seemed to find a way of justifying any convenient course of action. Father Dowling decided to go out to Holy Angels Home and have a talk with Father William Nolan, who had taught him moral theology at Mundelein. He had been known as Willy Nilly by the seminarians and was famous for his rigorism.

Holy Angels Home was up the Fox River Valley just below the Wisconsin border, a pleasant drive even if Willy Nilly could not provide him with information that would be useful when he had a talk with Nathaniel Green.

Is there any scenery more beautiful than the Fox River Valley, even in late winter? Father Dowling went north on minor roads, enjoying the rolling snow-covered hills, the copses of beeches and fir, the shimmering river visible from time to time as he drove. An hour and a half later he turned into the drive that led to the main building of Holy Angels.

At the reception desk, he was directed to the cottage in which Father Nolan was living out his twilight years. He found the old priest sitting on a glassed-in porch, his breviary on his lap, dozing. The sound of the car door stirred him into life. He sat forward, brought his glasses down from his bald head, and peered at his unexpected guest.

"Come in, Father. Come in. That door's not locked."

"Roger Dowling, Father. I hope you remember me."

"Of course I do. Sit down. This must be a visit. You're too young to be thinking of joining us."

"Not yet," Father Dowling said with a smile. "It seems pleasant enough."

"I always swore I would never end up in such a place. Chaplain in a convent or weekend work, anything but being put on the shelf. Vanity, of course. As it happens, although I was brought in kicking and screaming — metaphorically — I love it here. Let me show you my little house."

The brick cottage contained a bedroom, a study, a living room with fireplace, a dining room, and a diminutive kitchen. The window blinds were tilted and laid bars of winter sunshine on the furniture and floors. Every available wall space contained bulging bookshelves. It was as if Father Nolan had reproduced his suite of rooms at Mundelein.

"This is wonderful," Father Dowling said. Did such a future await him?

In the study a laptop computer nestled among books and papers and dozens of framed photographs. A statue of St. Thomas Aquinas looked down from atop a bookcase.

"You use a computer?" Father Dowling asked. He himself had resisted learning how to use this wondrous device.

"A very useful gadget. I am writing my memoirs."

"I can hardly wait to read them."

"Autobiography is the best revenge," Willy Nilly said. "Let's have a beer on the porch."

"Not for me, Father."

The old priest drew back in mock surprise. "Next you'll be telling me you don't golf. What kind of a priest are you?"

"Do you know Dr. Johnson's remark? 'I find abstinence easier than moderation.' "

The old priest chuckled. "The one I remember is 'Marriage has its pains, but celibacy has no pleasures.' "

Father Dowling accepted a glass of iced tea, and they went out to sit on the porch where he had found Father Nolan. It was there, surrounded by Christmas cactus, a large potted impatiens — "My middle name, Father" — and other plants, that they talked. Willy Nilly sipped his beer and nodded as Father Dowling told him the saga of Nathaniel Green.

"I came upon the distinction Pius XII made between ordinary and extraordinary medical means," Father Dowling said.

Father Nolan shook his head slowly. "That statement has been the cause of lots of arrant nonsense. Unintentionally, of course. Our friend Basil Spritzer considers water extraordinary means when a patient is in a coma."

"What would count as extraordinary means?"

"That is the problem," Willy Nilly said. "What were extraordinary means a generation ago have become ordinary. You mustn't think that I have become a relativist." He glared at Father Dowling.

Father Dowling laughed. "That would be extraordinary."

"Your thinking it or my becoming it?"

"In the case that concerns me, the means were a life support system."

"That's too vague, Father. Say it means just oxygen. Would you consider that extraordinary?"

"You're the moral theologian, Father."

The old priest sighed. "Medical ethics has become the last refuge of the scoundrel. 'Extraordinary' could characterize most of the stuff written in the field. Extraordinary nonsense."

Father Dowling presented the details of his problem to the moralist.

Willy Nilly sighed. "I don't think I could responsibly encourage you to believe that what that man did does not amount to depriving his wife of ordinary medical care. The circumstances are extraordinary, no doubt. I can sympathize with the wife's fear and the husband's anguish. But what he did, as you describe it, was kill her."

Father Dowling realized that this was the answer he had expected. He could not regret not having consulted Basil Spritzer.

"Tell him to pray for his wife," Willy Nilly suggested. "As she is undoubtedly praying for him. That is not sentimentality. I can give you a reference in St. Thomas."

"I'll take your word for it." He thought he

knew the passage in the *Summa theologiae* his old professor had in mind.

Willy Nilly nodded. "It was the realization that whatever I said in the classroom would become gospel for the men I taught that made teaching such a weighty responsibility."

"I think you bore it well."

"That is my hope," Father Nolan said.

So Father Dowling drove back to Fox River unable to enjoy the beautiful countryside on the return trip. Still, despite what Willy Nilly had told him, or not told him, he looked forward to talking with Nathaniel Green.

Back in the rectory he called Edna Hospers.

"Has Nathaniel Green become one of your wards, Edna?"

"I want to talk to you about him, Father."

5

Natalie Armstrong, a handsome widow in her early sixties, came reluctantly to St. Hilary's senior center, not considering herself a senior, but lonely and bored. Helen Burke's enthusiasm made her hesitant. The description in the parish bulletin held her attention, but she was certain she was not old enough for that. To her surprise, she found that the age range of the regulars included half a dozen her own age and then rose choppily up the scale until it reached such denizens as Leon Bartlett, pushing ninety, hunched over his walker as if it were a motorcyle threatening to get out of control, and Marlys Logelin, who would never see ninety again and was confined to her motorized wheelchair, in which she zipped around the former gym as if she were engaged in one of the basketball games that had been played there when she was a girl. Watching her, Natalie felt in the full flush of youth.

The very first day, Eugene Schmidt introduced himself. He was at least her age, with a head full of hair that might have been cotton wool and a dapper little mustache to match. His eyes twinkled at her over his half-glasses.

"You look lost," he said, as if he meant to do something about it. He did. He squired her around, introducing her — how on earth had he known her name?

"I asked." He actually squeezed her hand.

They kibitzed at bridge; they followed a shuffleboard match with Eugene whispering critical comments in her ear; they watched a little television, which was what Natalie had come to the center to escape.

"I found myself turning it on at breakfast and not turning it off until I went to bed."

Eugene shook his head, but there was sympathetic understanding in his bright blue eyes. "I know what you mean. Oh, do I know what you mean."

"How long have you been coming here?"

"Time flies when you're having fun."

At noon they went together up the walkway to the church and attended Father Dowling's Mass. To her surprise, Eugene sat through the Mass and did not go forward to receive communion. Afterward, he explained.

"I'm a heretic."

"A heretic!"

He made even that seem fun. "I mean I'm not Catholic."

"Then why would you come to the center?"

"Until today I wondered that myself."

Honestly. Natalie hadn't been at the center a week and she seemed to have acquired an admirer.

That night, she alternated between being pleased and being half ashamed. She had been a widow for three years; her children, both of them, were gone. One a Maryknoll missionary and the other a Poor Clare. She resolved that the following day she would avoid Eugene Schmidt. Then another thought came. Eugene wasn't a Catholic. Everybody should be Catholic. Perhaps God had thrown them together so that Eugene would come into the Church. The next morning she went off to the center with some of the zeal that had sent her daughter to a convent and her son into the priesthood.

Over coffee and a doughnut she did not need, she got right to the point. "What kind of heretic are you?"

"How many kinds are there?"

Natalie had no idea. "You just meant you're not Catholic, didn't you? You're really nothing at all, I mean religiously?"

"What are you getting at?"

They had wandered outside on this suddenly sunny day with their coffee and were sitting side by side on one of the benches along the walkway. Natalie hadn't liked the way Phyllis Pilgrim had talked to Eugene in a saucy way, as if she had some kind of claim on him.

"Perhaps you've already talked with Father Dowling."

"Of course I've talked with him."

Natalie looked away. Phyllis had come outside, and then she saw them. She didn't look happy when she went back inside.

"I think Phyllis is looking for you."

"You have to protect me," he said, grasping her arm. If it hadn't been for his devilish smile, she might have thought he was in danger. She said as much.

"The predatory widow, Natalie. They're the bane of my life."

"Poor you."

He nodded. "That, too."

It was difficult to get back to the subject that had led her to take him outside to this bench.

"Now, if you were Phyllis, I wouldn't be sitting here for a million dollars."

Whatever he said seemed to indicate that he considered her, well, unlike the other widows. As indeed she was.

"Do you ever think of your soul, Eugene?"

"I don't think I have one."

"Of course you do. An immortal soul. Eugene, we're no longer young. We have to be more serious about what it all means."

"What does it all mean?"

"Father Dowling could explain that better than I could."

"I do have a heart. I'm sure of that."

He just couldn't be serious a minute, and Natalie found she liked that. He was such fun to be with. After all those dreadful months watching television, being with Eugene was a tonic. Thank God she had decided to come to the senior center. Would she ever have imagined that coming here would mean meeting someone like Eugene? No, not someone like. Eugene himself.

That afternoon Phyllis followed her into the restroom, and when they were washing up, their eyes met in the mirror.

"Be careful, Natalie."

"What do you mean?"

"Don't be misled by our Don Juan."

"I don't think I've met him."

Phyllis dipped her head and looked at Natalie over her glasses. "A word to the wise."

Pooh. The word came from a woman who was jealous! Imagine. Did Phyllis think that life still lay before her? That she might meet someone she might want to marry? What silliness. Natalie had half a mind to tell Eugene what Phyllis had said. But she didn't. It would have seemed, oh, she didn't know what it would have seemed.

The next day there was an excursion to the mall, and Eugene was at the wheel of the center shuttle bus, the kind one saw at airports taking passengers off to rental car lots. He drove in an almost reckless fashion, laughing while his passengers rocked back and forth as he changed lanes and sped along.

"Why don't you sing?" he suggested.

The whole group burst into "Merrily we roll along," Eugene's beautiful tenor voice leading them. In a back seat, bracketed by Leon Bartlett with his chin on his chest and Lester Bernard, whose ears were plugged with the largest hearing aids Natalie had ever seen, Phyllis stared gloomily ahead. It was on that jaunt that Natalie was teased about stealing away Phyllis's boyfriend.

Then one day when they were again outside and sitting on a bench, Natalie noticed the man on a bench farther along on the walkway, reading a book.

"Who is that?" Natalie asked.

"Nathaniel Green."

"Really? He's some sort of relative of mine."

"He is being shunned."

"What?"

"Helen is his sister-in-law. She's convinced the others that Nathaniel doesn't belong here."

"What right does she have to do that?"

"He did kill his wife."

Natalie almost wanted to deny it. The sight of that lonely man, reading a book, unwanted inside, filled her with pity. "The poor man."

"According to Herman, Green doesn't really mind."

"Who is Herman, for heaven's sake?"

"Of course you haven't met Herman. Come, I'll introduce you."

"I'd rather talk to Nathaniel Green."

"Later. You must meet Herman first."

6

Tuttle heard of Nathaniel Green's release from Joliet in the newsroom at the court-house. Tetzel had an annoying habit of reading aloud, although to what audience it would be hard to say. The reporter had been alone when Tuttle came in, holding the printout of the wire service story a foot in front of his face as he read it. He turned to Tuttle.

"Good work, Tuttle. How long did he serve?"

When ignorant of the answer, silence is the best response. Tuttle took a chair next to the reporter and reached for the sheet. Tetzel moved it out of reach.

"You didn't answer my question," Tetzel said.

"Rephrase it."

Tetzel's barking laughter might have been

directed at the whole legal profession.

"How did you spring Greenbeard out of Joliet so soon, Tuttle?"

Tetzel spoke, if not with forked tongue, in a slurred voice. It was early afternoon, and he was either still sloshed from the night before or getting a head start on today's sunset. Or both. Tuttle had trouble with crossword puzzles but not with Tetzel's unimaginative reference to his former client Nathaniel Green.

"I asked to have him released to your custody, Tetzel."

"I wouldn't mind getting my hands on that SOB."

"Aren't you a member of the Hemlock Society?"

"He didn't claim that his wife asked him to do it."

"No," Tuttle said. "I did. Let me see that."

Tetzel yielded the news story, and Tuttle read it with feigned nonchalance. Nathaniel Green's release from Joliet was news indeed to his former lawyer. He was not mentioned in the story. Perhaps Tetzel could be induced to correct that omission before it went into the *Fox River Tribune.* He made the suggestion, keeping urgency from his voice.

"Tuttle, it would only be news if you ever got a client off."

"He might have rotted in prison if I hadn't persuaded Jacuzzi to change the charge to manslaughter."

"Careful, careful."

Tuttle tipped back his Irish tweed hat, an interrogatory gesture.

"Womanslaughter," Tetzel suggested.

"That would be language slaughter."

"That's good!"

"Use it."

Tuttle was adjusting his hat as he sought to make an exit on that high note when he ran into Rebecca Farmer in the doorway, toppling her to the floor.

"Jesus Christ!" Rebecca cried.

"I grant the resemblance. Here, let me help you up."

"Don't you touch me!" She actually shuddered. Nonetheless, she needed help in getting to her feet. Tuttle also picked up the knitting that had spilled from the cloth bag that had been and still was on her arm. She sidled to a chair, looking warily at Tuttle as she did so.

"Nathaniel Green has been released from Joliet," Tuttle told her, before Tetzel could ruin the news with sarcasm.

"Who in the hell is Nathaniel Green?" Rebecca asked.

"You should read the paper you write for,"

Tuttle advised.

This time he got safely out the door and went briskly down the corridor. He was peeved. Peanuts Pianone, his friend on the Fox River Police Department, should have given him a heads-up on Green's release. Tuttle eschewed the elevator and took the broad winding staircase beneath the building's dome to the lobby, where he moved across the checkered marble floor like the man who would be king and sailed through the revolving door. Standing in the weak March sunlight, he sought and found his cell phone and put through a call to his office.

"Tuttle and Tuttle," Hazel said. Her voice gave the impression that his was a thriving practice.

"Is Mr. Tuttle there?" he said, disguising his voice.

"Where are you?" Hazel asked.

"I thought you should know that my client Nathaniel Green has been released from Joliet."

"Your former client. I know. He called."

"He did!" No need to feign nonchalance with Hazel.

"He had to explain who he was. You lost that case before I was with you." She might have been trying to explain the verdict.

"Thank God for grateful clients," Tuttle said.

"Sure. Both of them."

"What did he say, Hazel?"

"I made an appointment."

"For when?"

"If you hurry you can get here before him."

"Hazel, keep him there if he gets there first."

He skipped down the steps to the battered Toyota parked in a handicapped spot. The door sounded as if it would come off in his hand when he pulled it open. He eased himself onto the ringlike cushion on the driver's seat. "I'm sitting on piles" was his answer to inquiries as to how business was. He started the car and entered traffic to the accompaniment of irate horns. Road rage was everywhere.

He made his mind a blank slate as he drove. No great feat that, but thoughts of Nathaniel Green kept chalking themselves on the board. He tried unsuccessfully to keep hope from rising in him. The Green case had been a bonanza, even if he had lost. If he had won, his client might not have paid the exorbitant bill Tuttle had presented.

Some scofflaw had parked in the spot behind the building clearly marked TUTTLE

& TUTTLE. He had half a mind to let the air out of the tires. Then it occurred to him that the car might be Nathaniel Green's. He put the Toyota in a space marked MANAGER and hurried into the building.

It was at times like this that he wished the building's elevator were still functional. Complaints about it had been useless. He had tried to turn the matter over to Hazel with the thought that she could intimidate Jenkins, the slack-jawed lout who spent the day napping in his basement office, but she shook her head. This motion did not disturb her tightly curled and hennaed hair.

"It's the only exercise I get," she said.

"You don't need exercise."

Hazel had taken it as a compliment and smiled her sweet and predatory smile. Tuttle had darted into his office. Hazel was a force to be avoided when memories of romance were awakened in her massive bosom.

Now, on the second landing, he stopped, huffing and puffing. If this was exercise, why was he overweight? When his breathing returned to something like normal, he continued up the stairs to his floor.

Hazel was banging away at her computer when he came in, in profile, looking very efficient and busy. She turned in her chair.

"Ah, Mr. Tuttle. This is Mr. Nathaniel

Green. I was able to squeeze him in."

Tuttle noted that she had divested Green of his topcoat and hung it in the corner.

"Mr. Green and I are old friends," he said to Hazel, and to Green, "Unavoidably detained." He shook Green's hand. "Come into my office." Before closing the door, he said over his shoulder, "No calls."

He hoped the chaos of his office gave the impression that he was swamped with work. He cleared a chair for Green, got him settled, and hung his own coat and hat on a stand that began to tip. He caught it and eased it toward the perpendicular. "The scales of justice," he said when equilibrium had been restored. Then he settled at his desk and looked receptively at Nathaniel Green.

The years had not been kind to Green. His Joliet pallor would persist if he did not get some sun. He still had the passive doomed air with which he had gone through the trial. When the verdict was read, he had stood with his chin on his chest. The only animation he had shown was earlier when Tuttle got the charge reduced to manslaughter.

"I murdered her," he had said to Tuttle.

"Not unless the law says so."

"Which law?" Green asked.

Tuttle had let it go. Never encourage religiosity in a client unless it could prove of use.

Now here, years later, was Nathaniel Green sitting across the desk from him in his office.

"So what can I do for you, Mr. Green?"

"I was told to come here."

Tuttle smiled as if beneficent hordes were forever directing clients to his door. "By whom?"

"Jerome Paxon."

Tuttle held his receptive smile. Who the hell was Jerome Paxon?

"My parole officer," Green said.

"Of course, of course." Paxon was a yo-yo who considered criminals innocent and the innocent criminals. Green was in good hands if he wanted to be treated like a victim of society and its benighted laws.

Tuttle began to talk about the time when Green had been his client, but let it go, silenced by the man's indifference.

"So what are your plans?" he asked Green.

Green seemed to have difficulty with the word. After a pause, he said, "I've been going to the senior center at St. Hilary's. That was our parish."

"Ah. Father Dowling. Good man. Give him my best."

50

The hope that Green represented income was fading, but then Green took an envelope from his inner pocket and laid it on the desk.

"That is my will. I want it rewritten."

Redoing Green's will might be a foot in the door. Tuttle reached for the envelope and took out the will. As his eyes went down the first page, he asked, "Who wrote this?"

"Amos Cadbury."

"Good man." Actually Fox River's best. He remembered a scary moment during his first interview with Green when he had said Cadbury was his lawyer.

"Why didn't you go to him?" Tuttle had asked.

Green had fallen silent, and Tuttle prepared for a reference to his own status in the local bar.

"He said I shouldn't plead guilty."

Tuttle had danced away from that. Of course Cadbury was right. It was then that he learned that his client had no wish to be exonerated.

"You've come to the right man," Tuttle said, then wanted to withdraw the equivocal remark.

Green had shown no interest in his own defense; he wanted to be executed for what he had done. Tuttle explained the Illinois ban on capital punishment. The ban was sometimes cynically referred to as the Illinois Investment Statute. He had to explain the feeble joke to Green.

His client's fatalism had lightened Tuttle's task. He could not lose by losing in this case.

Now Tuttle drew a legal pad to him, unearthing it from the debris before him. "Tell me what changes you would like in your will, Mr. Green."

"I want most of my estate to go to Helen Burke. My sister-in-law."

Tuttle was surprised. Helen had demanded Green's scalp for what he had done to her sister.

"A magnanimous gesture," Tuttle said.

"She hates me."

"I remember."

"It's mutual," Green said.

After the interview was over and Green was gone, Tuttle donned his tweed hat, pulled out a lower drawer, and put his feet in it. *It's mutual.* He pondered the significance of the remark. Could generosity be a form of revenge?

7

Edna Hospers attributed the treatment of Nathaniel Green by the others at the senior center to the fact that he was an ex-convict, and it was that, even if she might otherwise have been willing to ignore the shunning on the assumption that it would fade away, that enlisted her on Nathaniel's side.

"It's Aunt Helen," Madeline said. "Florence was her only sister."

"Florence?"

"Nathaniel's wife. He killed her, Edna."

Edna sank into the chair behind her desk. Most of the regulars at the center had known one another before coming here, some of them all their lives, and others were relatives of one sort or another, but it was an unwritten rule that newcomers unknown to the others must not be quizzed about themselves. Whatever they wanted to tell of their past lives — and few elderly people could be silent for long about that — okay, but there should be no pumping. In the case of Nathaniel Green, Edna seemed to be the only one unaware of his tragic history.

"Killed her?" Edna managed to say.

"His lawyer called it a mercy killing," Madeline said. "The actual verdict was manslaughter. Aunt Helen attended every session of the trial, sitting there like Madame Defarge. If he had been found innocent, I think she might have strangled him in the courtroom."

Edna's husband, Earl, had served a sentence in Joliet for what was called manslaughter, although how it could be seen as anything other than a bizarre accident had always baffled Edna. The trouble was that Earl had considered himself guilty of the death of Sylvia Lowry and almost longed to be punished for it. So it seemed to have been with Nathaniel Green.

"He confessed," Madeline recalled. "He wanted to plead guilty. His lawyer didn't dare put him on the stand or he would have confessed again in court."

Now Nathaniel seemed almost to welcome the cold shoulder the other old people gave him. It broke Edna's heart when the weather was fairly clement and she looked out her window to see him sitting solitary on a bench, reading.

"How long will this go on, Madeline?"

"Till hell freezes over. Helen is an avenging angel."

"She'll drive him away."

"That's her hope, Edna."

Still Nathaniel showed up almost every day. Edna made a point of talking with him, but she couldn't spend the day with him. Madeline looked bleak when Edna suggested she take her turn in making Nathaniel feel welcome.

"Helen would never forgive me."

So Edna asked Helen to come by her office. She entered bright as a button, looked around with a nostalgic smile, and sat. "I remember being summoned here for a scolding when I was a student in the school." She looked at Edna. "Is that what this is?"

"Helen, you have to stop treating Nathaniel Green this way."

"What way is that? I avoid him entirely."

"That's what I mean. Helen, whatever he did, he paid for it, and now he's back. He is here at Father Dowling's suggestion."

"It happened before Father Dowling was pastor. He doesn't understand."

"Understand what?"

"Edna, just look at the man. Woebegone, shuffling around like Oedipus, as if he were the victim. He adopted that role from the beginning, as if the tragedy were not one he had caused. He never once expressed the least bit of sorrow for what he had done. I was not impressed by his self-dramatization at the time, and am even less so now."

"What would you expect him to do?" Edna asked.

"If he doesn't know, my telling him wouldn't help."

"Then tell me."

Helen fell silent, working her lips. Suddenly tears began to leak from her eyes. "I know what I sound like. Who am I not to forgive a sinner? Who am I to judge him? What I'm doing is a sin and I know it and I blame it on him."

"Have you talked with him, Helen?"

"No!"

"Helen, I can't have this going on in the center. It is souring the atmosphere."

"Then tell him to stay away!"

"I can't do that."

"I understand." Helen lifted her chin and stared over Edna's head at the bookshelves behind her.

"What do you mean?" She was referring to Earl, Edna was sure of it.

"Is my scolding over?" Helen asked.

Edna was on the verge of exploding at this insufferably smug woman, but she managed to control herself, barely. "Go back to the others."

For five minutes after Helen had gone, Edna sat seething at her desk. She stood, looked out her window, then went downstairs and through the former gym. Voices seemed to die down as she went by. Outside, she slowed her walk as she approached the bench where Nathaniel Green sat, his coat collar up, engrossed in a book.

"What are you reading?" she asked, sitting beside him.

"Shelby Foote. This is volume two." He lifted the large volume, then let it drop on his lap.

"Shelby Foote."

"His account of the Civil War," Nathaniel Green explained.

"We have a little civil war going on right here, Nathaniel."

"How so?"

For a moment she felt something of Helen's impatience with his martyred air.

"You know what I mean, Nathaniel."

He sat silent for a while. "I don't blame them. I don't blame them at all."

What is more crushing than forgiveness? Nathaniel's response to the shunning could only make it continue. She remembered Helen's little bout of weeping. They had made him a pariah, and yet they all knew that what they were doing was wrong. Then, like Helen, they blamed that, too, on Nathaniel.

"My husband was in Joliet," Edna said.

Nathaniel Green nodded.

"Did you know him?"

"Oh, I only knew who he was. Everybody liked him. Herman is an alumnus, too."

Herman. Herman was the latest in a series

of ex-convicts Father Dowling had turned into what he called maintenance men. He was as useless as the others, but he was a cheerful incompetent, impossible not to like. His story of his arrest for breaking and entering was a hilarious tale of a plan gone wrong.

"So you've met him," Edna said.

"He looked me up. He seems to think we're part of a fraternity. He was the clown of the place."

"Now he's the clown of this place," Edna said.

"He loves it here. That's quite a little apartment he has in the basement."

It was sad to think that the only one who had welcomed Nathaniel to the center was Herman. Herman the German, as he styled himself, although his name was Wycinski. He explained that his family came from a part of Poland, Silesia, that had been taken over by Germany. "If it isn't the Russians, it's the Germans. Anyway, my family got out of there and came to America, where I became a criminal. Upward mobility."

Nathaniel seemed impatient to get back to his book.

"It can't go on forever," she said.

"I don't mind."

"I can't believe that, Nathaniel."

"I got used to solitude in Joliet. Ask your husband."

A fraternity. Edna hated the thought that Earl was part of a group with Nathaniel and Herman the German. She rose. She almost apologized for interrupting his solitude.

Back in her office, the phone rang. It was Father Dowling asking about Nathaniel.

"I want to talk to you about him, Father."

8

Jason Burke owned a shoe store — the Foot Doctor — in a mall north of town: a large rectangular room, one wall lined with boxes, rows of chairs, a little stool for the clerk to sit on when he helped the customer try on shoes, and a nice leathery smell that Madeline loved. She loved Jason, too, in the way you loved a cousin who hadn't amounted to much. The shoe store was the latest attempt at a business of his own that Aunt Helen, Jason's mother, had underwritten. He had one employee, a gangly young man named Eric, whose Adam's apple was disconcertingly prominent. His smile, revealing massive but regular teeth, made up for that.

"Is he in?" Madeline asked.

Eric looked up with that wonderful smile from the stool on which he sat. A woman with three young boys was getting them shoed. Eric bobbed his head toward the back. In the back were a stockroom with more shoes, a break room, and Jason's office. Dangling aslant from the knob of his door was a sign: DOCTOR IS IN. Inside, Jason sat, or lay, in a Barcalounger tipped back so as to be horizontal with the floor. His desk was clean; there was a computer on a stand beside it, one file cabinet along the wall, and Jason in his chair, sleeping.

Madeline went up to him, grabbed his stockinged foot, and jiggled. He sputtered awake.

"Geez," Jason said. "You could have given me a heart attack."

The air was redolent of alcohol, but there was no sign of a glass or bottle. Jason drank with consummate furtiveness, most often alone, never observed. Never completely sober, either. He grabbed a lever and shot himself into an upright position. Even now, Jason retained a vestige of the debonair manner and good looks that had made him stand out as a young man.

"What can I do you for?" he said.

"Have you seen your Uncle Nathaniel since his release from prison?" Madeline asked.

Jason jerked with alarm. "Shut that door,

will you?"

Madeline obliged.

"Do you have anything to drink, Jason?"

"Drink? What do you mean, coffee, Coke, what?"

"Booze."

She had startled him. He seemed glad the door was closed so that the matron with her kiddies could not hear what his depraved visitor had said. "Booze," he repeated.

"Oh, a beer would do."

"A beer?" He adopted a thoughtful expression. "Let me look."

There was a little refrigerator in the break room, and he got out of his chair and pattered in his stockinged feet from the office. Madeline followed him, and he tried to block her view of its contents when he opened the refrigerator and cried, "By gosh, there is beer. Two! I'll join you."

Madeline felt manipulative. She did not want a beer, she hated beer, but Jason would be far more at ease if he were topping off the alcohol content of his blood.

"What do you think of the sign?" he asked proudly, adjusting it before he closed the door. In the store, Eric was waiting on more customers.

"You should wear lab coats," Madeline suggested.

"Good idea! I suppose stethoscopes would be too much?"

"Oh, I don't know. But it would be more convincing if you wore shoes."

He had put the cans of beer on his desk and now looked over his shoulder at her. "I'd go barefoot if I dared. I hate shoes."

"How is business?" Madeline asked.

"We sell a lot of shoes."

"Good."

Jason snorted. "Do you know what the retail markup on a pair of children's shoes is?"

Madeline felt that she had led a charmed life, never having to worry about money. Once she had started teaching, she had a job that would last as long as she wanted it, and the retirement plan ensured a comfortable and modest afterward. Being single helped, of course, but then Jason had been single ever since Carmela left him and his whole life became one try after another at something that would become permanent. By contrast, her life, with its steady income, seemed one of ease and security.

"Nathaniel is out of prison?" Jason was whispering.

"I see him every day at St. Hilary's."

Jason's eyebrows went up. "Every day?"

She told him about the senior center then.

Hadn't his mother told him about it? He had poured their beer into clear plastic cups and sipped while Madeline told him how she was spending her day.

"What's it pay?" Jason asked.

"Oh, I'm just a volunteer. Apparently the prison chaplain told Nathaniel to look up Father Dowling, and he did, and that's why he comes to the center. Your mother is furious."

Jason lifted his eyes and then his cup. "What a battleaxe." A smile broke out. "Battleaxe! That's what Dad called her."

"Why is she so unforgiving, Jason?"

"Guilt. She almost never visited Florence in the hospital, and when she did it was just in and out. She stood the whole time, kept her coat on. She can't stand hospitals. I can't say that I blame her."

Jason had been a nurse's aide before opening a lawn service, his business before the Foot Doctor. Nursing had been a stopgap job between private enterprises.

"Did Nathaniel ever complain about Helen?"

"Why would he? He preferred being alone with Florence. When you looked in, it was difficult to tell which one of them was dying. Anyway, he and Helen hated one another."

Jason considered the ceiling. He took a long swallow from his plastic cup. "This is just speculation, you understand."

"Tell me!"

"Well, as I piece it together, long ago when Nathaniel came calling at the house, Helen assumed it was to see her. It turned out it was Florence he was interested in. Helen was as willin' as Barkis, but Florence had to be wooed. Eventually, Nathaniel was successful. Helen never forgave him that."

"She bore a grudge all those years?" Madeline asked.

"I think it was refueled when Florence fell ill." He finished his beer. "I don't claim it makes sense."

"Did you ever visit Florence, Jason?"

"My dear, I was on the staff in those days, delivering tasteless meals, swabbing the floors, resolving never to get sick. Working in a hospital squeezes the cheerfulness out of life. I understand my mother's attitude. People step into a hospital out of normalcy and are confronted with the grim facts of fragility and terminal illness."

"That hardly explains Helen's vendetta against Nathaniel."

"Vendetta?" Jason asked.

"She has all the other old people shunning Nathaniel. A killer in our midst."

Jason rubbed his already messed-up hair. "That is bad," he said.

"Could you talk to her?"

"Anybody can talk to her. Changing her mind is something else."

"Will you try?" Madeline put her hand on his arm.

Jason shrugged. "It won't do any good. How are you fixed for shoes?" He leaned forward and examined her ankle-high boots.

"Not today."

She had a closet full of unwanted shoes, bought in a gesture of solidarity with Jason.

"You might talk to Nathaniel, too, Jason."

"Madeline, you should have married. You have a compulsion to organize other people's lives."

Sometimes Madeline imagined that, when they got a little older, she and Jason might share a house. She would like to bring order into his life. At the store he had Eric, but out of it he was on his disorganized own. He lived in one of the condos abandoned by public housing and sold dirt cheap to anyone foolish enough to buy them. Madeline got a glimpse of the chaos inside whenever she picked him up to take him to dinner.

"Are you free tonight?" she asked.

Jason brightened. "The Great Wall?"

"If you like. Meet me there at six."

"Done." He said it as if she had overcome his reluctance.

He walked her through the store, his stockinged feet not seeming unusual there. He stood in the open door as she went through and squinted at the sky.

"Looks like snow," he said.

"So wear shoes tonight."

Out she went to her car for the drive to St. Hilary's. It did look like snow.

9

The parking lot at St. Mary's Hospital was chock-full of cars. Cy Horvath did not avail himself of one of the official spots by the emergency ward but parked in the main lot and threaded his way through the other cars in the slushy snow toward the main entrance. Business was good, meaning things were bad for a lot of people.

The revolving doors were huge, to accommodate wheelchairs and the like, and they moved with glacial slowness. Cy came into the entrance hall and walked past the great circular reception desk, wondering if he would be challenged. He wasn't. Some security — but a hospital was a place people wanted to get out of, not into. He continued, took a left, and found the elevators. A very wide nurse entered it with him.

"What floor is cancer?" Cy asked her.

"Oncology?"

He nodded. She looked at her clipboard as if for directions. "Five."

He had thought it was four. At five, she bustled out before him and then went in the twinkle-footed way some overweight people have to the nurses' station. Cy went on down the hallway and found the waiting room he remembered. A place for people to sweat it out while loved ones went through who knows what hell. On the wall hung a huge sylvan scene by some Sunday painter, chairs in a row beneath it, plastic seats, stainless steel arms, looking like an ad for the death penalty. He eased himself into one. It was here that he had done a lot of interviewing after the death of Florence Green.

The chubby nurse looked in, sans clipboard. "Can I help you?"

He showed her his badge, and she backed away. "Is something the matter?"

"No."

He waited. He was used to the fact that his expressionless face prompted people into telling him whatever was on their minds. She said she had thought he was a funeral director. She nodded as if he had expressed surprise. "Ghouls. Do you know Dickens's *Christmas Carol?* They can't wait until it's all over. Meanwhile they butter up the family."

"How long have you worked here?" Cy asked.

"Going on seven years."

Not long enough. He nodded as if in approval of her longevity.

"Anything I can get for you?" she asked.

"How about some recent magazines?"

She smiled when she decided it was a joke, then scampered away. Some of the tattered magazines in the room looked as if they could have been lying with curled corners on the table since the last time he was here.

Cy had come to the hospital directly from a visit with Father Dowling, who had asked him to drop by and tell him about the investigation of Florence Green's death. That had been almost ten years ago, but Cy only had to refresh his memory. Of course, his memory had been stirred by the release of Nathaniel Green from Joliet.

What an enigma that guy had been, Cy remembered. Green had sat right here in this waiting room and said in a flat voice, "I killed her."

"Wasn't she dying?"

"What difference does that make?" Green had asked.

"Not a lot. How did you do it?"

"She was on a life support system. All I had to do was pull the plug."

"And you did?"

He looked pleadingly at Cy. "I couldn't take it anymore. More important, she couldn't. The loss of all hope is a terrible thing."

"I understand she was in a coma," Cy said.

"She might have come out of it. Now she won't."

Green didn't call it a mercy killing. That had to wait for the trial, when Tuttle brought it in as if it were an item from the Sermon on the Mount.

"When did this happen?" Cy had asked Green.

"When?"

"What time? The nurse went into your wife's room when she noticed the monitors on your wife were down. That was at 2:17."

"It was before that," Green said.

Cy observed a half minute of silence. "How long before?"

"I didn't look at my watch."

"How long had you been keeping vigil in

your wife's room?"

"Ever since I had to bring her back here."

"I meant today."

"All day."

"There's no bathroom in your wife's room," Cy said.

Nathaniel Green had looked blankly at him.

"Most people have to go once in a while. You must have left the room in order to go to the john."

"I was only gone a few minutes," Green said.

"How many times?"

"What are you getting at?"

"The way the nurse described it, you were practically on a liquid diet. Ice water, soup, juice. There were half a dozen plastic cups with sipping straws angling from them on the bedside table."

"I don't see what this has to do with anything," Green said impatiently.

"Probably nothing. I'm just trying to establish a timeline."

"Officer, I confess. I did it. What's the point of an investigation?"

"Mr. Green, I want to determine when you pulled the plug."

Green gave it some thought. "The nurse said she came in at 2:17? It was after two."

"Good. So we have fifteen minutes, maybe a little more. Where is the restroom?"

"I don't believe this," Green said, shaking his head.

"How many times have you confessed to murder? This is just routine. Come, show me where the restroom is."

"Don't you believe me?"

"I want to know what it is I'm believing."

Green didn't want to help. He just wanted to be hanged, and as quickly as possible. He was learning it wouldn't be quite that easy.

Cy had clocked Green on the way to the restroom and back, maybe a minute each way, adjusting for a hurried going and more leisurely return. Give him a few minutes to do his business. That was when Cy told Green he had been observed going toward the restroom at maybe 2:10. No need to tell him it was just a maybe identification.

It had taken a while to get used to the gradations among the staff, doctors, nurses, nurse's aides, various helpers of a lesser sort, some voluntary, janitors. The grades seemed color coded. It was a volunteer wearing one of the off-blue pajama-like outfits who had answered Cy's routine question with the statement that she had seen Green going off to the restroom at maybe 2:10.

"That's pretty pinpoint," Cy had said to the woman. For answer she displayed an enormous wristwatch. "I was taking magazines around. I do this wing at two o'clock."

"Do you suppose anyone else saw him at that time?" Cy asked.

"Is this important?"

"I doubt it."

The point of routine is that you don't decide about importance before the fact. For all the apparent fuss he had made about it, Nathaniel Green's trip to the restroom before the plug was pulled on his wife, and the exact time of each, dissolved into vagueness. Yet sitting here again in the creepy waiting room brought it all back. Of course, he was consulting his old notes as he sat here.

He had been less informative with Father Dowling. Remembering all those years ago, all the questions he had asked, noting them down, writing it up when he went downtown, all that recorded trivia retained somewhere in the great maw of police records, he had a fleeting sense of the futility of detective work. By and large. What difference did it make to establish as precise a timeline as he could to determine when a man who was eager to be punished had killed his wife? Cy had sat through the trial in the courtroom. Jacuzzi the prosecutor had asked him to, on the off-chance he might need his testimony. He didn't. How many hours had he sat in courtrooms for no eventual reason? He had almost longed to be questioned by Tuttle.

Cy realized too late that he was responsible for Green's choosing Tuttle. The little lawyer had slipped what looked like a used business card into Green's hand, and Green had asked Cy about him.

"Not a fastball pitcher," Cy said carefully.

"What do you mean?"

"That you could do better with anyone else."

That had amounted to a recommendation. After all, Green hadn't wanted a lawyer at all; he thought he could go into court, tell the judge he was guilty, and be sentenced then and there. If he had to have a lawyer, he didn't want a fastball pitcher. Cy should have realized that. Tuttle, to give him credit, had tried. Mercy killing. Well, it probably saved Green from the far longer sentence he deserved.

"They destroyed him," Jerome Paxon, the parole officer, said to Cy. "They broke his spirit. He's like a zombie. His only interest is in writing a will and leaving everything to his sister-in-law."

"Helen Burke?"

Paxon nodded vigorously. "His nemesis. The harridan. Madame Defarge. What a virago." Paxon might have been consulting a book of synonyms. But he was right about Helen. She had acted as if Florence Green were in the pink of health and Nathaniel had cut her off in the bloom of youth. Cy felt that he himself had been consulting a book of clichés.

"It sounds as if her grudge is with death, not her brother-in-law," Father Dowling had commented when Cy gave him a short version of those long-ago events.

"You may be right. Every doctor called to testify said that Florence had been dying, that nothing could save her."

"Then why would her husband kill her?" Father Dowling reasonably asked.

None of Nathaniel Green's explanations made sense. He wanted to save her further suffering, but she was already in a coma. To which he had replied that she might come out of it. Why hadn't he waited to see if that would happen? An oddity of the circumstances was that the oxygen petcock on the wall had been turned off. Green had been annoyed when Cy pointed this out. Then he made a face and said he had done that after he took the mask from his dying wife's. Lest oxygen be wasted? Green asked Cy if he had ever sat by a deathbed. A rhetorical question, but Cy could have answered yes. He had stood by his father's bed when he breathed his last breath; he had been holding his mother's hand when her eyes widened, her grip tightened and he watched her wondering eyes dim as she slipped into eternity.

"What ever happened to the nephew?" Cy asked Paxon.

"Jason?" Paxon shrugged. "At least he tried to get his mother to shut up."

"How does Nathaniel Green spend his time?"

"Do you know the senior center at St. Hilary's?"

Yes, Cy already knew of Nathaniel's persistent attendance there, despite the shunning engineered by Helen. His nemesis, his Madame whatchamacallit. The virago. Paxon was contagious.

When he left the parole officer's cluttered quarters, Cy thought he might see if Jason was still in town. It was a slow period in the Fox River detective bureau.

10

Herman the German was surprised that Eugene Schmidt had never been in Joliet or a place like it in another state. Eugene said that he had moved to Illinois from Michigan, but he seemed to have lived in lots of places, if you could believe him, something about which Herman was not sure. The guy reminded him of several in the place, bunco artists, con men, sure they were smarter than everyone else until finally they were outsmarted themselves. Herman thought of Wendel, who had sold forged lottery tickets and thought that nickel-and-dime operation put him in the big time. Well, it put him in Joliet, where he spent all the time he could trying to apprentice himself to real con men.

"Wendel, think of it. They're here. Why do you think they're smart?"

"A fluke. Do you know how much Mc-Gough made before he got caught?"

"A lot of good that does him now."

Wendel leaned toward Herman, his whisper emerging with exhaled smoke. "He stashed it. It'll be waiting for him when he gets out."

Oh, the stories one heard. Listening to Eugene Schmidt, Herman was reminded of all those guys, mad to make money any way but honestly, for whom a term at Joliet was just a bump on their road to unheard-of wealth. One stay in Joliet was all Herman wanted, which was why he had jumped at this job at St. Hilary's.

"So what did you do before you retired?" he asked Schmidt, making conversation.

Eugene liked to come down to Herman's apartment for a smoke, and up to a point Herman enjoyed his company. If only to find out what made him tick.

"Who said I'm retired?"

"Come on. You're here every day."

"Ah, these widows." Eugene rolled his eyes and sent a series of perfectly formed smoke rings across the room.

Herman laughed.

"A cat among the pigeons, Herman." He frowned at his own remark. "I'm kidding, of course. The luck I've had with women, I should join the monastery."

"Pretty bad?"

"A trail of broken dreams."

The guy talked that way, half shutting his eyes, looking sad, but his eyes never lost their twinkle.

"Tell me about Nathaniel Green, Herman."

"It's all in the papers."

"Did you know him . . ." Eugene delicately

left the question unfinished.

"Not really. You don't really get to know anyone in a place like that."

"Cellmates."

"Cellmates least of all. Most of them are trying to rob you blind."

"What did you have to steal?"

You couldn't explain it to an outsider. Stuff that wouldn't mean a thing anywhere else loomed large behind those walls, and thieves never lost their habit of wanting what they did not have.

"Tell me about the widows," Herman suggested, wanting to get off that subject.

Eugene developed his theory for Herman. People grow older, sure, but they never grow up. Particularly women. Good-looking women, and not only the good-looking ones, never got rid of the idea that they were women. And what do women want? A man. That never stops.

"I'll tell you what this place is, Herman. We're in a school, right? Outside is a playground. Okay, we're all kids again. The women think they're girls. They can't help it."

"And you're a boy?"

A boyish grin. "That's what they tell me."

Already Eugene and Natalie were the talk of the place, either chuckled over or envied or both. Herman had to admit that Natalie was a fine-looking woman, that silver-gray hair, that unlined face, the nose with a little hump in the bridge. He felt half in love with her himself. That was why he kept an eye on Eugene, to see what progress he was making.

"Everything's on schedule," Eugene said. "She's interested in my soul."

"You don't have one."

"That's what I told her. She's determined to save me."

"From what?"

"We haven't gotten around to that yet."

What a guy. Just like some at Joliet, Eugene found anywhere he was a stage on which to perform. The senior center at St. Hilary's wouldn't attract many men Eugene's age, but, as he said, here he was a cat among the pigeons. Herman couldn't believe that Natalie Armstrong didn't see him for the little con man he was.

"You play them like a fish, Herman. Why am I down here? Absence makes the heart grow fonder. Keep them off balance, that's the thing."

Herman felt like a snitch when he asked Edna Hospers what she thought of Eugene.

"Everyone seems to like him."

"A real ladies' man."

She laughed when he said it. Well, if she wasn't worried, why should Herman be?

11

After a couple of hours' effort in the courthouse pressroom, Tetzel got an opening paragraph that he liked and went down to the paper to get a go-ahead from Menteur the features editor. It would take a little digging and footwork to do the piece on Nathaniel Green, and Tetzel was unwilling to undertake it without assurance that it would be used.

"Who would be interested?" Menteur asked. He must have had a full package of gum in his mouth, which he chewed ferociously in the now smoke-free premises of the *Fox River Tribune*.

"I'll make them interested," Tetzel said.

"All this took place, what, eight, ten years ago?"

"The story is his release. The past as prologue."

"That's catchy," Menteur said with weary sarcasm. He was always finding clichés in other people's prose.

"The Return of Nathaniel Green." Tetzel might have been reading the headline off the ceiling above them.

"What's he doing now?"

"You see? You're curious. What does a man who killed his wife do when he gets out of prison?"

"Remarry?" More sarcasm. You had to know Mrs. Menteur to understand the features editor. "Any other Pulitzer possibilities, Gerry?"

"Is that no?" Tetzel asked, annoyed.

Menteur chewed his cud, then shrugged. "Write it. But it better be good."

"With me, that's second nature."

Heads turned throughout the room at the unfamiliar sound of Menteur laughing.

The laughter stopped abruptly when Menteur screamed, "Don't light that!" Tetzel had unthinkingly plucked a cigarette from one pocket and a plastic lighter from the other. "We can't smoke here anymore."

"Just chew gum?"

Menteur shook his head and hunched over his desk. "I never thought I'd live so long. Honest to God, I think Prohibition will be back before I die."

"We can smoke in the courthouse," Tetzel said.

Menteur lurched into an upright position. "But it was the city council that passed the ordinance!"

"They exempted the courthouse."

Menteur fell back, his open mouth revealing the pink wad of gum. He turned and spat it into a wastebasket.

"Write *that* up, Tetzel. Skewer the hypocrites."

"Watch your language," Tetzel said.

"I mean it, damn it. I want a piece on the danger of secondhand smoke to anyone who enters the courthouse."

Tetzel rose. "Good idea. Right after I do the Nathaniel Green story."

"Skewer them, Tetzel. Skewer them."

Wondering eyes followed his departure, Menteur's vindictive commission ringing in his ears. Fat chance he would complain about being allowed to smoke in the courthouse pressroom. That would be like fouling his own nest. He wondered if they let the inmates at Joliet smoke. He would put the question to Nathaniel Green.

For two days, Tetzel pursued his project furtively, lest Rebecca learn what he was working on and steal his thunder. Not for the first time, he felt that he had hit on a story that would captivate his readers and make his name a household word among the dwindling subscribers to the *Fox River Tribune*. The one story that would never run in the *Tribune* was the paper's falling circulation. Menteur might see the demise of newsprint before he saw Prohibition return.

In the pressroom, Tetzel angled the screen of his computer so others would not see that he was consulting decade-old issues of the *Tribune*. He had been a callow youth in those days, and sitting in traffic court and other courtrooms was part of the apprenticeship. So it was that he had sat through the trial of Nathaniel Green, his unattributed reports moving from the front page to page two, then three, always heavily edited, until the verdict came and he was briefly back on page one, and above the fold.

He read his youthful prose with the eyes of the craftsman he felt he had become, and found it good. Not that there wasn't a lot of Menteur in it. Even so, the story on the verdict bore his name, Gearhart Tetzel. It was the first time other reporters learned what "Gerry" stood for, and he was teased mercilessly. "What *is* the heart of a gear, Gerry?" That sort of thing. He brushed this minor assault aside. He knew jealousy when he saw it in others. Now an older, less naive Tetzel read his early story with a moist eye. By God, he'd been good.

It was reading his magnanimous tribute to Tuttle's efforts on Nathaniel Green's behalf that sent Tetzel now to the little lawyer's office.

At the building, he wasted five minutes punching the button for the elevator before giving up and mounting the stairs to the door bearing the legend TUTTLE & TUTTLE, ATTORNEY AT LAW. He pushed through, and a bosomy Amazon turned from her computer, her face radiant with expectation.

"Is Tuttle in?" the reporter asked.

"Do you have an appointment?" Sweet but firm.

"I'm Tetzel of the *Tribune.*"

Her radiance increased. "The *Chicago Tribune?*"

Tetzel did not correct her. "Just tell Tuttle I dropped by."

An inner door opened, and an unmistakable tweed hat was visible in the crack. Then the door opened completely, and Tetzel was looking into the wary gaze of the little lawyer.

"Got a minute, Tuttle?"

"Mr. Tetzel is from the *Chicago Tribune,*" the receptionist gushed.

"Thank you, Hazel. No calls. Come in, Gerry."

The inner office was unbelievably chaotic. Presumably there was a desk beneath the debris over which the now seated Tuttle regarded his caller; the floor was littered with open law books, newspapers, magazines, and old Styrofoam containers.

"I like a neat office," Tetzel said, having sat on a container that had once held fried rice. He threw it into a corner, spread his handkerchief on the chair, and sat.

"*E pluribus unum,*" Tuttle said mysteriously. "As the poet says."

"I want to talk about Nathaniel Green," Tetzel said.

Tuttle pushed back from the desk, and his chair continued to the wall. When they collided, Tuttle grabbed his hat and managed to stay in the chair. He put the hat on again. "You, too?"

"What do you mean?" It was Tetzel's turn to be surprised. Although how could other reporters fail to see the human interest in the Nathaniel Green story? Tetzel looked abjectly at Tuttle. "Who else?"

"Cy Horvath," the little lawyer said.

Relief flooded through Tetzel. Cops didn't write for newspapers. Then second thoughts brought back anxiety.

"What's Horvath up to?" he asked.

"A little nostalgia, I think. He was young when he worked on that case. Maybe he's trying to regain his youth."

"Since when did you become a counselor, Tuttle?"

"What else is a lawyer?"

"Don't get me started. Tell me about Horvath."

"He wanted to talk about the trial. He wondered if I had a transcript. I was lucky to find one for him." Tuttle looked benevolently around his office.

"What would he want with that?" Tetzel asked, excited.

"I suspect that law students study my defense in that trial."

"You say Horvath was on that case?"

"He never missed a day in court," Tuttle said, as if cherishing a fond memory of better days.

"I don't remember seeing him there," Tetzel said.

"You would have been concentrating on what was going on in the front of the courtroom. Of course, Horvath had to be there on call," Tuttle conceded.

"Why would the detective division still care about a case like that? The guy was guilty from the word go."

"So it seemed."

"What do you mean?"

Tuttle tipped back his hat and then, with great carefulness, his chair. He clasped his hands behind his head. "It was all circumstantial evidence."

"Circumstantial evidence!" Tetzel cried. "He was sitting there with the tubes in his hand, he said he did it, no one else could have done it."

"So it seemed." Tuttle smiled mysteriously at Tetzel. "I wouldn't be surprised if Horvath gets the case reopened."

"On what basis?"

"So far it's all confidential," Tuttle said dreamily.

"Bullshit."

"As you wish."

Half an hour later Tetzel left, feeling strangely excited. Of course, he knew all about Tuttle. Normally he wouldn't credit anything the little lawyer said, but the suggestion that Horvath was reviewing the case with an eye to reopening it was preposterous enough to be plausible. In any event, Horvath's interest in Nathaniel Green after all these years, after his trial, imprisonment, and now release, promised material for the feature he was writing. Cy Horvath wasn't much of a talker, but whatever he said could be believed.

The return of Nathaniel Green had caused a stir — or better, a hush — at the senior center at St. Hilary's, and it had given the pastor reason to ponder as well. Father Dowling had talked with Nathaniel a few times since their luncheon on Ash Wednesday, but they had amounted to scarcely more than exchanges of greetings. Father Dowling wanted Green to come to him; only then could he have the conversation he now realized he longed to have. But it had to be initiated by Green.

Father Dowling had talked with Cy Horvath again and been told more of the investigation into the death of Florence Green. Cy had brought along the notes he had taken at the time, and he had been checking things out.

Cy said, "If there ever was anything to find out, the trail has long since gone cold."

"What does Phil think of your going over all this again, Cy?"

"Father, at the time, neither of us could figure out what Green gained from what he claimed to have done."

That was always the basic question: *Cui bono?* Who benefits from the deed under investigation? All Green had gotten for his pains was a stretch in Joliet — and he very nearly didn't get that.

Jacuzzi the prosecutor had insisted that the police look into the matter when Crawford the coroner made out his report and classified the death as natural.

"Natural!" Jacuzzi was shocked. "By his own admission the husband killed her, and that idiot calls it natural. Look at that gobbledegook."

Jacuzzi was excited, his normal condition. His narrow bald head seemed to have pushed through the bushy hair that still adorned its sides and covered the prosecutor's outstanding ears.

"All he did was copy things from her medical chart," Jacuzzi had said with disgust.

The cause of death, according to Crawford, was the cancer and its attendant effects. Tuttle had been as alarmed as the prosecutor by this judgment since it threatened to deprive him of his client. It was Tetzel, prompted by Tuttle, who had saved the day, running a story on the man who had killed his wife in St. Mary's Hospital. The death certificate had not been brought up during the trial.

Were there ever any uncomplicated deeds? What seemed as simple as could be, a husband removing his wife from life support, became ever more complex. Father Dowling paid another visit on Willy Nilly.

When he had parked at Holy Angels and was walking to Father Nolan's cottage, Father Dowling wondered if he should disturb the old man's retirement like this. Father Nolan dismissed the objection when he knew why Father Dowling had come to him a second time.

"How would you characterize what he did, Father? Morally?"

"Ah." Father Nolan nodded for a minute, as if in consultation with his once professional self as moral theologian. "One could say: He killed his wife. True, but that's not yet a moral description. You can kill another by accident, you can kill another in combat, you can kill another as public executioner, you can kill another in self-defense."

"If the hospital had taken her off the life support apparatus, wouldn't they have killed her?" Father Dowling asked.

"Of course. In the sense that they had stopped preventing her from dying."

"That is all Nathaniel Green did."

Willy Nilly hummed and nodded some more.

Father Dowling said, "If the hospital

would have been justified in doing that, wouldn't it be because the husband asked them to?"

"I suppose all this was argued at the trial," Willy Nilly said.

"His lawyer was more interested in portraying the man as a mercy killer."

They went on through the labyrinthine ways of moral appraisal. The gap between the moral absolute that one may never kill an innocent person and the singular deed done that day long ago in a room in St. Mary's Hospital seemed to widen as they talked.

"What did the man intend to do?" Willy Nilly finally asked. "In the end, that is the heart of the matter, morally."

The answer to that at least was simple. Nathaniel Green had intended to bring about his wife's death.

"That brings it under the moral absolute, Father Dowling."

"So he is a murderer?" Father Dowling asked.

"Are we talking legal description or moral?"

They were talking about a man's soul.

Finally Nathaniel Green came to bare that soul to Father Dowling.

"Can a lapsed Catholic go to confession, Father?"

"Do you want to?"

Nathaniel Green looked at Father Dowling with his haunted eyes. "Do you know what you miss most about going to confession? Being able to reveal yourself to another and know it will go no further."

"You're revealing yourself to God when you confess," Father Dowling said.

"You know what I mean."

Father Dowling nodded. "I know what you mean. How long has it been since your last confession?"

"Are we beginning?"

For answer, Father Dowling opened the drawer of his desk and took out a stole. Nathaniel Green watched as he put it on. Father Dowling waited. Some minutes are longer than others, but then time is a measure, and what was being measured here was a man's deciding to do what he had avoided doing since the death of his wife. That established how long it had been since his last confession.

"I never stopped believing in God, Father. I tried to, but I couldn't." A crooked smile. "I even prayed that I could stop believing."

"You and your wife were practicing Catholics, Nathaniel?"

"Oh, yes. Mass every Sunday and holy day, confession every month or two. Florence said the rosary."

"Did you?"

"I took it up again in Joliet."

"You're a strange lapsed Catholic, Nathaniel. Why didn't you take up confession again? There's a chaplain at Joliet."

"I attended his Mass, Father. Lots of us did, just to break the routine."

"Was that your only motive?"

"Not really."

"You'll have to state the serious sins you committed."

"Mortal sins?" Green said it as if bringing up an old memory.

"We'll start with those."

"Father, I think it would be harder to figure out what I've done right."

"Why don't I just run through them?"

So he went through the capital sins, feeling that he was starting at the top of Mount Purgatory and descending to the level where Dante's souls were doing penance for murder. For all his self-reproach, Nathaniel's life was not that of a hardened sinner, or of much of a sinner at all. Then Father Dowling put the question that explained why they were here.

"Murder?" he asked.

A long silence. "You mean Florence?"

"Yes."

"I didn't murder her, Father."

Father Dowling had the sinking feeling that he was being drawn into the maze he had gone through with Willy Nilly.

"But you killed her?"

"No."

"I don't understand," Father Dowling said.

There were tears in Nathaniel's eyes as he went on. "It's why I didn't want to go to confession, didn't want to be in the Church. That would have separated me from her more than her death had."

"Did you remove her life support system, Nathaniel?"

He shook his head vigorously. "No."

"But then who did?"

Nathaniel looked at the priest from the melancholy depths he had occupied all these years. He spoke in a whisper.

"She did."

■ ■ ■ ■

PART TWO

■ ■ ■ ■

1

The human mind is a marvel and a mystery.

"Where do thoughts come from?" Tuttle asked Peanuts Pianone as they sat in a booth in the Jury Room, the pub across from the courthouse. Peanuts gave him a feral look over his mug of beer and said nothing.

Tuttle did not really expect his old buddy to say anything. Whenever Tuttle felt depressed by his status in the local bar, he was heartened by the realization that Peanuts was even less esteemed in the police department. After a dozen years there, Peanuts was still a patrolman. He was unlikely ever to rise higher. So there was affinity between them, but also a comforting hint of Tuttle's somewhat superior status.

Needless to say, Peanuts did not meditate on his station in life. His family — the term had a Sicilian ambiguity in this case — having found Peanuts useless in any of their enterprises, had, thanks to the Pianone on the city council, palmed Peanuts off on the Fox River Police Department. There he had vegetated ever since, shuffling toward retirement. If the Pianones had thought Peanuts might be a source of inside information on any investigation into their activities, they would have been disappointed. Peanuts had a very limited interest in his surroundings. One thing only had stirred him into resentment at his status, and that was the coming of Agnes Lamb to the department. At first, Peanuts and the young black officer had been paired, a sufficient prod to Peanuts's racism, but when Agnes was taken into the detective bureau and soon became the rising star of that division, Peanuts was devastated.

"They're all dumb," he protested to Tuttle.

"I'm told she scored highest on the entrance examinations."

"A fix! You ever hear of affirmative action?"

Tuttle was surprised that Peanuts had. In any case, he had been a beneficiary of it. When after an hour of trying Peanuts had failed to find the right indentations into which to fit the different-shaped wooden blocks, this elementary intelligence test was waived. No one intended to rely on Peanuts's mind. Tuttle was amused, but did not show it, that Peanuts should consider himself a member of the master race.

"You will wonder what idea I have in mind," Tuttle continued. He was drinking a shandy, a drink he had trained Wilma, the bartender here, to make.

"Where'd you ever hear of it?" Wilma asked.

Tuttle laid a finger alongside his nose. He had learned that gesture along with the recipe for shandy from a 1930s-era English movie shown on television during one of his insomniac nights.

He sipped his drink and half aloud, half in his mind reviewed his great idea. It was bound to get him a mention in the story.

Peanuts finished his beer and shook his head at the offer of another one. "Gotta go."

It was a strange thought that Peanuts had some sort of private life.

"Who is she?"

Peanuts just looked at him, then got up and shuffled toward the exit, one of the bit players in the drama of life. Tuttle still hoped to emerge from the spear-carriers and sing a song or two.

The thing about a shandy was that you could make it last. An hour after Peanuts left, Tetzel came in. Of late, the reporter had adopted an air of importance. He stopped inside the door and waited as if for applause. Tuttle hailed him, and, having no better offer, Tetzel joined him.

"How's it going?"

"What?" Tetzel asked, almost alarmed.

"Rebecca told me," Tuttle lied.

"Bullshit."

"That's what she said. I may be able to help you."

Tetzel couldn't decide whether or not Tuttle actually knew of the great feature he was writing on Nathaniel Green. The mention of Rebecca had been an inspiration. Tuttle had overheard her on the phone in the pressroom trying to convince her editor that a story on the paroled wife killer made sense.

"We're already doing one?" she said in her husky voice.

After a while, she hung up, obviously disappointed. Tetzel was her rival. Tuttle put two and two together. The plus sign was the visit Tetzel had paid to Tuttle's office.

Tetzel took a pew and tried to get the attention of Wilma. He shouted his order to her twice before she got it.

"Nathaniel Green has made a new will," Tuttle said in a lowered voice.

"Yeah?"

"Leaving everything to Helen Burke." This was a flagrant breach of confidentiality, but he could always claim that Tetzel must have got the information as a result of journalistic digging because the will was registered. Green had insisted on that, as if to prevent himself from changing his mind. Tetzel's reaction was everything Tuttle had hoped. Not that he was surprised. After all, it was he who had been able to tell Tetzel that Cy Horvath was reviewing the long-ago investigation of the death of Florence Green.

"Save my seat," Tetzel said and went to the bar to get his double bourbon and water, unwilling to wait. When he returned with it he was trying to adopt a nonchalant expression. "Did you say *everything?*"

"The whole kit and caboodle." Well, almost.

"Why the hell would he do that?"

"Ah. That's the story behind the story."

Tuttle had Tetzel's undivided attention when he told him of the efforts of Helen Burke and her son, after the conviction, to take possession of the money that Florence had brought to her marriage. Nathaniel had killed Florence; he shouldn't be allowed to benefit from his crime. At the time, it had sounded like a good argument to Tuttle. Unfortunately the Burkes had first tried to enlist Amos Cadbury in their cause.

Cadbury had pointed out that the money was Nathaniel's before and independently of the crime he had been convicted of. That was when Jason Burke came to Tuttle, wanting a second opinion.

"The claim has merit," Tuttle said carefully.

"You think we can win?"

"Only if the case is properly handled."

Helen Burke had been furious with her son when he told her he'd taken their case to Tuttle. Jason called to tell Tuttle it was all off.

"It's only money," Tuttle said. He was thinking of his fee.

Jason groaned.

"Now, of his own volition, the paroled killer is turning his fortune over to Helen Burke and her son." Tetzel seemed to be composing the sentence as he pronounced it.

Tuttle shook his head. "Just the mother. Helen."

"What'll he live on?" Tetzel wondered.

"Nathaniel? What does everybody else live on?"

"Tell me."

"Social Security. It may not be much, but it's certain."

Tetzel looked as if he were about to dispute that.

Even without the bourbon, Tetzel would have been excited by learning this new twist in the story he was writing. It wasn't just about the past. The future had intervened in the form of a will. The bar was getting noisier and noisier, and Tetzel cocked his good ear toward Tuttle, trying to hear.

"We could go to my office," Tuttle suggested. Hazel would have left by now.

"You got anything there?"

"Pepsi."

"Let's go the pressroom."

That was closer, and Tetzel had a bottle in his desk. Tuttle refused the offer of a drink. He took one taste of the coffee he had poured, then put it on the desk. Rebecca's desk. He was in her chair and swung toward Tetzel.

Tetzel put down the glass after taking a long pull. He turned to his computer. "Now tell me the whole thing again."

"In my own words."

"Monosyllables will be fine."

Like Tetzel earlier, Tuttle felt he was composing as he talked, Tetzel banging away at the keyboard with a minimum of fingers.

"Meanwhile Nathaniel has possession of

103

the money?" At the thought, Tetzel stopped writing.

"While he's alive," Tuttle conceded. "He said he wouldn't touch a penny of it."

"He could change his mind."

"He could die in his bed tonight."

Tetzel thought about that, then nodded. "It doesn't matter. He's still doing now what he's doing."

"Done," Tuttle corrected. "The will is registered. That's how you found out about it."

Tetzel nodded. "What's his motive?"

"I told you. He doesn't want to benefit from his wife's death."

"Who'll believe that?"

Tetzel was obviously thinking what Tuttle himself had thought. This was Nathaniel's way of getting back at Helen, for her attitude during the trial, for her attempt to take from him her sister's money, for the shunning at the St. Hilary parish center.

"Tell me about that."

Tuttle told him what he had heard from Herman the German.

"Who the hell is Herman the German?"

"Janitor at St. Hilary's. A classmate of Nathaniel's."

"Joliet?"

Tuttle nodded.

Tetzel shook his head. "How does Father Dowling get these guys paroled to him?"

"The chaplain at Joliet. Jerome Paxon is their parole officer."

"Both of them?"

"You might talk to him."

Tetzel said something noncommital.

"Tell me how your story is shaping up."

"I have to protect my sources," Tetzel said pompously.

"I don't want protection."

Tetzel understood. He nodded.

"What's the name of Helen Burke's son?"

"Jason."

That had been two days before, and now Tetzel's story had appeared. Tuttle liked it. If only Tetzel had claimed to learn of the will because it had been registered.

After he had read the story, Tuttle took the paper to the outer office and dropped it casually on Hazel's desk. He returned to his own office and waited at his desk, tweed hat pulled over his eyes. Suddenly there was a great whoop from the outer office and then Hazel appeared in his doorway.

"Prominent local attorney!" she cried. "Do you realize how often you're mentioned in this story?"

Tuttle tipped back his hat and tried to

repress the foolish grin that spread across his face. "I tried to be of help to Tetzel."

"He's the man who was here in the office, isn't he?"

"The same."

"How on earth did he hear about the new will?"

A small cloud on the horizon, that. "You know how thorough investigative reporters can be."

"You told him!"

Hazel had once worked for a large firm in Chicago, where she must have picked up some rudiments of legal ethics.

"Nathaniel Green insisted that I register the will. That made it more or less public."

Hazel thought about it. It was a delicate moment. Would she go back to her normal contemptuous attitude toward him? Apparently she found her earlier elation more attractive.

"I am going to clip this," she said. "For the files."

"Good idea."

Tuttle was left to enjoy his ambiguous pleasure. It was annoying that she had made such a point of Nathaniel Green's new will.

2

Jason was already at the Great Wall, sipping a Chinese beer, when Madeline arrived precisely at six. He pushed a copy of the *Tribune* toward her when she sat across from him.

"What's this?"

"Read it."

It was a feature story on the return of Nathaniel Green written by Gearhart Tetzel. Madeline let her eye run through the story, her lips moving in disbelief.

"Reopen the case?" she asked.

Jason turned the page half toward himself and pointed at a paragraph.

"Good Lord!" Madeline cried.

According to Tetzel, Nathaniel had rewritten his will, leaving everything to Helen Burke.

"Does he have anything to leave?"

"Plenty." Jason finished his beer. "You want one of these?"

"I'll have tea. Hot tea. How much is plenty?"

"It's not the amount."

"Have you talked to your mother?"

Jason closed his eyes. "Not yet."

The waitress arrived, and Madeline folded the paper and set it aside. No need to consult the menu; she knew what she wanted. Jason took his time, considering the menu.

"Could you bring the tea?" Madeline asked.

"Another of these, too." Jason flicked a finger at the empty bottle before him, his eye not leaving the menu. Madeline picked up the *Tribune* again, read a paragraph or two, then put it away.

The waitress returned with the tea and another bottle of beer, and Jason ordered. Then he hunched toward Madeline.

"Florence and my mother were the only beneficiaries of my grandfather's will. Fifty-fifty."

"Of what?"

Jason mouthed the amount, then said it aloud. "A couple of million. Apiece."

Madeline just stared.

"Of course, a million now isn't what it was then," Jason said.

Was Jason thinking of the mega-million-dollar lottery jackpots he dreamed of winning? Not only did he buy hundreds of dollars' worth of lottery tickets, he was a member of Gamblers Anonymous. When Helen wasn't financing Jason's newest business venture, she was bailing him out of his gambling debts. He was always genuinely contrite when he had to take a maxed-out credit card to his mother. Madeline thought he found it easier to admit to his gambling than to his drinking. What is there about men like Jason? He brought out the mother in Madeline, too.

Why should she be surprised to find that Helen was so well off? Jason had told her that his father's money had increased exponentially under Carter interest rates and from that point had been coaxed to ever larger amounts. After all, Helen had always been able to rescue Jason from his losses; she had set him up in business time and again. She herself lived a simple life. How many women with that kind of money would spend their days at the St Hilary parish center?

"Nathaniel can always change his will," Jason said.

"After making a public announcement?"

"He didn't make it. I know Tuttle, Madeline. What kind of lawyer would reveal work he had done for a client?"

"Well, you're certainly philosophical about it."

"What do you mean?"

"Whatever your mother has will go to you."

Jason thought a minute, then looked sad.

"I'd just gamble it away."

"Jason, what in the world attracts you to gambling?"

"I wish I knew. It ruined my marriage."

Madeline thought drink had been the major cause, but gambling had certainly played a role. "Do you ever see Carmela?"

Jason shook his head, then looked at her. "Do you?"

"Infrequently."

Jason sat forward. "When's the last time you saw her?"

Madeline found this an unwelcome turn in the conversation; she wasn't sure why. The three of them had been in the same class at St. Hilary's years ago, she, Jason, and Carmela. Jason had been sent off by his mother to a military school in Wisconsin, then to another in Indiana; next she managed to get him into Jesuit prep; after that, giving up, she let him finish at Fox River High. Madeline and Carmela had gone on to an all-girls Catholic high school in Chicago and then to Loyola. In those years, there were still school dances, and when Carmela broke up with the boy she had been going with just before the big spring dance, Madeline, asked if she knew a substitute, thought of Jason. Who would have thought it would be a fatal meeting?

Jason's hair was already thinning, and he was overweight, but he could dance like a dream. His checkered school career had lent him a certain devil-may-care dash, and an enlistment in the navy contributed an exotic veneer. Carmela was smitten by her former grade school classmate. Flattered, Jason had danced away the night with Carmela while Madeline looked on with foreboding. Should she tell Carmela about Jason?

It wouldn't have mattered. That was what she always told herself later. The attraction between the two — it was soon mutual — would have been impervious to cautious reasonableness. Fulton, the boy Madeline was with, thought he had a vocation, and that pretty well defined their relationship. Over Cokes, Fulton asked Jason what he did.

"I'm getting acclimated to civilian life."

"Were you in the service?"

That was when Jason talked about his time in the navy — he called it the Battle of California — and soon he had Carmela in stitches.

"Then what?" Carmela asked.

"I may rob banks."

Who would have seen an omen in his tales of payday card games in the barracks where a month's pay could be lost in hours? He had a flask with which he bolstered his Coke. The others put their hands over their glasses. Alcohol was strictly forbidden at these interschool dances. Madeline found herself as fascinated by Jason as Carmela clearly was. Her cousin had been transformed into a dashing charmer.

"Don't you just love him?" Carmela had asked Madeline in the powder room.

"I could, you know. We're not first cousins."

A silly answer. How could you have a crush on a cousin, second, third, whatever Jason was? From then on Carmela treated Madeline as a rival rather than the friend who had come through in a fix with a date for the big dance.

It was a month later when Madeline learned that, unbeknownst to her, Carmela was seeing a lot of Jason. Fulton had just told her that he would indeed be entering the Dominicans after graduation. Madeline felt abandoned, and now she found that Jason and Carmela had become inseparable.

"Have you met his mother, Carmela?"

"I don't think she likes me."

Madeline was on the point of saying that Aunt Helen didn't like anybody, but she let it go. Her aunt now seemed an insuperable obstacle to any further development.

She was wrong. A week after graduation, Jason and Carmela eloped, returning from a weeklong foray into Indiana man and wife. Madeline, as chance would have it, was there when they sauntered into the house and informed Aunt Helen.

"Married! When? Where?"

She seemed to drop into her chair from the ceiling as the grinning Jason told her. She looked pleadingly at her son, but for Carmela there was only an icy stare.

"A civil ceremony? That doesn't count."

Jason was angered by the remark. "What do you mean, it doesn't count?"

Aunt Helen explained patiently that they were Catholics, that Catholics got married in the Church. How could a son of hers have ever forgotten that? "Or did you?" she murmured.

"What's that supposed to mean?"

Somehow, without actually saying it, Aunt Helen conveyed the thought that such a pseudo-marriage could easily be dissolved. The suggestion had the opposite effect than the one she might have intended. That very day, Jason and Carmela were at the St. Hilary rectory petitioning the Franciscan who was then pastor to bless their marriage. They could not have been luckier in the priest they spoke to. He asked a few questions, smiling all the while, as Jason later described it to Madeline, and the next thing you knew they were in the sacristy having their marriage blessed. Now they were husband and wife enough even for Aunt Helen.

And lived happily ever after? The following years were a tale of woe. Belatedly Carmela came to see the character of the man she had married. What had once seemed charm was now revealed as irresponsibility. He couldn't keep a job. Helen appealed to Amos Cadbury, the family lawyer, and he did what he could. If getting a new job was fairly easy at first, keeping it was something else. Madeline worked; Helen grudgingly subsidized the marriage. There were separations, then reunions. After a while, Madeline tried to know less and less about the doings of the star-crossed couple. It didn't help that she felt responsible for their having met again after years of not so much as remembering one another.

"It's impossible," a tearful Carmela had finally confided in Madeline. Dear God, no intimate revelations, please. No, the problem was more mundane, money.

All Madeline could offer was sympathy, and what good was that?

"His mother is urging him to get an annulment!" Carmela said. "Him! As if it's all my fault."

"Oh, Jason wouldn't do that."

"Maybe he would if he had thought of it first."

They reunited, there was another miscarriage, their second, and then — was it ten years ago? — Carmela had had enough.

She didn't want a divorce, she didn't want an annulment, she just didn't want anything more to do with Jason. Aunt Helen consulted Amos Cadbury and decided this was the best solution that could be hoped for. Money on which Carmela could draw was deposited with Amos Cadbury, and then she was gone from Jason's life.

They kept in touch, Madeline and Carmela. Carmela became a financial advisor, and it seemed obvious she was good at it. It was a little disturbing the way she spoke so fervently of money when they got together from time to time. They were the same age, but only Madeline looked middle-aged.

At the time of Florence Green's death, Carmela dismissed the idea that Nathaniel had killed his wife.

"Do you know him, Madeline? He is the sweetest man, and they were like newlyweds. I could always go to Florence and Nathaniel with my troubles."

"She had cancer."

"And he was at her side during the whole ordeal. Would a man like that kill his wife?"

Madeline didn't want to say how easily it supposedly would have been. Just detach her from the life support system and let her drift into painless peace.

"You know how Helen acted through it all, Madeline. If anyone killed Florence, Helen did."

The absurd accusation seemed excused by all the years Carmela had endured as the daughter-in-law of Helen Burke.

Now all that was in the past. Florence was long since dead, Nathaniel had spent nearly a decade in prison, and now he was back. It pained Madeline to think that Helen's intimidation had prevented her from making Nathaniel welcome at the St. Hilary center.

"When was the last time you saw her?" Jason was asking now.

His eagerness was almost pitiable. It seemed a time to lie.

"I can't remember when," Madeline said.

3

Dogs go willingly and with wagging tails into houses hardly larger than themselves.

Herman had seen it with his own eyes when Paxon his parole officer took him home to dinner. The Paxon dog was big as a bear, and Herman tried to hide his fear. He hated dogs. Then Mrs. Paxon lifted the door on a wire cage right there in the kitchen, and the dog scooted inside. It kind of brought back the Place, as Herman did not tell Paxon. This invitation to the Paxon home was meant to be a glimpse of normalcy.

Well, maybe. Paxon himself was a bit of a nut, a nice nut, but still a nut. He seemed to think he was obliged to believe anything an ex-con told him. He leaned toward you while you talked, forehead wrinkled, eyes full of sympathy, feeling your pain. Mrs. Paxon, Kate, was tall and skinny and oozed a lot less, but she was a good cook. Afterward, while she cleaned up, Paxon and Herman watched hockey on TV. Herman was glad to leave and beat it back to St. Hilary's and his little apartment in the basement of the school. When he shut the door behind him, he felt as happy as the Paxon dog in its cage.

He realized that he had learned to like being alone. Solitude. It was a word from an old song that, like the tune, stuck in his mind. It made enjoying his apartment even better to call it solitude. Solitude, not solitary. Sometimes he thought of it as Command Central.

Scattering sweeping compound, pushing his broom around, Herman kept up on all the parish center news. It wasn't that he was invisible, but his janitorial tasks made him anonymous; people didn't feel they had to drop their voices until he went by. Of course, they thought he was a dumbo. He encouraged that. He always had. It was like a protective coat. He liked telling them of the way he had been sent up. The story had improved over time, of course. Talking with Nathaniel Green was different.

"The truth is I was left holding the bag," Herman admitted.

"They just left you there?" Nathaniel asked.

"Inside the damned bank, with alarms going off. When I got to the door it was locked or jammed, I don't know. Outside the car just took off, leaving me to take the rap."

"Were the others caught?"

"Not for that. Remember Zappia, the big swarthy guy?"

"He was in for murder."

"That was later."

In the Place Herman had kept clear of Zappia. The guy would be a great-grandfather by the time he got out. Such a thought could mellow you, but not Zappia.

Nathaniel sat in silence. He always had a book with him. Herman had often promised himself that he would take up reading. He had even worked for a while in the library in Joliet, hoping to catch the bug. Maybe later.

"What are you reading?"

Herman had never heard of the book or author. He lit a cigarette and directed smoke at the ceiling. The seniors upstairs always stepped outside for a smoke. Life was getting as organized outside as it was inside.

"What's she got against you?" Herman asked.

Nathaniel looked at him for a moment. "Helen Burke? She's my wife's sister."

Herman's head lifted as he raised his eyebrows. "Even so. Why do you take it?"

"I understand her."

He could understand her at a distance. Why come to the center day after day and be treated that way? Did Nathaniel enjoy it? Herman decided that wasn't it. Then the newspaper story appeared, and he began to wonder which of them, Helen or Nathaniel, was the torturer.

Neither Nathaniel nor Helen came to the parish center the day after the story appeared in the paper. It had been hard for Herman to get hold of a copy. The first several he grabbed brought shouts of protest.

"Just cleaning up," Herman said in self-defense.

"That's today's paper."

Finally he got one into the trash cart he wheeled around and retired to his apartment, where he settled down to see if the remarks he had been picking up all morning matched the story in the *Tribune.*

It was the amount of money that impressed Herman. You'd need a Brinks job to get that much. It was funny thinking that he'd had a multimillionaire sitting here in the apartment. A multimillionaire who wanted to give it all away to a woman who didn't need it and had been giving him one helluva of a time since he showed up at the center.

Herman knew that Edna Hospers knew about the treatment Nathaniel was getting. She had called Helen in, but nothing had changed. Herman knew that Edna didn't want him getting too friendly. He understood. Earl was doing fine, running Flanagan Concrete. That made Herman a reminder of where Earl had spent some time. He understood. He even kept away from his own family, now that his mother was dead. Mothers and parole officers will forgive anything.

But the main one for him to keep clear of was Marie Murkin, the rectory housekeeper. The problem was that he couldn't always do that. It was his job to get the rectory trash out to the curb on Wednesdays and check the level of the salt in the water softener in the basement of the rectory. In the area behind the furnace was an old easy chair, one that tilted back. Herman tried it out, closing his eyes and listening to the hum of the water heater, the whir of the furnace. Once he had actually fallen asleep, and Marie woke him.

"You're just like the others," she said. "Do you think we pay you for sleeping?"

We? "You're not my boss," he said, getting out of the chair.

"When you're in this house I am."

"Thanks for the warning."

He thought she was going to shoo him from the house with the broom she clutched in one hand. Or maybe take a little flight on it. Herman got out of there.

Paxon had told him that he had had predecessors in his job, other graduates from Joliet.

"How long did they stay, on the average?"

121

"Until they got fed up with the house-keeper."

Maybe if it hadn't been for Father Dowling, Herman would have been fed up already. Still, it was a good spot for him — the apartment, food, and what Father Dowling called a token salary that seemed enormous to Herman.

"We don't want to put you in too high an income bracket," Father Dowling said.

"Income tax. I've never paid income tax."

"Well, you'll have to start now. But don't worry about it. Amos Cadbury will take care of it."

Herman had his lunch at the parish center but came to the rectory for his evening meal, having it in the kitchen. Father Dowling had wanted Herman to join him in the dining room, and that was one time he appreciated the support of Marie Murkin. Not that she was doing him any favor. Imagine having to serve the janitor at the pastor's table.

"Come just after five," Marie said. "So I can get you out of the way."

Poison? Actually, it was a good arrangement. Marie put his meal on the kitchen table and then disappeared, leaving him to himself. If he saw anyone then, it was Father Dowling.

The rectory was fragrant with pipe smoke. Sometimes strains of music came from the pastor's study, not Herman's kind of music, but pleasant as background. Sometimes he thought that Father Dowling enjoyed solitude the way he did.

The day Marie caught him snoozing in the basement behind the furnace, Father Dowling came into the kitchen while Herman was having his evening meal.

"Do you mind?" he asked, pulling out a chair and sitting across the table from Herman.

"Be my guest, said the guest."

"Would you like a beer?"

"Do you have any?" Herman was surprised. His own drinking was a little secret between himself and Miss Solitude. Father Dowling turned without getting up, plucked a bottle of beer from the icebox, and handed it to Herman.

"So how are you finding things, Herman?"

Oh-oh. Was this going to be like one of his sessions with Jerome Paxon?

"Can't complain, Father."

"I suppose it takes a while to get used to the excitement around here." Father Dowling smiled as he said it. A pause, and then, "You knew Nathaniel Green before, didn't you?"

"Only in the way you get to know someone there. I knew who he was. He was the guy who had the beautiful visitor once a month."

"Really?"

Herman was going to go on about the way they all hung around on visiting day for the woman's arrival, but then he remembered that Father Dowling was a priest. Herman busied himself opening the beer.

"I suppose you knew the chaplain."

Father O'Connell. He was called Barney, after the character in *The Flintstones*. Herman nodded.

Father Dowling said, "We were classmates."

"At Joliet?"

Father Dowling had a sense of humor, all right. He tipped back his head and laughed.

Marie Murkin bustled in the back door and stopped, looking at the pastor and Herman at her kitchen table.

"Well, this looks cozy." She was staring at Herman's bottle of beer.

Herman lifted it to her in a toast and took a long swig. Marie made a face and busied herself with the dinner she was preparing for the pastor. Father Dowling lit his pipe, and soon the room was a cloud of wonderful pipe smoke. Marie coughed and waved her hand, but if she wasn't used to the

124

pastor's pipe she wouldn't be here.

Herman hurried up with his meal, chug-a-lugged what was left of the beer, and stood. Father Dowling did, too. He came out on the back porch with Herman. From inside, Marie called, "Now don't go running off. Dinner's in fifteen minutes."

4

Later that night, Phil Keegan stopped by. Once he and the pastor were settled in the study, Marie went up the back stairway to her apartment.

Phil was scowling as he unwrapped a cigar. "You see the paper?"

Father Dowling knew he was referring to Tetzel's story on Nathaniel Green. "Tuttle must be pleased. I don't know about Nathaniel."

"Helen Burke wants to sue him."

"Tetzel?"

"No, Tuttle." Phil got his cigar going, one of the cheap ones by the smell of it.

"Whatever for?"

"The new will. Tuttle made it out, and she claims he committed a breach of legal ethics by revealing it."

"How did you learn that?"

"She came downtown, mad as a wet hen.

She seemed to think I would hurry out and arrest Tuttle. I suggested she go have a talk with Amos Cadbury."

Father Dowling nodded in approval. "Amos will calm her down."

"Tuttle is just a target of opportunity."

Father Dowling pondered that, drawing meditatively on his pipe. The new will, public or not, certainly put Helen Burke on the spot. The man whose conviction she had wanted, attending every session of the trial, the man whom, after his release from Joliet and appearance at the St. Hilary center, she had ostracized, enlisting the others in her campaign, now turned the other cheek and delivered over to her everything he had in the world.

It is one of the paradoxes of Christianity that following its maxims can sometimes amount to the sweetest revenge rather than charity. There was a text in St. Paul suggesting that. Turn the other cheek, for another instance. Nathaniel had certainly done that, during the long shunning campaign, accepting it with a meekness that was edifying, unless, of course, his motive had been to infuriate his sister-in-law. Now this public news that he was making his chief tormentor the beneficiary of his will could be an instance of almost heroic virtue, or . . .

It occurred to Father Dowling that the will was a kind of threat, a future rather than a present humiliation for Helen Burke. Still, how was it possible to think of it as the mild Nathaniel Green's revenge?

Phil wasn't interested in such fancy speculation. "Cy is still looking into the death of Florence Green."

"What's the point?"

"That we don't have a lot of work at the moment."

The idea that Cy Horvath would devote himself to a pointless task rather than loll around the detective division, catch up on paperwork, doing the dozen things daily officialdom called for, seemed out of character and quixotic.

"Quick what?" Phil scowled. "We gonna watch the game?"

Spring training had begun, and the Cubs were on in an intersquad practice game. Sometimes it seemed that all the sports would overlap, football, basketball, hockey, baseball all in one season. The bread and circuses of modern man. Father Dowling was enough of a modern man to tell Phil to turn on the television.

"Get yourself a beer, Phil."

"I'm giving it a rest."

"Oh."

"Last night I counted up the drinks I've had in the past week." Phil shook his head. "I was drinking at the time. It's the danger of living alone. I cleared everything out of the apartment. From now on, I only drink in the line of duty."

Father Dowling smiled. "I thought that's when you don't drink."

"That's what I mean. Look, I'm not taking the pledge or anything."

It might have been an allusion to Father Dowling's own onetime problem with drink. As a member of the archdiocesan marriage court, one of the bright young priests, a doctorate in canon law, apparently destined for higher things, he had become so weighed down with the futile appeals for annulment at a time when they were still more or less unthinkable that he had sought relief in drink. It was solitary drinking that was the real danger, Phil was right about that. Phil stood.

"Maybe I will have a beer. You want anything?"

"A Diet Pepsi."

Phil made a face and went off to the kitchen. Father Dowling doubted that Phil had any real problem, but he was wise to be careful. In any case, beer in the rectory while he watched television with the pastor was in line with Phil's apparent resolution.

"Has Cy come up with anything new?" he asked when Phil was back and settled.

"He said he'd let me know."

That didn't sound promising.

The things that stick in your mind. The following day, Father Dowling found himself remembering Herman's remark about the woman who had visited Nathaniel Green every month while he was in Joliet. Then he remembered that Madeline, the woman who was helping Edna at the center, was a distant relative of Nathaniel's. He went down the path to the school, through the former gym, waving and acknowledging greetings, and up the stairs to Edna's office. As he went up, he met Madeline coming down.

"Hello, Father."

Father Dowling stopped, one hand on the stair railing. "Edna has nothing but good things to say of you, Madeline."

She grew flustered. "I wish I could think I deserved it. I do like being here."

"You should be on the payroll."

"Oh, there's no need for that."

"I suppose that newspaper story has everyone talking."

Madeline lifted her eyes. "My Aunt Helen

hasn't been here for several days."

"And your uncle?"

She seemed surprised. "Oh, you mean Nathaniel."

"I understood you were his niece."

"Oh, nothing so close. My mother married his cousin. I don't really know what that makes me."

"The daughter of Nathaniel's cousin."

"Does that make me his niece?"

"I have no idea."

Madeline started down the stairs, and Father Dowling continued up. Madeline didn't strike him as the femme fatale who had visited Nathaniel monthly at Joliet according to Herman, but then the pastor was celibate. And he'd never been cooped up in prison, not a thought flattering to Madeline.

Edna looked up from her desk, and her face broke into a smile. Father Dowling took a chair facing her.

"Madeline tells me Helen Burke isn't here."

"Not for several days."

"And Nathaniel?"

"Wasn't he at your noon Mass? He said he was going over there."

Had he been? Father Dowling was not in the habit of checking the congregation while he said Mass. In any case, he was now saying Mass *ad orientem,* facing away from the people, in the way he had said Mass as a young priest. It had come as something of a surprise to see that the rubrics for saying the *Novus Ordo* assumed that the celebrant was facing away from the congregation, leading them in prayer, addressing God, rather than smiling out at them, seeking eye contact, and checking who was in the pews. Nathaniel had yet to come forward for communion, which was the only way Father Dowling would have known he was in the church.

"I didn't notice. How do he and Madeline get along?"

5

The realization that two of those who came to the St. Hilary senior center were not just comfortable but well off, rich, caused mixed reaction. That Nathaniel Green, the man they had shunned, possessed the amount of money he was leaving to his sister-in-law Helen Burke brought on sheepish second thoughts from those who had fallen in with Helen's treatment of her brother-in-law. Who could contest her reason? Nathaniel by his own admission had killed his wife,

Florence, Helen's sister. Not only did he not deny it, he insisted that he was guilty; he was tried and convicted and had spent long years in Joliet. As long as he could be thought of, when he was thought of at all, as a wife killer, there had been little unease. And Nathaniel kept to himself, as often as not reading, either outside the building or in one of the classrooms that lined the main corridor of the school. Now all that had changed.

Nathaniel's new will suggested an indifference to money, and that money added to what Helen already had made her a far less sympathetic creature.

"He hasn't given it away yet," Eugene said to Herman.

"It's in his will."

"He's probably counting on her going first."

Eugene found little sympathy for such cynicism, and he dropped it. Natalie was stunned to learn that her relatives were so wealthy.

"Your relatives?" Eugene asked.

"We have the same grandfather. On my mother's side."

Eugene figured that in the end everyone was related to everyone else, if Adam and Eve were indeed the parents of us all.

Eugene, at Natalie's urging, had been visiting Father Dowling, learning about the faith.

"What stumps me is the Trinity," Eugene said.

Father Dowling took his pipe from his mouth. "The Trinity."

"I just don't get it. Three persons, one nature." He shook his head.

"No one understands it, Eugene. It's a mystery. We believe it, not because it makes sense to us, or as if we would have thought of it eventually anyway, but because it was revealed." The pastor reviewed the scriptural texts that were at the basis of the belief.

"We acknowledge that mystery every time we make the sign of the cross. You know the words? 'In the name of the Father, and of the Son, and of the Holy Spirit.' "The priest traced a cross on himself as he said the words. Eugene followed suit.

"Eugene, you don't have to be a Catholic to come to the center, you know."

"Oh, I know that."

"What prompted your interest?"

Eugene dropped his eyes. "Natalie Armstrong."

"Ah." Father Dowling seemed to be waiting for more, but Eugene let it go at that. He wasn't sure he had made the right choice with Natalie. But how was he supposed to know that Helen Burke was loaded? Relatives. Apparently money didn't run in the family. From what Natalie had let him know, not really knowing she was, her life suggested a comfortable widowhood and not much more. Not that he was dropping her. That would have been difficult in any case, given how much time the two of them were spending together. It had all been at the center; Eugene had yet to carry his campaign farther afield.

When he couldn't get away to Herman's apartment, Eugene went off to the noon Mass with Natalie. Most of those who came to the center went. Sitting beside Natalie, who knelt and stood and rattled off the prayers, Eugene didn't know what to make of it. The first time, he had started toward the front at communion time, but Natalie had put a hand on his arm and shaken her head. When she returned, she knelt and put her face in her hands and didn't stir for minutes.

The newspaper story made Eugene curious about Nathaniel, and he began to seek the man out, joining him on his bench, lighting a cigarette. It took a while to break the ice, but Eugene got around to telling

Nathaniel that he was impressed by his generosity.

"You can't take it with you," Nathaniel said.

"I suppose you must have thought of spreading it around."

"How do you mean?"

"Well, leaving everything to a woman who really doesn't need it."

"She probably thinks it's hers anyway."

"I would have left something to St. Hilary's," Eugene said. "Maybe I will."

"Oh, I've done that, and there are other relatives who will benefit, but the bulk will go to Helen."

"I suppose you've got a lot of relatives."

"You'd be surprised."

Well, Eugene had been surprised, pleasantly, by what Nathaniel had said. Would those other relatives include Natalie? Eugene rose. "I'd better get back to my beloved."

"Your beloved?"

"A manner of speaking. Natalie Armstrong. Do you know her?"

"Know her? I'm related to her."

It was all Eugene could do not to sit down again and ask Nathaniel directly if he had remembered Natalie in his will, but the whole conversation seemed to assure him that Nathaniel had indeed done that. Eugene went off down the path toward the school with a springy step.

6

To the imagined strains of "Hail the Conquering Hero," Tetzel strolled into the pressroom at the courthouse. He sat at his desk, he flicked on his computer, he lit a cigarette, he was ignored. Rebecca went on knitting, looking at him over the rims of her glasses. McGonagle, a storklike teenager from the Fox River High School paper, sat squeezing his pimples as he read the *Sun-Times*. On a Naugahyde couch, Peanuts Pianone, with a Styrofoam cup of coffee in his meaty hands, stared straight ahead. Tetzel felt his balloon slowly deflate before this indifference.

His story on the return of Nathaniel Green was the talk of the town, certainly of the courthouse. On his way to the pressroom, Tetzel had heard the buzz, was certain he was the cynosure of every eye. He was on top of the world. He had just come from Menteur, his editor.

"I hardly changed a word, Gerry."

This was high praise from Menteur.

There was actually a ripple of applause when he left the city room. He could have floated to the courthouse, where his sense of having scored a ten-strike with his story was strengthened when Bennie, the blind man who ran the newstand off the lobby, told him he was all sold out.

"They been buying them by the armfuls."

Did he imagine that room was made for him in the elevator, a special deference shown? A little lady in the back of the car was reading his story as they rose. So to the pressroom and this cold and churlish response. Rebecca seemed ready to pounce if he brought up his story. Tetzel was about to ask her if she'd had any responses to her ad in the personals when Tuttle arrived.

The little lawyer came directly to Tetzel, genuflected, grabbed his hand, kissed it, then, struggling to his feet, swept off his tweed hat, and cried out.

This story shall the good man teach his
  son
And Crispin Crispian shall ne'er go by
From this day to the ending of the world
But we in it shall be remembered.
We few, we happy few, we band of broth-
  ers.

The paper from which he had been reading fluttered from his hand.

McGonagle, openmouthed, had stood during the recitation.

"What's that from?" Rebecca asked.

"The Internet," Tuttle replied, not looking at her. "You look dry, Gerry. Do you have time to wet your whistle?"

Tetzel was on his feet, glad for an excuse to get out of the pressroom.

"Come on along, Peanuts," Tuttle said as they left the room.

To many, the Jury Room, the bar across the street, seemed an extension of the courthouse, integral to its effective operation. Tuttle stepped back, to let Tetzel enter first and be greeted by a standing ovation. Friends, acquaintances, strangers clapped, banged glasses on the table, whistled. Tetzel was all but overcome. By God, this was more like it.

"Order up," Wiley, the smiling proprietor, cried, and soon waitresses were scooting about in response to eager calls. Wiley himself brought Tetzel's usual, a triple bourbon with very little water. Tuttle and Peanuts had to wait for the waitress to come around.

"I don't know what to say," Tetzel said.

"You can afford it."

It was then that Tetzel realized that this

celebratory round was on him. The hell with it. It was worth it. He took a long salubrious pull on his drink. Over the next fifteen minutes happy drinkers came to congratulate Tetzel, and he held court with dignity. The waitress had trouble getting Tuttle's root beer and Peanuts's brown ale onto the table.

When the tumult and the shouting subsided, Tuttle said, "I hear Helen Burke wants to sue."

"No kidding." The prospect of further fallout from his story pleased Tetzel, and his pleasure did not diminish when Tuttle explained that he was the object of her wrath.

"Get a good lawyer," Tetzel advised.

"Hey."

A day begun like that had nowhere else to go but down. Tetzel remained when Tuttle and Peanuts took their leave. The thought of the tab he had already run up by that round for the house and what he added to it during the following hours filled him with an odd elation. The bar emptied, then filled again, over and over, and still Tetzel stayed on, his soggy whistle wetted to a fare-thee-well.

In midafternoon, the melancholy thought occurred that this could be the high point of his journalistic career. He had scored a coup, no doubt of that, but with familiarity the thought began to lose its power to lift his spirits. He lifted the spirits in his glass, but they no longer brought on a renewal of his sense of triumph. An idea grew in him. He must follow up the Nathaniel Green story with another equally impressive. But what would it be?

His thoughts were jumbled now. He decided to leave and half an hour later acted on this resolve. Outside, sunlight and the chill in the air lightened his head. He stepped into the street but was pulled back from the path of a careening taxi. Then he went with the crowd across the street to the courthouse.

The ride up in the elevator was a solitary one. He emerged from the car and walked with careful deliberation to the pressroom. Only McGonagle was there. Tetzel sat at his computer. There was an e-mail message from Menteur he could not make out, even when he closed one eye.

"Hey, kid," he said to McGonagle. "Come here."

McGonagle came.

"Read that to me. I got something in my eye."

McGonagle leaned toward the screen and

read. Would the message have seemed less annoying if it had not come in the piping tones of the teenager?

"Get going on the story about smoking in the courthouse."

7

Dr. Pippen, the assistant coroner, was in the cafeteria, a cup of yogurt in one hand, plastic spoon in the other, and the *Tribune* open before her. Cy sat down across from her, and she looked up, distracted, and then her eyes brightened and he got the big smile and toss of the head he needed.

"What do you think of it?" he asked. Of course she was reading Tetzel's story.

"Where did he take creative writing, Cy?"

"Tuttle."

"Will there be a retrial?"

"There might have been an appeal, years ago, I suppose."

Pippen folded the paper and pushed it aside. "Is it true that you're reexamining the whole thing?"

"It's a slow time."

Pippen sat back, and a ray of sun caught her golden hair. "That's what you think."

"What do you mean?"

"Bring your coffee. I'll show you."

Cy followed her out of the cafeteria, and they took the elevator down to her office in the morgue. Lubins, the nominal coroner, wasn't there, of course. Some years before, Lubins had been defeated as county commissioner and then, all unqualified, been given the nomination for coroner. He had had the good sense to hire Pippen to do the job he had been elected to do.

"You ought to oppose him in the primary," Cy said.

"And end up on one of these slabs?"

She had taken him into a frigid room, the centerpiece of which was a kind of operating table over which hung various instruments suggestive of the Inquisition. Cameras were trained on the table, and a microphone hung over it. Pippen went to one of the drawers along the wall and pulled it out. The body was blueish, shriveled, an overweight middle-aged man.

"Where was he found?"

"In the river, in a pizza delivery car. The light on the roof was still on."

"Was the pizza still warm?"

She punched his arm.

"What a way to go," Cy said.

"What do you mean?"

"Drowning."

"If only he had rolled down a window, he

might have escaped. I don't suppose you think too clearly in such circumstances."

"Got any more bodies?"

She leaned toward him. "Do you know, I almost wish there were. I don't know what I'd do without crossword puzzles."

"Are you still in the reading group?"

She crossed her eyes. Cy could have hugged her. Sometimes it was difficult to think of Pippen as if she were his little sister.

"We're actually reading *The Godfather.* All we do is compare it to the movie."

Cy shrugged. Maybe even the Pianones could be turned into sympathetic characters with the right treatment.

After he left Pippen, Cy checked out the body in the pizza delivery car. The case was still being treated as an accident. He had Phil Keegan have everything transferred to the detective bureau. He began reading the reports of the patrol squad that had been at the scene when the car was discovered and pulled out of the river. Apparently it had not submerged. No doubt that was why the roof light was still burning. It was the light that attracted attention and triggered a 911 call. Cy had shaken the victim's effects onto his desk when Agnes Lamb came in.

"The guy in the river?" she asked.

"How did you know?"

"Pippen told me."

Agnes pulled up a chair and watched as Cy dealt money and plastic-encased cards and other odds and ends from the wallet onto the table. The change had probably been in the man's pocket. Along with the rosary. Agnes picked up the driver's license.

"The family been notified?"

Cy looked at her. "Check with accidents."

She pulled his phone toward her and made the call. Her eyes widened, and the corner of her mouth went down. She shook her head at Cy.

"Thank you. We'll take care of it."

She picked up a pencil and made a note of the address on the driver's license. Then she just looked at Cy. "They said they called several times and no one answered."

"We'll go together," he said.

If nothing else, it was a change from stirring up the ashes surrounding the death of Florence Green. Reconstructing events that had occurred that long ago wasn't easy, especially if you weren't sure it was even remotely important. Nathaniel Green had been tried and convicted, which was what he had wanted; he had served his time and was now out. His release might have passed without notice if it hadn't been for that idiot

144

Tetzel, no doubt urged on by Tuttle. What really irked Cy was the suggestion in Tetzel's story that the Fox River police, specifically Cy Horvath, were determined to get to the bottom of the matter at last. The implication was that Nathaniel had been wrongly accused and sentenced and a reversal was in order.

It was old Gleason, the doctor who had been the Green family physician and stayed close even after his patient was turned over to the oncologists, who cast a kind of light on things. When all hope had gone, the experts disappeared, and Gleason had checked on his patient daily, sometimes several times a day.

"They were friends as well as patients," he explained to Cy, lighting up a cigarette. He noticed Cy's surprise. "Nine out of ten doctors smoke Camels."

"I remember that."

"So does the surgeon general." He shook his head. "Where do they find these people?" He meant the surgeon general.

"Did Nathaniel take his wife off the life support system?"

"Maybe."

"Why?"

"Are you Catholic?"

Cy nodded.

"Okay. Florence is moribund, despondent, close to despair. When the hospital chaplain came by, she just waved him away. Nate told me this. Finally he got her to agree to the last rites, from their parish priest. So now she was ready to go through the pearly gates. I think Nate feared another bout of despair."

Gleason drew deeply on his cigarette and then expelled inhaled smoke from his nostrils as well as his mouth. Cy watched the old doctor's ears to see if any smoke would come out of them.

"Nate would have thought he'd bought her a first-class ticket to heaven."

It was fanciful but to a Catholic plausible. Of course, his wife's inevitable death provided motive enough to just get it over. If Nathaniel had pulled the plug, that is. One of the curiosities was that the oxygen petcock had been turned off. Before or after the mask was taken from Florence Green's mouth? How, after all these years, could you find the answer to that? Did it matter, since Nathaniel took responsibility for both?

"Do you know Helen Burke, Doctor?"

"She was my patient, too. Maybe impatient would be the best word. Her husband, too, poor devil."

"Tell me about him."

"What's there to tell? A completely bland character, a financial wizard who was beaten into submission by Helen Armstrong, as she once was. She only married him because Nathaniel married Florence. Life is a soap opera, Horvath. Never forget that."

Cy promised to keep it in mind.

"Some people just will themselves to die. Burke was one of them."

"What did he die of?"

"He had a cold. He went to bed. It developed into pneumonia. He said nothing, and by the time Helen noticed it was far advanced. He was a goner by the time I got him to the hospital."

"What did he do for a living?"

"Clip coupons. I think that was their main recreation."

"Money of his own?"

"Piles. Do you remember Burke Cleaners and Dyers? The buyer changed the name of the chain."

"And Florence had money of her own?"

"Money is never the answer." Gleason was full of epigrams.

"What's the question?"

Gleason squinted through the smoke. "Why did God make me?"

The only thing going against the consensus of those who still remembered that Nathaniel had done what he said was the chronology Cy had drawn up. If it was accurate — and who could be sure of memories after all this time? — Nathaniel must have been down the hall in the bathroom when the alarm went off at the nurses' station, indicating that Florence's life support system had been detached. The pizza car in the river, its driver drowned, was a welcome distraction from all this ancient history.

The name on the driver's license, James Thomas, and the address brought Cy and Agnes to an ancient apartment building in the middle of Fox River. The outside door was open; in the entryway was a bank of mailboxes, each with a button to push and a little grid to speak through. Agnes ran her finger over them and stopped at the last one. She pressed the button. There was no name on the little slip on the door of the box, only MGR. It took three pushes on the button before a voice crackled through the little grid as if it were coming from outer space.

"Police," Agnes said.

Fifteen seconds went by. "Again?"

Cy leaned toward the speaker. "Police," he said in a very loud voice.

"Okay, okay."

They waited by the locked inner door, but it was the street door that opened. The man weighed about a hundred pounds. He wore corduroy pants and a sweatshirt with NOTRE DAME on it. He kept the street door open as he looked over Agnes and Cy.

"I don't see Thomas's name on any of the boxes."

"You from bankruptcy court?"

"Why would you think that?"

"Talk to Mrs. Thomas. If she's in." He let the door close behind him, went to the bank of mailboxes, and pressed the button on unit four. "Better let me talk," he said to Cy.

A woman's voice was heard, and then the manager was telling her there was someone here to see her.

"The police?" came a voice.

"How did you know?"

"I called them. Send them up."

The manager shook his head and unlocked the inner door. "My place is downstairs," he explained.

"What's your name?" Agnes asked.

"Charlie Brown."

"Come on."

"It is. And it was before that damned cartoon."

■ ■ ■ ■

Apartment four was on the first floor. Why had she said to send them up? Probably because she thought Thomas was calling from the basement. The door was open. Mrs. Thomas stood in it.

"Well, that was fast," she said, stepping aside and waving them inside. "I hope you can find Jack as quickly."

The apartment was filled with a delicious aroma. Cy let Agnes do the talking. Mrs. Thomas had just called in a missing person report on her husband.

"When did you last see him?"

"He took out an order two nights ago."

"An order?"

"We started a pizza business." Apparently in the kitchen, by the aroma. She seemed to be waiting for Agnes's reaction. "It was Jack's idea."

"How long have you been at it?" Agnes asked.

"A month, a little more. So far, we're relying on flyers and word of mouth."

"How's it going?"

She looked from Agnes to Cy and back again. "We've had threats."

"Tell me about it."

"A phone call. Then someone let the air out of the car's tires. Can you imagine anyone thinking of us as a threat?"

"Why pizza?"

"You ever taste one of mine and you wouldn't ask." She slumped inside her voluminous dress and took a hankie from the pocket of her apron. "We declared bankruptcy."

"I thought you said you were doing okay."

"Oh, not the pizza thing. We're doing that because Jack is determined he is going to pay back every penny we owe. Even though the court wiped it all out."

Cy marveled at the way Agnes managed to turn the conversation to the fact that they wanted Mrs. Thomas to come along with them.

"Where?"

"Downtown."

Her eyes became wary. "You've found him."

She began to weep then, as if she knew what lay ahead. Agnes comforted her and not long after was leading her out to the car. Cy followed, thanking God he had not come alone. Good old Agnes.

After Mrs. Thomas had identified the body and been sustained by both Pippen and Agnes, Cy escaped to his office. The

151

pizza was in a kind of thermal satchel. That was when Cy noticed where the order was meant to go. The Foot Doctor.

8

Eric, the salesman at the Foot Doctor, had discovered the break-in only after he opened up the store and began getting ready for the day. When he went back to the stockroom he noticed that Mr. Burke's office door was open. Drawers of the filing cabinet were pulled out; the lounge chair had been pushed over, the wastebasket emptied on the desk.

Cy Horvath and Agnes Lamb listened to this tale from the young man, whose Adam's apple seemed proof of the inerrancy of Scripture.

"What's missing?" Agnes asked.

Cy could see that she was still trying to figure out why he had decided that they should respond to the patrol car report. Cy had sent Mintz, the officer who had responded to Eric's call, on his way. "We'll take care of it."

Eric didn't know what was missing. "But just look at this office."

"You call the boss?"

"It's not yet noon."

Cy let it go. He had Jason's address, and it seemed a good idea to call on him in his native habitat.

"Lock the door of the office," Cy said. "We'll be back."

"I can stay open?"

"Of course. And don't mention this to any customers."

"Are you kidding?"

Agnes was driving, and Cy gave her directions.

"That's public housing," she said.

"It used to be. The units are up for sale."

"Being gentrified?"

"If you say so."

Gentrified? Agnes was full of surprises. She had put in a couple of years at the community college before applying to the police department. She had to take the tests twice, to prove she hadn't been cheating. Given her score, it was a pardonable suspicion, but there was probably a trace of prejudice in it, too.

"Why do you want to be a cop?" Cy asked her, when she was assigned to the detective division after a stint patrolling with Peanuts Pianone.

"Know your enemy." But she smiled when she said it.

"Peanuts?"

"Is he retarded?"

"Just a cop."

The area was several blocks of row houses that still bore the effects of residents who hadn't really given a damn about their condition. The buildings had declined to the point where the city had to make a decision between spending a lot of tax dollars to fix them up or putting them on the market. If there had been no takers, they would have been torn down, but there had been takers. The units could be had for a pittance, and a lot of remodeling had gone on, but the row house in which Jason Burke lived was still untouched.

The storm door hung askew on its hinges and was unlocked. Cy opened it, tried the bell, figured it didn't work, and pounded on the door. He had to pound twice more before there was the sound of a key turning. The door opened slightly, and Jason Burke looked out over a chain.

"Good morning," Cy said.

"What do you want?"

"Police."

"I didn't call the police."

"Eric did."

"Eric?" The door closed, there was the sound of the chain, and then the door opened again. Jason was wearing pajama bottoms and a T-shirt. The hair on the sides of his head was wild; his eyes were puffy.

"Can we come in?"

He clearly didn't want to ask them in, but he did. He stepped aside, and Cy and Agnes walked into chaos. There are kinds of messiness. Some kinds make sense, a sort of haphazard order, but Jason's place was not of that sort. This was just a mess. Clothes, newspapers, books, plates, and cups. Glasses. The glass beside the couch — a sagging four-cushion affair — still had an inch of drink in it. A nightcap or a morning eye-opener? The place had the feel of a lair.

"What's this about Eric?" Jason demanded.

"Your store was broken into."

He absorbed that. "What did they take?"

"You'll have to tell us that. Why don't you go back there with us?"

"But I'm not up yet." It was ten of eleven.

"Thieves wait for no man," Agnes said. "Nice place you got here."

"It's temporary."

"What isn't?"

For the first time he smiled and looked like a human being. A nice guy, actually. Agnes had made a conquest.

"We used to live here," she said. "The next row house, middle unit."

"No kidding."

"Why would I kid about a thing like that? We all wept when we moved out."

"That sad to leave?"

"That glad to go."

"I've gotten used to it," Jason said.

Cy was trying to figure out why the son of Helen Burke was living in such squalor.

Jason tried to smooth down his wild side hair. "I have to take a shower."

"We'll wait."

He shrugged and disappeared, pulling a door shut behind him.

"You think he's got someone in there?" Agnes whispered.

"Shame on you."

"He's kind of cute."

"His family has money. This doesn't make sense."

"He fits right in."

Agnes had picked up an ashtray with a casino logo on it. "Gambling as well as booze," she said.

"They go together."

"Like a horse and carriage."

She walked around the room, avoiding the mess, an odd expression on her face.

"Boy, does this bring it all back."

"How long did you live here?"

"I don't like to think of it."

All the residents would have been black then, Cy thought. It was odd how you learned things about people you worked with. Well, what did Agnes know of him?

Jason wasn't quite transformed when he emerged, but his appearance had improved. You could almost mistake him for a man who owned a shoe store.

"We'll follow you," Agnes said when they went outside. "You didn't lock the door."

"I only lock it when I'm inside," Jason said enigmatically.

He drove a clunker whose motor had to make up its mind to respond to the starter. Finally it clattered into life. He put out a hand and waved and then started off.

"His family has money?" Agnes asked.

"Lots."

"Maybe he's just eccentric."

"Being gentrified does that to you."

When they entered the Foot Doctor, Eric was sitting on a stool watching a kid try on tennis shoes. He started to rise, but Jason told him to go on with what he was doing. Eric seemed disappointed.

Jason unlocked his office, stood in the doorway, and looked around. "What's the problem?"

Agnes looked at Cy. Well, considering the

condition of the place in which he lived, the office looked almost neat.

Jason went in, pushed the file drawers shut with his hip, and righted the chair. "I should have done that before I left."

"You tipped the chair over."

"I'm kind of clumsy."

"The wastepaper basket?"

"I was looking for something, and I thought I might have thrown it out."

"You're saying this is a false alarm?" Agnes asked him.

"Eric is a good kid, but excitable. Did he say the door was locked when he got here?"

Agnes said, "I'll ask him."

When she came back, she said, "It was locked."

"There you are," Jason said, giving her a big smile.

It would be pretty hard to persuade someone who denied it that his place had been broken into.

Cy said, "What's in back?"

"The stockroom. A john. Another room."

"Show me."

The stockroom was just metal shelving filled with shoe boxes. The john was a john. In the other room Jason checked the little fridge.

"Nothing missing," he said. He had hesitated.

"You sure?"

"This is a false alarm, Lieutenant." He was addressing Agnes. "I'm sorry."

"Your tax dollars at work," Agnes said.

He came with them to the front door and stood in it while they went out to the car. Before she got behind the wheel, Agnes waved good-bye. Jason waved back. She settled behind the wheel.

"Why is he lying, Cy?"

"Good question."

9

Amos Cadbury was now seventy-eight, and aging had seemed to move him ever further from the era of rectitude, civility, and sanity in which his career had begun. There had been a time when the back cover of the telephone directory was not aglitter with the advertisements of law firms eagerly seeking business, usually from those with alleged injuries from accidents or complaints against the products they freely bought and consumed and then turned on in remorseful wrath. Gluttons sued the fast-food chains that catered to their appetites, likening the multicolored photographs of cholesterol-filled offerings to criminal and culpable temptations. Eventually someone would sue God rather than blame his troubles on his own weakness. Lawyers could be found who were not only willing but eager to aid and abet such nonsense. Against this background, Nathaniel Green's new will, leaving all but everything to his vindictive sister-in-law, carried a note of nobility that cheered Amos. Helen had come to him demanding that he bring a suit against Tuttle.

"What would be the charge, Helen?" Amos asked patiently. What a contrast the woman was to her brother-in-law.

"Don't lawyers have an ethical code? He told that reporter about work he had done for Nathaniel. Confidential work."

"Are you sure of that?"

"What do you mean?"

"Nathaniel might have released Tuttle from confidentiality in the transaction."

It was an odd position for Amos to occupy, defending the ineffable Tuttle. The little lawyer frequently skated near the increasingly fuzzy line that separated ethical from unethical behavior. He had often been brought before the local bar, threatened with the loss of his license. Amos had served on those boards. In another time, he might have landed on Tuttle like a Torquemada, but now Tuttle's behavior scarcely differed from that of many of his fellow lawyers. In the dark of night all cats are black.

"You don't know that," Helen said.

"Would you like me to find out?"

Helen threw up her hands. "I suppose he would lie."

"Putting that to one side, what do you think of the provisions of the new will? Of course, I know only what I have read in the paper."

"He wanted it made public, Amos Cadbury," Helen said, undermining the claim that had brought her to his office.

"He is being very generous," Amos said.

"Generous! It's Florence's money."

"Isn't this what you once demanded he do?"

Helen looked around the office with wild and angry eyes.

"That's what makes it so. . . ." She could not find the word. "He wants to humiliate me."

Amos had heard from Father Dowling of the treatment of Nathaniel that Helen had enforced at the parish center. He had heard, too, of her tearful admission to Edna Hospers that her conduct was reprehensible. Amos felt a wave of sympathy with Helen that was strengthened when he thought of her son.

"How is Jason? This will affect him, too, eventually."

"When I am dead?" Helen said in the mournful tones of one who did not seriously believe in her own mortality. "Can you imagine what he would do with money, without restraints?"

"How is the shoe store going?"

"The Foot Doctor!" Helen cried. To such disfavor had the Burkes come.

Amos had done the legal work for this new enterprise, as he had for Jason's earlier entrepreneurial efforts. The location was good; people would always need shoes. With an accountant and reliable help even Jason should be able to make a go of it.

"Has he overcome his weaknesses?"

Helen seemed about to deny that her son drank and gambled. "As far as I know," she said finally. It was as good an answer as any. If things went bad, she would be the first to know, confronted by a contrite Jason in need of maternal bailing out. Helen had reacted with horror to Amos's suggestion, after Jason's last debacle, that she simply leave her son to his fate.

"They'd put him in jail!"

"Helen, that might frighten him into serious resolution."

"If I could believe that, Amos, I would be tempted."

Unblessed by children of his own, Amos alternated between envying those with children and grandchildren and seeing the benefit he derived from not having any. Of course, that was selfish. Annoying as Helen Burke was, she continued to support her wayward son.

"Perhaps, if he and Carmela . . ."

"No! I trace all his troubles to her."

"I don't think that's fair, Helen."

"You don't know her as well as I do."

Actually Amos knew Carmela a good deal better than Helen did. At first, Carmela had drawn sparingly on the money that had been placed in Amos's care for her when she and Jason separated, but in recent years, once she had become a financial planner, she had become, if not a frequent, then a regular caller. It was usually an investment prospect that brought Carmela to Amos's office.

"You might want to invest in it yourself, Amos."

He smiled.

"Who does handle your investments?"

"You make that sound like a task. I take care of things myself, Carmela."

The years of wanting to amass more and more wealth were long behind Amos. He had never fully accepted the thought that money should earn money, at least in the way that was done in the stock market. One of his professors at Notre Dame had reviewed medieval theories on the matter and ended by asking if the class thought the ban on usury had been abrogated. The consensus was that the medieval economy and the modern economy were so different that those old strictures no longer applied. Amos had neither agreed nor disagreed, but throughout his long life he had often surprised in himself a medieval disdain for the antics of Wall Street. In his private restroom here at the office he had hung a framed photograph of Wall Street traders frantically waving slips, buying, selling. They all looked mad, in both senses of the term. Now Amos had almost everything in tax-free municipals. It simplified his income tax and gave him the comforting sense that he was benefiting communities rather than profiting from their debts.

Carmela's career seemed to be going smoothly, insofar as Amos understood it. At first, he had found it improbable that people would entrust their money to this beautiful young woman. Beauty can seem an alternative to brains, but Carmela had both.

"It's a shame you can't control Jason's finances."

Her reaction surprised him. The veneer of the professional woman seemed to drop away, to be replaced by the sadness of a woman separated from her husband. "How is he doing?"

"Don't you ever see him?"

"I don't dare."

"Dare?"

The thought that Jason Burke represented a fatal attraction to Carmela surprised Amos at first, but, of course, they had been married. They were still married.

Amos said, "You really should see him."

It was the kind of unsolicited advice he almost never gave.

10

Carmela Rush — for professional purposes she had resumed her maiden name — shared offices in Schaumburg with two other financial advisors. They called themselves the Avanti Group, the name suggested by Augie Liberati, who had also been the one to invite Carmela to join forces with Andrew Baxter and himself.

"A partnership?"

"Limited. We will share rent, insurance, utilities, office help. From then on it's to each his own."

"So what's the advantage?"

"You'll pay a lot less for rent. We can pool quite a bit of equipment. Of course, if economizing means nothing to you . . ."

Carmela joined the Avanti Group, armed with the experience she had acquired working for someone else. Baxter was the oldest member of the group, a retired economics professor who had decided to try practicing what he had preached. He had an annoying habit of explaining how he operated as if he were giving a lecture, but that had been a one-time event and Carmela came to like him and his fat, nagging wife. Their kids were grown and gone, and Mrs. Baxter took to dropping in unannounced as if to surprise an office orgy in progress.

This was Augie's interpretation. "I know the type."

"Your wife?"

"I'm not married. You?"

She had been aware of him trying to get a good look at her rings. Her wedding ring was not on the appropriate finger. That was in her apartment, left behind like her married name when she came to the office.

"Once bitten, twice shy," she said.

"Ah."

That had been meant as information as well as a warning. She had remained faithful to Jason, only saying it that way made it sound like a chore. Carmela felt that the years with Jason had cured her forever of the mating impulse. Now she just wanted to make money, lots of it, for her clients, for herself. Her goal was to have more money than her mother-in-law; why she didn't know. Still, one needed investment goals. That was the creed she preached to her clients and thus had to practice herself.

Augie had taken classes from Baxter in the long ago, as Augie put it, but now their roles seemed reversed. Gradually Baxter shed his theories and took his cue from the swashbuckling approach of Augie. As far as Carmela was concerned, they were both too deep in hedge funds, their clients as well as themselves. To her the whole thing looked like a bubble bound to burst, and she steered between the Scylla of excessive caution and the Charybdis of moderate speculation.

Augie dipped his chin and looked at her over his glasses. "I'd ask you to explain that to me, but I'm afraid you would."

"The Strait of Messina. The *Aeneid.*"

"Where did you go to school?"

"Loyola."

"You're Catholic?" He brightened as he asked the question.

"Once."

"That's all it takes."

"Are you?"

"Only on Sundays."

The three of them sometimes had lunch together, when they didn't have something brought in. Augie preferred eating out. He worked like a Trojan mornings and then liked long liquid lunches in which he could savor the accomplishments of the morning. From time to time, Carmela accepted his invitation to come along.

"Dutch," she said.

"I voted for the other guy."

He had to explain that to her. She kept the lunches to the minimum because she didn't like to drink in midday and because the lunches were too much fun. In another world she could have liked Augie, a lot, but she was in this world, a disillusioned wife who blamed the troubles of her marriage on her mother-in-law. The way Helen babied Jason was disgusting, and he claimed not to know what Carmela was talking about when she brought it up. The fact that it was still going on, Helen paying off Jason's gambling debts, setting him up in one enterprise after another, kept the flame of Carmela's resentment bright.

"My husband drank," she explained once when she had to refuse Augie's repeated offer that he join her in a drink during lunch.

"Your husband?"

"It's a long story. And it's all over."

"I'll drink to that."

"I'm sure Jason does, too."

"Jason."

"My husband."

"Your former husband."

"Former human being would be more like it."

Eventually, to lighten the burden of Jason's guilt, Carmela told Augie about her mother-in-law. She talked too much. When she mentioned Florence's death and Nathaniel's insistence that he had killed her, Augie's eyes widened.

"In Fox River?"

She nodded. She might just as well have a drink, the way she was babbling.

"O'Hara," Augie said, searching for the name. "Bourke." Then he had it. "Burke."

"That's right."

"I have a sister in Fox River," he said.

"Lots of people do."

From his sister he got all the details. Carmela liked that better than being the one to tell him the whole sordid story. His sister was married to a Pianone.

"*The* Pianones?"

He laughed. "That's how they think of themselves."

Did he know their reputation in Fox River? "What's your sister like?"

"You should meet her."

They left it at that.

When Nathaniel was released from prison, Augie knew of it before she did.

She was delighted. "I used to visit him, in Joliet. Once a month. He is the sweetest man in the world."

"I resent that."

That kind of kidding was becoming a habit. A warning signal. Carmela resolved to see less of Augie, but she saw him every business day whether she liked it not, and she couldn't help liking him. She promised herself to be careful. For a week she worked with such intensity that even she marveled at the results. *Eat your heart out, Helen,* she would say to herself. Sometimes she thought her plan was to make a bundle, resettle in Fox River, and be a standing rebuke to Helen.

"The poor woman," Nathaniel had said when she expressed this thought during one of her visits to Joliet.

"How can you say that?"

"Who better? Carmela, look at her life. Surely you don't think she's happy."

"Why shouldn't she be?"

"She was unlucky in love," Nathaniel said.

"But she was married."

"That's what I mean. She had hoped to marry someone else."

"Who?"

"Me."

"Nathaniel! Are you serious?"

"I'm afraid so."

"Tell me."

So he told her of his courting days, visiting the house with the two lovely sisters, Helen the elder, Florence the younger. He himself hadn't been sure which one he was after.

"What decided it?"

"My appendix."

He had had an appendicitis attack, during a visit when only Florence was there. She took him in charge, called an ambulance, and waited through the operation, not telling her family where she was. In the recovery room, she sat beside him, holding his hand. It seemed destiny.

"We were engaged before I was released from the hospital."

"That's romantic!"

"Yes. And ours was a wonderful marriage, as you must have noticed."

She had. She had thought more than once that if only she and Jason could be like Nathaniel and Florence everything would be right. But Nathaniel didn't drink, he didn't gamble, and he had no mother to smother him with a protective love that prevented him from growing up. Helen, of course, had become his implacable enemy, something she could barely conceal at family gatherings. She had married Burke, had Jason, buried Burke, and been left with no one but Jason to care for and no one but Nathaniel to hate.

The downside of Nathaniel's release was that Carmela no longer saw him. Joliet had been a neutral site, but she couldn't show up in Fox River without running the risk of seeing Jason and his mother. Particularly his mother. When she telephoned Nathaniel, he told her of the St. Hilary center and Helen's constant attendance.

"You should stay away from there, Nathaniel."

"I like it. And my parole officer approves."

His parole officer. During those years that Nathaniel had been in Joliet, Carmela's conviction that he was innocent of Florence's death strengthened.

He discouraged talk about it. "The important thing is that Florence received the last sacraments and died in the peace of God."

Hearing him say that, she wished desperately that she could share his simple faith.

Her main source of news of Nathaniel — and Jason — was now Madeline. Poor Madeline. She still had a crush on Jason, making light of it by saying that he was her cousin, for heaven's sake. Carmela learned of the Foot Doctor, of the sign on Jason's office — DOCTOR IS IN — and it was too good not to pass on to Augie.

"Is he a podiatrist?"

"No!"

"A pedophile?"

"You're awful."

"Hey, I like mature women."

Was that what she was? Sometimes she felt like the foolish girl she had been when she became infatuated with Jason.

Then she did a stupid thing. She went to see Nathaniel. It was a weekday, so he was at the St. Hilary center. She drove there. She parked, wondering if she dared go in and ask for him, and then she saw him sitting on a bench. She got out of the car and went to him, just sitting beside him on the bench. He turned, and his reaction seemed all the justification she needed to be there.

"What are you doing out here?" she asked him.

"Reading."

"Can't you read inside?"

"It's better out here. Quieter."

They had such a nice reunion after what, months, just chattering away on the bench, happy as larks until Madeline came along.

"Carmela!"

"Hello, Madeline."

Madeline sat on Nathaniel's other side. He asked, "Is Helen inside?"

"I won't tell."

"Tell what?" Carmela demanded.

"About you two lovebirds cuddling here on a bench in sixty-degree weather."

Nathaniel chortled at this, but Carmela thought she detected an edge in Madeline's voice.

"Are you going to visit Jason, too?"

"Not this time."

Carmela had given Nathaniel one of her cards, showing off, and Madeline saw it.

"Can I see that?"

Nathaniel handed it to her.

"Could I have one?"

Carmela opened her purse and got out another and gave it to Madeline. She should have remembered what a snitch Madeline was. Two days later Jason showed up at the offices of the Avanti Group and asked if his wife was in.

11

Ever since Ash Wednesday, Marie Murkin had been brooding over the way she had treated Nathaniel Green when Father Dowling had brought him over for lunch. At the time, she had thought that, apart from his annoyingly Christian behavior that contrasted so pointedly with her own, Father Dowling just didn't understand what Nathaniel Green had done. Done and then admitted he had done, been tried, convicted, and all the rest. Forgive and forget? What kind of world would it be if murderers rubbed shoulders with the rest of us?

As Lent progressed and Marie got used to fasting and abstinence, these practices began to exert their intended result. She consulted her soul, she examined her conscience. She did not like what she saw. As matters went on as they had at the parish center, with the shunning of Nathaniel Green, Marie had the upsetting thought that she was as bad as Helen Burke.

This muddied her motives, of course. Helen had always rubbed Marie the wrong way. When Florence was dying and Nathaniel was at his side, Helen had been an infrequent presence at the hospital, in and out, just a pro forma visit. Of course, she had never liked Florence.

Florence was the sister whom Nathaniel chose when Helen thought she was the reason for his visits to the Burke home. How did she pick up gossip like that? No matter. Marie knew it was true. The man Helen had married, God rest his soul, had been a wimp, dancing to whatever tune Helen chose to hum. Marie could still remember them arriving at Sunday Mass. Helen would sit erect in the passenger seat until her husband scooted around to open the door. Then she would emerge and proceed to the church door, head high, ramrod straight, with poor Burke toddling along behind. Portrait of a mismatch. By contrast, even Marie's rocky marriage seemed an idyll.

Oh, admit it. During the trial, Marie had been as eager as Helen allegedly was to see Nathaniel sent away for good. Like Helen, she lamented the softness of a state that had abrogated the death penalty. When Nathaniel was sent away, it all might have drifted out of Marie's consciousness if Helen had not been such a constant presence in the rectory during the reign of the last Franciscan pastor.

If Helen ever asked to have Masses said for her dead sister, Marie did not know of it. It was during that time that Burke, too, died. Helen briefly tried to play an Italian widow, but then her usual crustiness returned. The Franciscans loved her. Her husband had been a member of the Third Order, and she had him buried in the habit. Marie couldn't believe it when she saw him laid out at the wake. What kind of woman would want her husband buried in a religious habit? Of course Helen doled out pittances to the friars, who were as grateful as mendicants ought to be.

The coming of Father Dowling had meant the eclipsing of Helen. She just disappeared. Marie heard she was going to Mass at St. Patrick's downtown, but Marie suspected that she just couldn't face the St. Hilary parishioners when her son, Jason, began disturbing her peace of mind. The boy was a drunk. He was a gambler. He was a bad husband. When they married, Marie had been astonished at the beauty of Jason's bride, radiant, ignorant of what lay ahead. Well, what bride isn't? But Carmela Rush would have a very tough row to hoe. The marriage hadn't lasted five years. No divorce or anything, Carmela just decided to make a life of her own. By all reports, she had.

Eventually, when the scandal died down and Father Dowling had decided to turn the parish school into a center for older parishioners, the retired, the widows, Helen was back.

The majority of those who attended the parish center came to Father Dowling's Mass. Helen had not been among them until Lent started. What a shock it must have been to her when Marie escorted Nathaniel over to the center after his lunch with Father Dowling.

Then scooted back to the rectory to tell Father Dowling all about the man. Remembering that now, her behavior seemed as bad as anything Helen was capable of. And then the idea came.

Given her longtime service in the parish, it was pardonable in Marie that she from time to time assumed a pastoral role. The continued harassment of Nathaniel in the center called for action. She was about to insist that Father Dowling do something about it when the idea came. Marie was not the type who thought that the Holy Ghost spent his time whispering in her ear, but this seemed a genuine inspiration. Father Dowling seemed content to let the shunning wear itself out. Edna Hospers seemed helpless to do anything about it. Clearly this was a problem that required the skills of Marie Murkin.

There was, of course, a problem. Since Helen now came to the noon Mass, she could easily be waylaid when she started back to the center with the other seniors, but that was when Marie had to serve Father Dowling's lunch. She could prepare something beforehand, a cold lunch, salad, a sandwich, and put it on the table before going over to the church herself. No, that went so deeply against her grain, it pained her even to think of it. She intended to give a hundred percent to her job until they carried her out of the rectory. Contrive to get Father Dowling to invite Helen to have lunch with him? That would be to put the problem back on the pastor's plate, and thus far he had shown no inclination to deal with Helen Burke. There was no alternative but to go over to the school.

As she came along the walk from the rectory, she met a dapper little man who might have been waiting for her.

"Mrs. Murkin?"

He came up to her and took her hand before she could stop him. "Eugene Schmidt. I've never formally introduced myself."

Marie had seen him in church, sitting through the Mass, in the same pew as Natalie Armstrong, and wondered who he was. His smile had the same trained look as that of a church-goods salesman. She knew he had spent time with Father Dowling in the study, coming to the rectory when Marie was out shopping. Father Dowling had said nothing after the man left, and Marie refused to make inquiries, fearful that the pastor would begin teasing her about her interest in the man.

"I've heard all about you, of course," Eugene Schmidt said.

Not from Father Dowling. From Edna Hospers? Marie continued on her way to the school, and Eugene Schmidt tagged along. "From Natalie Armstrong," the man explained.

Marie nodded. The thought of entering the school with this persistent little man brought her to a stop. "You come regularly to the center?"

"What a great idea it is."

"Father Dowling has done wonders for the parish."

"Oh, everyone sings his praises, Mrs. Murkin." The smile became shy. "And yours, of course."

How could she not respond to that? It was

a pleasant thought that her own contributions to the flourishing of St. Hilary's were recognized — and talked about. Then the reason for her coming to the school drove such thoughts away. She stopped. "Have you been taking part in this awful treatment of Nathaniel Green?"

"Me?" He splayed a hand upon his chest. "Nathaniel and I have become friends."

"How has Helen Burke browbeat so many into doing her bidding?"

"So you know about Helen."

The idea came quickly. "Would you go inside and tell her that I want to speak to her?"

With a little wave, he headed for the door of the auditorium. Watching him go, Marie wondered if she had acted on an inspiration or done something very stupid. Now she had no alternative to just waiting out here to see if Helen came out.

Minutes went by, and Marie was feeling increasingly foolish. Then the door opened, and Helen Burke came out, shielding her eyes from the weak sunlight. She saw Marie and came right to her. She stood before her, saying nothing, just waiting.

"Helen, you know why I want to talk to you."

"Tell me."

"This treatment of Nathaniel Green has to stop."

"Is that an order?"

"No. It's an appeal to your good nature."

Silence. Then, "You don't understand."

"Tell me." She led Helen to a bench, and they sat.

Helen joined her hands on her lap and looked across the parish grounds. All the snow had melted now, and the lawn looked soggy, but there was the beginning of buds on the trees.

"He is a hypocrite."

Without pause, Helen went on, talking about the supposedly abject Nathaniel beside Florence's hospital bed. A tragic figure. Helen snorted. And then to show up at St. Hilary's, still trying to look like a tragic figure. Helen ran out of air.

"Jealousy is a terrible thing, Helen."

"Jealousy! What do you mean?"

"I know that you expected Nathaniel to choose you rather than Florence."

Helen jumped to her feet. She was speechless with anger.

Marie uttered her ultimatum. "Either you stop persecuting him or I will make sure all the others know what your real motive is."

Marie stood and started toward the rectory. That wasn't what she had meant to say to Helen — she had planned to tell her how incompatible her behavior was with her Christian faith and with her daily attendance at Mass — but now she had no doubt she had hit on the right means to get through to Helen. She inhaled deeply. She almost smiled. What is so satisfying as a job well done?

12

When Carmela was told that her husband was in the reception area, she just nodded, avoiding her secretary Emily's quizzical expression. No one in the office, except Augie, knew that she was married.

"Show him in."

Emily left, and Carmela waited, realizing that she was posing. Pinstriped suit, pink blouse, her glasses still on, sitting upright and businesslike in her chair. Jason appeared in the doorway, looked across the intervening space at her, and then came toward her, saying, as if nothing had ever gone wrong between them, "Nice place."

Carmela took off her glasses and sat forward. "Do you like it?"

He let his eyes go round the room. "No fridge?"

"That's down the hall in our lunchroom."

"I wanted to thank you for the beer."

She sat back. "What do you mean?" The question brought back one of the main reasons they were living apart.

"I found the fridge in my office chock-full of beer. Thanks."

"Jason, it wasn't me. Why on earth would I supply you with beer?"

"I wondered about that."

"I didn't do it. Are you saying someone filled your fridge with beer?"

"It really wasn't you?"

"Jason, no one who had the least concern for you would encourage your drinking."

"I've cut down."

Carmela had heard that before. She had also heard him say that beer wasn't really drinking. She had heard a dozen excuses, but Jason remained Jason. All in all, though, he looked good.

Then he said, "Are you concerned about me?"

"What a silly question."

He seemed genuinely surprised. Good Lord, did he think she hated him? If she had, leaving him would have been a lot easier than it had been. Helen Burke had made it seem necessary.

"A wife should be able to manage her husband," Helen had said, her voice heavy with reproach.

"I want my husband to manage himself."

"I think you encourage his weaknesses."

Oh, the things she might have said to that insufferable woman. But she never had. Was it fear or just the sense that you didn't say out loud the things she thought about her mother-in-law? Still, it was good to have it out in the open that Helen thought Carmela was responsible for Jason's troubles.

"Do you think I should leave him?" Carmela asked.

Helen was silent for a moment. "Jason's great mistake was having your marriage blessed by the Church."

How had that dreadful conversation ended? Looking back on it, Carmela was sure her mother-in-law was asking her to leave Jason. Did she really believe he would grow up if left to himself? From everything she had heard since their separation, that hadn't happened.

"How is your mother?" she asked Jason.

He wrinkled his nose. "The same."

"She is backing you in your new enterprise?"

"What else? And waiting for me to fail."

"Will you?"

"I really don't think so. People will buy shoes, you know. As long as I keep away from the casinos . . ." He grinned like a boy when he said it.

"Why on earth gamble? You don't need money, Jason. That can't be it."

"If I did, the last place to get it would be in a casino. That's where you leave it."

One of the theories Carmela had entertained was that Jason's destructive habits were aimed at his mother. Helen thought she had ruined Jason; well, two could play at that game. Did Jason enjoy the thought of going back to his mother with bad news?

"Have you seen your Uncle Nathaniel?"

"Not yet."

"Do you intend to?"

"We could go together."

He had spoken softly and then looked away. What on earth had brought him here?

"Jason, why did you really come here?"

"To see you."

"And ask if I had put beer in your fridge? When you thought I had, what else did you think? That I wanted you to start drinking again?"

"I haven't opened a bottle."

"You've quit?"

"I'm not into dramatic resolutions. But it's been a while. Ask Madeline."

Madeline! "Do you see her often?"

"It's a way of getting news of you."

Carmela smiled. "And she keeps me up to date about you."

"We could just talk to one another."

"Well, here we are talking," she said brightly.

"You know what I mean?"

Did she? It had been a long time since she had thought that Jason could change his stripes. Still, if his shoe store was flourishing . . . The thought of Helen Burke brought Carmela back to earth.

"We can have lunch. Sometime."

"Lunch."

"You know, the midday meal."

Her phone rang, it was a client, and she had to take it. Jason started to rise when she picked up the phone, but she waved him back into his chair. He looked around the office while she talked, but she knew he was aware of the rapid-fire advice she was giving her client. What the client needed was an okay. He got it. "I'll take care of it immediately." She hung up. "Sorry."

"If I had money I would put it in your hands."

"The day will come when you will have plenty. I read about Nathaniel's new will."

"It's driving my mother crazy. It didn't help when I told her Nathaniel might outlive her."

Are there omens in such everyday exchanges? The mention of the money he would inherit, his mother's assumption that she would outlive the brother-in-law who had left everything to her . . .

She was walking to the door with Jason when Emily hailed her. Another phone call.

"Get the number. I'll call back in a minute."

She went outside with Jason and stood beside his car while he got behind the wheel. The motor took a while to start. "Like me in the morning," he said, grinning at her.

For a moment, everything she had ever felt for him came rushing back, and it was all she could do not to kiss him. She turned and hurried back to her office.

The call had been from Madeline. Carmela had Emily dial the number.

"Carmela? Awful news. Helen is dead."

Taking the phone with her, Carmela ran into the outer office, but Jason's car was gone.

"Did you hear me?" Madeline asked.

"I was just seeing if I could stop Jason. He just left here. Tell me what happened."

Madeline's description of the auto accident was hurried, and then, "Did you say

Jason was there?"

"My husband," Carmela said.

■ ■ ■ ■

PART THREE

■ ■ ■ ■

1

Agnes Lamb was angry, a mood she might have described more graphically. John Thomas, the pizza delivery man found in the river in his half-submerged car, had died violently, and when they talked to his wife it was clear that he had been threatened.

"I thought you were interested in the break-in at the Foot Doctor," she said to Cy. It might have been an apology.

"Because he's connected with John Thomas."

"You think Jason did away with the man when he didn't bring the pizza?"

"Agnes. I think someone did away with him before he brought the pizza."

"It's always best to get clear on the time-line."

She knew that Cy was kidding with her because he didn't find it a damned bit funny himself. He knew what she thought explained the body in the river; he would think it himself. But all he could do was try to kid it away.

When they had responded to the alarm Eric had put out about a break-in, they hadn't pursued what brought them to the mall in the first place. They were agreed that for some reason Jason denied that there had been a break-in. He was sloppy, sure, but his office looked vandalized, not messy. Just like that, though, Cy seemed to have lost all interest in the the Foot Doctor.

Agnes hadn't. If she weren't saved, thanks to the exhortations of the Reverend Jones and total immersion right up there in front of the whole congregation, she would have said that she was damned if she would let John Thomas and his wife fade into the oblivion of unsolved mysteries. Many of them were unsolved because of possible connection with the Pianones. Both Cy and Captain Philip Keegan had explained to her that, hot as any trail that led to the local Family might be, it was cold to them.

"Agnes, Jacuzzi wouldn't touch it, and even if he did, one of the Pianone judges would make sure it ended in acquittal."

"When was the last time you tried?"

"Look, Agnes. Let's keep to things we can handle. You want to reform local politics, the police department isn't the means."

The detective bureau, to which thank God she had been assigned, was, Agnes came to see, the one division of the department that was not infested with Pianone influence. Peanuts? Even the Pianones must have seen that he was a joke, but the thought occurred to her that he was in a way their insurance policy, giving the illusion that the influence of the Pianones extended even into the detective division.

So Agnes came to understand the restriction under which the division worked. That didn't mean that she agreed. Which is why she took a day of her sick leave and went back to the mall.

"Did you complain when your pizza didn't arrive?" Agnes asked Jason.

He was big in a soft way, bald on top but not on the sides, the belly of an umpire, and seemed puzzled by the question. Here in his office at the Foot Doctor, it was difficult to think of him living in a unit in the development that Agnes's family had managed to free themselves from.

"I didn't order any pizza. Pizza? If I want food brought in, it'll be Chinese."

"You never ordered a pizza from . . ." Agnes read off the name from her pad. "John Thomas Pasta."

"Never heard of it," Jason said.

"I did."

It was the clerk, Eric, looking into the office.

"You ordered a pizza?" Agnes asked him. For the first time Jason seemed interested.

"How did you hear about John Thomas Pasta?" Agnes had looked in the yellow pages. There was no ad for John Thomas Pasta, nor was it listed in the column of addresses and numbers squeezed between the ads.

"Their flyer," Eric said. "They distributed flyers around the mall."

"You still have it?"

"Geez, I don't know. I could look."

Agnes went away with him, into the little room with the table and folding chairs and the little fridge. Some customers came in, and Jason excused himself and went into the showroom.

Eric found the flyer in the wastebasket in a corner of the little back room. Agnes took it into Jason's office. Smoothing it out, she was reminded of that poor woman making pizzas in her own kitchen so her husband could pay off debts he was no longer held legally responsible for. The flyer had been done on a computer, several changes of font, one color. Not even a picture of a pizza.

"Why did you call them?" she asked Eric.

"Look at those prices."

"They're low?"

If these flyers were their only means of attracting customers, the Thomases would starve to death. No, they could always eat pizza.

The tinkle of the bell announced more customers, and Eric left her. Agnes looked around Jason's office. The chair had been righted and the file cabinets closed, but the debris that had been dumped on the desk was now back in the wastebasket. Feeling like a bag lady, Agnes rummaged around in the contents of the basket. Most of it looked like lottery tickets of various levels, attempts at the jackpot and then down through the lesser layers of hopefulness. Why would a man with a nice little business like the Foot Doctor waste time on the lottery? The lottery was for losers. There were also tabs from the tops of cans. Soda, beer, how could you tell? It had to be soda, with all these tabs.

She went again into the little room in back and opened the fridge. It was so full of beer one of the bottles started to roll, and she slammed the door shut.

"Have one, if you'd like."

Jason smiled in the doorway.

"Not while I'm on duty."

"I keep those for visitors."

He said it dismissively, but Agnes knew what drinkers were like, and, even if she hadn't seen how he lived, she would have pegged Jason as a drinker.

Outside, she sat in her car and told herself this was a stupid way to spend a day off. Of course, she had called in sick, and maybe she was. Sick in the head. Her interest was in John Thomas and his wife, and it was pretty clear the explanation of that was not to be found at the Foot Doctor.

The door of the store opened, and out came Jason, wearing a jacket that flapped as he walked. Of course, he couldn't have buttoned it if he tried. He seemed to be coming right toward her, and Agnes wondered if he had thought of something he wanted to tell her, but he walked right past the passenger side of the car to the clunker in the row behind. Agnes heard the complaint of the starter, and it brought back memories of the first vehicle her dad had brought home, proud as punch. The starter had sounded like that at first, but her dad had it fixed. Jason apparently was willing to take the chance that his car would start. Well, he was a gambler. This time he won.

When he pulled out of his space and headed for an exit, Agnes followed. Call it her crazy day.

She couldn't believe it when Jason got onto the interstate with his bucket of bolts. I-90 had been designed for motorized lemmings heading pell-mell for the Loop, changing lanes, all of them at least twenty miles over the speed limit, wearing the crazed look of Luddites with only their cars as tools of destruction. There was no lane for slower drivers, and Jason settled into the lane farthest to the left and kept it at forty-five miles an hour. When he wasn't nearly run over by the irate drivers behind, he was cut off when they passed, swooping in ahead of the clunker, nearly taking off its fender. Agnes took a lot of flak herself, trying to keep behind him.

Then Jason entered the express lane! Agnes was two cars behind him. Soon there were a hundred cars behind him, their drivers furious to be kept to the speed that Jason set. They couldn't get around him in this express lane, which was like a chute, narrow and bordered by concrete barriers four feet high. Agnes turned on the radio to drown out the sound of infuriated horns.

As they approached the Schaumburg exit, Jason's signal lights went on. His right turn signal. He got onto the regular lanes, and the signal kept flashing. He was going to have to cross six lanes of traffic to get to the exit. Somehow he did it, just edging over at his infuriating forty-five miles per hour, seemingly impervious to the chaos he was creating. Following him, Agnes felt some of the fury of the other drivers, but at the same time she admired his guts. Forty-five was the minimum speed limit, and Jason kept religiously to it. Maybe he couldn't exceed it.

Once they were on the exit ramp, Agnes felt the tension drain from her. Schaumburg was spread over what had once been choice Illinois farmland and was still growing like corn in July. Jason's speed, or lack of it, was less of a problem now. Agnes wondered where they were going.

Jason's turn signal went on, the left one, and he crossed a lane of cars going in the opposite direction and entered a driveway. Agnes went on by, entered a large parking area, drove through it, exited, and returned the way she had come. When she turned in where Jason had, she could see his parked car. It stood out among the other sleek expensive vehicles.

Agnes didn't smoke. She didn't even chew gum. She began to wonder if there was a restroom she could use in the Avanti Group. But she couldn't take the risk of running into Jason. This madness was between herself and God.

There was a sign in front of the building, and after a while Agnes changed parking places, wanting to get nearer so she could read it. Under the legend THE AVANTI GROUP, in smaller letters was, FINANCIAL ADVISORS, and then three names.

Financial advisers. She could have kicked herself. According to Cy, Jason was loaded. At least his mother was, and he was the son and heir. The thought that she had followed him all this way so he could check up on his investments stirred her proletarian soul. What a bundle of contradictions the man was.

He lived in a squalor few could tolerate, but he had a nice little business. So he gambled and drank; he could afford it. Agnes sat there trying to despise him, but it was herself she was angry with. After all, she was the one who had decided to waste a day off following Jason Burke around on the off chance that she would discover something that would cast light on the murder of John Thomas. Now she was sitting like a dope in her parked car in a lot in Schaumburg reading the sign of the Avanti Group. If she weren't so stubborn, she would have taken off, got on the interstate, and barreled back to Fox River at an appropriately maniacal speed. Instead she was still sitting in her car, God knew how much later, when Jason emerged. With a woman.

They stood for a moment outside the door, and it did not seem just a business relationship to Agnes. The woman came with Jason to the clunker. Agnes had rolled down the window, and their voices came to her, audible but not intelligible. Tilting her side mirror, she could watch them. After Jason got behind the wheel, the woman looked about to give him a kiss, but she didn't. When she walked back to the entrance of the Avanti Group, she no longer gave the impression of the levelheaded businesswoman her outfit suggested.

Jason pulled out, and Agnes let him go. She wasn't going to follow him anymore. Then the woman burst out the door again, a phone in her hand, looking desperately in the direction that Jason had gone. She slumped, and then, talking into the phone, went back inside.

On the way back to Fox River, Agnes got their police band on her radio. That was how she learned of the death of Helen Burke.

2

Edna called the rectory, relaying a cell phone message from Kevin Brown, who had been on the shuttle bus, and Father Dowling, grabbing the oils, ran out to his car. This took him through the kitchen, and Marie came to the back door and called after him, "Where are you going?"

He just waved at her. Minutes could mean everything. Once he got going, he brought the old Toyota up to almost maximum speed, roaring along Dirksen Boulevard. Where is a cop when you need one? He could have used a police escort. He went through several yellow lights — at least, they were yellow when he approached the intersections, but as he shot through cars were coming at him from left to right. He commended himself to St. Anthony of Padua and kept the accelerator depressed. At last he could see the flashing lights of an ambulance as he approached the accident scene.

The effort to extricate Helen Burke from behind the wheel of her car was still under way when Father Dowling came up. The firemen paused and let Father Dowling through. The engine of the car had been driven into the front seat, pushing it back. The steering wheel seemed embedded in the woman's chest. It was Helen Burke. Father Dowling lifted his hand to bless her and absolve her from her sins. The eyes fluttered open. Could she see him? He continued with the blessing, and despite the still-growling sirens, the flashing lights, the general pandemonium of the scene, Father Dowling heard Helen sigh. It was more than a sigh. It was her last breath. But he had uncapped the oils now, and he traced a cross on her forehead, her half open eyes, her mouth . . .

He stood then and stepped back so that the grim and now pointless rescue could continue.

The parish center shuttle bus had careened onto the shoulder of the road and had come to a stop, slightly tipped. Its passengers now huddled in a horrified group beside it, looking toward the demolished car. As Father Dowling went to them, Kevin Brown came forward.

"I called the center, Father."

"Thank God you did. That's why I'm here."

"Is she still . . ."

He shook his head.

"Then it was too late?"

"Just in time, Kevin. Just in time."

Kevin seemed relieved. "I only hope someone does as much for me."

Father Dowling decided not to ask Kevin what had happened. Eugene Schmidt was talking with a police officer. When Father Dowling came up, Schmidt turned and stared at the priest.

"I was driving, Father. Some guy just swerved in front of me. I don't know how it happened."

Father Dowling looked at the officer, an expressionless young man he didn't know. He took Father Dowling aside.

"How did it happen, Officer?"

"He says someone swung into his lane and forced him over." And that in turn had forced Helen from the lane?

Schmidt had come along with them. "I didn't see her in the mirror, Father. I didn't have time. Oh my God."

Out of a dozen fragmentary and incoherent remarks, something that had taken seconds in the occurrence was pieced together. It came down to the fact that the shuttle bus had forced Helen to swerve, and that had taken her into the bridge abutment and her death.

"Why wasn't she in the bus?"

"She insisted on showing me the way," Schmidt said. "She never rode in the shuttle bus." The object of the trip had been a park overlooking the river. In the bus were the baskets packed with the lunch they had meant to have there. Schmidt tagged along with Father Dowling, keeping to his side, as if anxious to hear how the others would describe what had happened. Monica Garvey had been seated in the center of the bus, on the right side, and had seen it all.

"I tried to call out, but I couldn't. I couldn't make a sound."

Everyone had his or her account, what they had or had not seen, emphasizing the reaction of the speaker. Few had realized what had happened when it did. Most spoke of the terror they had felt when the bus left the road and bumped to a stop on the shoulder, twenty-five yards from Helen's demolished car.

Encircled by the seniors, Father Dowling suggested that they say a prayer for Helen.

"Is she . . ."

"Yes." And he began the Hail Mary. They were asking that Helen's and the souls of all the faithful departed might rest in peace when Father Dowling saw Cy Horvath. He was with the group by the car, where an acetylene torch was being used to gain access to the body. Father Dowling hesitated. The old people should be taken back to the center. But how? In the bus? He doubted that many would care to board it now. He beckoned to Kevin.

"You have a cell phone?"

"That's how I called Edna Hospers."

"I think you should call for taxis to take everyone back to the center."

Kevin nodded. The suggestion turned him into a figure of authority. He began barking orders, moving the huddled group away, his cell phone at his ear. Father Dowling went to join Cy Horvath.

Helen's body was removed with some difficulty, placed on a gurney, and rolled away to the open doors of a 911 ambulance. Before it got there, Dr. Pippen, the assistant coroner, stopped it and made a swift examination. Then she waved the paramedics on, and Helen's body was put into the ambulance. A minute later, with periodic warnings from its siren, it started toward the road. Traffic had been halted; the ambulance bounced onto the pavement and then, its siren going at full blast, disappeared up the road.

Photographs continued to be taken. A tow

truck was now backing toward the crumpled car in which Helen Burke had departed this Vale of Tears.

Eugene Schmidt had hung back and was in the last little group awaiting a taxi to take them back to the center. He was holding a slip of paper in his hand that rippled in the slight breeze.

"He insisted he be given a ticket," Cy explained to Father Dowling.

"For what?"

"That was left blank."

Was Cy amused or annoyed, neither, or something in between? His facial expression never changed and had to do duty for whatever he might be feeling. Dr. Pippen, having seen the body off to the morgue, joined them.

"Did you get here in time, Father?"

"Just. One of the passengers in our shuttle bus called the center on his cell phone."

"Who'll give me a ride downtown?"

Cy looked at her. "How did you get here?"

"In the meat wagon."

"I'll take you."

They went off. The last group was getting into taxis. Father Dowling stood for a moment, looking at the bridge abutment. How quickly everything had been returned to normal. Going back to his car, he thought of the verse following the account of the burial of Jesus. *And all withdrew.*

3

Helen Burke's funeral was one befitting her status in the parish, and her means. Jason insisted that all stops be pulled out and his mother get the send-off of the half century. Not that he put it that way. His great moon face was a tragic mask, his eyes red from weeping. All the remorse for the trouble he had caused his mother sat heavily on his shoulders now, and an elaborate funeral seemed a way of easing the burden. McDivitt the funeral director nodded through Jason's instructions, the soul of discretion and good taste, not quite rubbing his hands at this bonanza.

Cars were at the disposal of Helen's old friends at the senior center — no one could bear the thought of getting into the shuttle bus; it stood now in a far corner of the parish parking lot, a memento mori of sorts. The viewing room at McDivitt's was almost festive, flowers everywhere, and a portable organ had been rolled in to provide lugubrious music while people took their places in preparation for the recitation of the rosary. A reluctant Eugene Schmidt was led in by

Natalie Armstrong, but she couldn't get him past the last row. Schmidt looked as if the whole assembly would rise as one and point an accusing finger at him.

"What will they do to me?" he had asked Father Dowling earlier, waiting for Natalie to sign the visitors' book.

"Eugene, it was an accident."

"But she's dead. And it's my fault."

"We are not responsible for what we just happen to bring about." He left it there. This was no time to give Eugene Schmidt a lecture on the nature of contingency. Accidents, by definition, just happened. If they had causes, the event could not be traced to those causes as if they were necessary results. Father Dowling felt that he would sound like Willy Nilly if he tried to console Eugene Schmidt in this way.

Kevin Brown was lobbying for a requiem Mass in the old manner with Latin and black vestments; Monica Garvey was on the side of the angels, saying that only the Mass of the Angels, with white vestments and the vernacular, was appropriate in this day and age.

"This day and age," Kevin growled.

The two went off to carry on their dispute.

Amos Cadbury came in, black suit, crisp white shirt with a beautiful tie with stripes of gray and black. He took his place in the line of those waiting to inscribe their names in the book that awaited on a little lectern with a hooded light illumining its pages.

"The Book of Life," Amos murmured when he joined Father Dowling.

"Let us hope so."

"I would like to talk with you, Father."

"Of course."

"Could we have lunch at the University Club on Thursday?"

Father Dowling nodded. "After the noon Mass."

"I'll be there. We can go off in my car."

That settled, Amos went into the viewing room, Father Dowling watched him advance to the closed coffin with the portrait of Helen Burke propped atop it. He knelt on the prie-dieu before the casket and blessed himself with great concentration.

Just before Father Dowling entered the viewing room, a final figure appeared. Nathaniel Green. Madeline was with him. They went past the visitors' book, Madeline nodded to Father Dowling as they passed him. Nathaniel wore an indescribable expression. They sat in the back row, at the end opposite Natalie and Eugene Schmidt.

When Father Dowling went up the little aisle between the groupings of chairs, everyone stood. There are always unlooked-for variations at wakes, and this was one of them. He knelt on the prie-dieu, and behind him the gathering took their seats. So the rosary was said, Father Dowling beginning each prayer, the mourners finishing it. At the end, as he had done at the scene of the accident, he prayed that Helen's soul and the souls of all the faithful departed might rest in peace.

"Amen," came the response.

When Father Dowling turned, he caught sight of Natalie and Eugene exiting. They were followed close behind by Nathaniel and Madeline. Jason stood and turned his great mournful face on the others.

"Thank you all for coming," he said, sounding as if he were going to burst into tears. "God bless you."

He came to Father Dowling and took his hand and shook it vigorously. The woman at his side looked on. Father Dowling looked at her receptively.

"I'm Carmela, Father."

"My wife, Father. Of course you haven't met."

Marie Murkin had her comment on that. She had not come to the wake — "I'll come to the funeral Mass" — and dipped her head when Father Dowling told her of the presence of Carmela Burke.

"Burke? She's been going by her maiden name."

Father Dowling then expressed the thought he'd had when confronting the couple.

"Tragedy?" Marie said. "And a pile of money."

"You're becoming a cynic, Marie."

In his study, lighting his pipe, he acknowledged that Jason's suddenly altered financial condition might indeed have magnetic properties for his estranged wife. He had been told that she was a financial counselor.

In the funeral Mass the next day, Father Dowling followed the *Novus Ordo,* but in Latin, and the vestments were white. Thus neither Kevin nor Monica was completely pleased or displeased. At Jason's insistence, Nathaniel Green sat with the family in the front pew, between Madeline and Carmela. Natalie Armstrong was there as well. Eugene Schmidt was nowhere to be seen.

4

"You don't like funerals?" Herman asked Schmidt.

"I'll go to my own."

That was all on that subject, thank God. Herman had heard how Schmidt was going around blaming himself for what happened, expecting any moment to be taken into custody. When he tapped on the door and looked in on Herman after all the others had gone off to the church for the funeral Mass, Herman feared that he was going to be a one-man audience for Schmidt's crocodile tears. To his relief, Schmidt seemed his usual cocky self.

"You got anything to drink?"

It was ten in the morning. Herman was an over-the-yardarm man, putting off drinking so he could get a mild buzz on while he watched television and then fall quickly asleep when he went to bed. Or sometimes before he got to bed.

"A bottle of water?"

"Ha."

"All I've got is beer."

"I want a real drink."

"Well, you'll have to go for it."

"Where's the nearest place?"

Schmidt was serious. Herman told him of the liquor store two blocks away. Schmidt was on his feet. "I'll be back before you can say Jack Robinson."

When he was gone, Herman sat there wondering who the hell Jack Robinson was.

Oh, he knew the expression, but how had it got started? He considered asking Schmidt when he came back, but he knew the answer — of course there would be an answer, sharp and quick — would have to be checked. Not that Herman really gave a damn about Jack Robinson, whoever he was.

Eugene returned with a bottle of scotch. Herman told him there was ice in the fridge. Eugene looked shocked.

"Neat, Herman. It's the only way to savor it. Of course, if you want ice in yours . . ."

Herman didn't want a drink, but he thought he might have a light one, with water and lots of ice, just to be good company even if he was the host.

Eugene lifted his glass with the ounce or so of scotch in it, let it slide toward his mouth, and then took a little on his tongue. "Ah," he said, resting the glass on the arm of his chair. "Always sip scotch." Herman's drink didn't taste weak enough, but he wasn't the sipping sort. Anyway, he was going to hold himself to the one drink.

"Life is like a billiard game, Herman. You hit one ball, it hits another, that hits a third, and then on and on."

"Where do you play billiards?"

"Okay. Have the third ball hit the first, which hits the second, on and on."

Herman nodded. If they were going to talk billiards, he wanted accuracy.

Schmidt wasn't interested in billiards, the game, he said, but the way one thing happened and then another and another, but if the first hadn't happened none of the rest would have. Herman nodded. He'd had a cellmate who talked like that.

"I run Helen Burke into the abutment — that was an accident, a pure accident, Herman, just ask Father Dowling — and look what follows. I've made all kinds of people rich."

Schmidt seemed to have acquired a lot of knowledge about Helen Burke and Nathaniel Green and all their shirttail relatives.

"Not only does Jason get what his mother had, he's in line for what Nathaniel will leave her."

"Nathaniel will change his mind now."

"Don't say that." Schmidt had been speaking as if he had endowed Jason; now he was alarmed.

"Why leave a pile to a dead woman?" Herman asked.

"He wants to get rid of it. I know it sounds crazy, but I've talked to him. He sits out on his bench like a monk and says he thinks Helen was right, what would he have if he hadn't married Florence?"

"What did he do?"

"For a living? Not much, I guess. He never mentioned it. Anyway, he thinks of what he has as ill-gotten gains. The solution? Turn it over to his sister-in-law."

"Who's dead."

"She's got an heir. Jason."

"What a loser," Herman said, as if his own life had been an uninterrupted series of triumphs.

"Some loser. He's rolling in it. Why do you think his wife came back to him?"

"Did she?"

"She was hanging on his arm at the wake as if she were afraid he'd get away."

"You take credit for that too?"

"Billiards, Herman. Billiards."

Schmidt's glass was empty. Full of his subject, he had forgotten to sip and get the savor of the scotch. He replenished his glass and looked inquiringly at Herman. What the hell, why not? Herman extended his glass. He would settle for the ice still in it.

Schmidt wasn't through. "There'll be others, too. Other relatives. What a family. They're related to one another in ways even they can't explain. Nathaniel told me there are other provisions in his will, but most of it goes to Helen."

"Who's dead."

"Damn it, I explained that."

"So who are the others?"

"Madeline Clancy, for one."

"No kidding."

"She's some kind of cousin to Jason. Nathaniel knows that. I'm sure she's in the will."

"Lucky her."

"And Natalie. Natalie Armstrong."

"Your girlfriend?"

Schmidt smiled smugly. Well, he was a ladies' man, no doubt of that. Even if Herman believed only a fraction of the conquests Schmidt had ticked off, he'd had a pretty interesting career.

"Why didn't you marry them?"

"Some of them I did."

"Come on."

"Twice. They didn't last, of course. I'm a rolling stone."

"How come you rolled in here?"

"I might ask you the same."

Herman explained the path he himself had taken to this snug little apartment in the basement of the school. The chaplain at the place, Barney O'Connell, had told him of the way Father Dowling helped graduates of Joliet get settled.

"My parole officer convinced me to accept. I'm glad I did."

"Who could blame you?" Schmidt said, looking approvingly around at Herman's habitation. He toasted the place, then tossed off his drink. He seemed to have forgotten his theory about sipping scotch.

They both had another. And another.

"An Irish wake," Schmidt said.

"You Irish?"

"Helen Burke is."

"I'm Polish."

"Herman the German?"

"It's a long story."

Schmidt wasn't interested. He sat there, wearing his smug smile, obviously very pleased with himself. Well, he considered himself a benefactor to all Nathaniel Green's and Helen Burke's relatives, shirt-tail or not.

"You forgot one thing, Schmidt."

"What's that?"

"You left yourself out. So all those others got lucky, what's it to you?"

Schmidt seemed about to say something, but he didn't. He just went on raising his glass to that smug smile.

5

When Father Dowling told Marie that he was having lunch with Amos Cadbury at the University Club after the noon Mass, she couldn't understand why they couldn't eat in the rectory. He told her it was Amos's suggestion that they eat in Chicago, and then wished he hadn't. Marie expected and received unstinting praise from Amos whenever she fed him at the pastor's table. She clearly thought Amos's decision to take Father Dowling elsewhere for lunch was an implicit criticism of her culinary skills. Father Dowling couldn't think of anything to say that would not make her feel worse. In the end, it was Amos who mollified Marie and left her purring

"In Lent, it seemed only fitting to deprive myself of your marvelous skills, Mrs. Murkin."

"A Lenten meal," she said dismissively, trying not to smile.

"That's just it. A Lenten meal prepared by you would be a feast anywhere else. No, Father Dowling and I will do penance at the University Club."

As they were driven away in Amos's elongated car, Father Dowling asked the lawyer if he had ever considered diplomacy. Amos professed not to understand the question. Roger Dowling let it go.

On the drive, they talked of Helen Burke's funeral. "Sometimes I feel like a doctor,

Father. Always burying clients."

"You were Helen's lawyer for a long time?"

"And her father's before her. Helen was like her father, Florence favored her mother."

"And now you will have to sort out her estate?"

Amos laid a hand on Father Dowling's arm. "After we've eaten."

Amos had reserved his favorite table, next to a window and away from the conversation and sounds of cutlery and china in the center of the room. Crab casserole and white wine for Amos and fantail shrimp for Father Dowling, no wine. During the meal, Father Dowling entertained Amos with stories of Herman, the current parish janitor.

"You're rehabilitating him, Father?"

"Only if leaving him alone has that effect."

"He's still on parole, I imagine."

"Paxon."

Amos's eyes rolled upward. "When do virtues turn into vices, Father?"

"When they abandon the golden mean."

Amos was delighted. "*In medio stat virtus.* Isn't that the phrase?"

"Aristotle."

"Have I ever told you about the ethics class I had from John Oesterle?"

Amos was a double domer, as he put it, holding both an undergraduate and law degree from Notre Dame. His loyalty to his old school had been put to severe tests in recent years, and he sought refuge in memories of a better if distant past. The ethics course he had taken from Professor Oesterle was one of his most consoling memories. "You should have heard him on double effect, Father."

"I've been hearing a version of it from Eugene Schmidt."

After finishing their meal, they stood and went into the club library, where they could have the talk that was the reason Amos had invited Father Dowling.

"Tell me about Eugene Schmidt, Father."

Father Dowling was surprised, and it must have shown. Or was Amos merely continuing from his guest's last remark at table?

"Natalie Armstrong seems quite taken with him," Amos said after he had his cigar going satisfactorily. Father Dowling was filling his pipe. "She sent him to the rectory for instructions, Amos."

"Did she?"

"I don't think he's serious."

"I am afraid she is. What I am going to say may sound like a strange extension of the obligations I owe that family, professionally but also personally. Anything you can tell me about the man, I would appreciate learning."

Father Dowling felt suddenly inadequate. When Schmidt came to the rectory with his doubts about the Trinity, he had seemed a familiar type. Someone who enjoys chattering about religion as long as he can keep it at a safe remove. Marie, of course, was curious about the dapper little man who seemed to be the darling of the senior center, but Father Dowling had not quizzed Schmidt about his past.

"Has he been coming to the center long, Father?"

"A month or two."

"Just showed up?"

"Amos, I have to confess I really know nothing about him."

The patrician lawyer nodded. "No reason why you should probe into everyone who comes to the center, of course." It sounded like a criticism. "Let me tell you what I propose to do."

What Amos proposed doing was hiring a private investigator to find out all he could about Eugene Schmidt.

"Is it really that important?"

"I'm afraid so."

Because of Natalie Armstrong's interest in

Schmidt, and vice versa.

"It will all be done with a maximum of discretion, of course. I have no idea what Maxwell will learn and what I might or might not do with what he tells me."

"Maxwell."

"The firm has used him in the past. An utterly trustworthy fellow, despite the unsavory nature of his craft."

"You might just ask Cy Horvath to look into it."

"I'd rather not. He would be bound to think that I have grounded suspicions about Schmidt."

Thus it was that Father Dowling seemed to have given his blessing to hiring Maxwell to check up on the past of Eugene Schmidt. That done, Amos turned to financial matters. Here the great worry was what Jason Burke might do with his soon-to-be-acquired wealth.

"He is the principal beneficiary of Helen's will, of course. That alone will provide him with a considerable fortune. And, unless recent events cause Nathaniel Green to change his mind, there will be a good deal more coming to Jason when his uncle dies."

The problem was caused by Jason's dual weaknesses, drink and gambling. "Madeline tells me that he hasn't darkened a casino door for months. But he has stayed away for months before and then returned with a vengeance. She also says he has confined his drinking to beer."

The two men exchanged a look, as if each of them knew of the alcoholic's claim that beer does not count as drink.

"That is why I spoke to Carmela, Jason's wife. Do you know her?"

"I met her at the wake and funeral. She was at the cemetery with him, too."

"She is a very impressive woman, Father. She put up with a good deal, from Helen as well as from Jason. Finally she could take no more."

"She left him?"

"They separated. Helen arranged a sum of money with me, on which Carmela could draw as needed. But she has been very successful in her line of work. Financial counseling. She manages other people's money. That is what gave me the idea."

Father Dowling waited.

"I can appoint her as the custodian and guardian of Jason's money."

"You can?"

"I persuaded Helen to write an equivocal clause in her will that can be interpreted as giving me that authority. It doesn't mention Carmela, of course. Helen would never have agreed to that." Amos puffed on his cigar. "I allowed her to think that I would be the one exercising that role."

"Won't Jason object?"

"I nurse the hope that he will welcome it. He knows his weakness; he knows how fragile his resolutions at reform have been in the past. Helen was of little help to him, that has to be said. Now, with her safely gone to God, a great motive for Jason's profligacy is gone."

"And if the couple doesn't reconcile?"

"That is not a necessary condition of the plan," Amos said carefully.

"Will Nathaniel's money, when it comes, fall under the same plan?"

"It will."

"Imagine, just leaving everything to his tormentor."

"Not everything, Father."

"Oh?"

"Others will be handsomely taken care of."

"Madeline Clancy?"

Amos nodded. "And Natalie Armstrong."

"Ah. Hence the interest in Eugene Schmidt?"

"Exactly. What was the point of your remark about double effect, Father?"

"Schmidt has been saying that as a result

of the accident, he has become the benefactor of Helen's and Nathaniel's heirs."

"He should be careful. People will wonder if he swerved into Helen's lane accidentally."

6

Cy got all the feminine intuition he needed at home and didn't want it raising its lovely head while he was working. Unless that lovely head belonged to Dr. Pippen, she of the golden hair worn in a ponytail, the enormous green eyes, a young woman vibrant with life who served as assistant coroner. She had taken the job while her husband the ob-gyn finished his residency and then stayed on when he opened his office in Fox River. She herself had qualified in pathology at the Mayo Clinic. Lubins, the coroner, had been a medic in the army and held the post as a gift from the local political powers.

"Look at the similarities, Cy," Pippen urged. They were seated across from one another at one of the very small tables in the cafeteria. She had taken her ponytail from behind her head and was holding it as she talked.

"And the dissimilarities."

"Cy, in both cases, the car was forced over

at great speed."

He had told her the results of the examination of the car in which the body of John Thomas had been found. The driver's side of the car told the tale that Pippen was now feeding back to him.

The young woman posed a moral problem for Cy that no one would have guessed. He tried to think of her as his little sister; he tried to find flaws in her that he could magnify in order to protect himself from the attraction he felt. There had never been any overt expression of this, and there never would be. He told himself that with time he would just get used to Pippen and not even remember feeling this goofy about her. That hadn't happened. He would have liked to be annoyed at her playing detective if he hadn't encouraged it in the past as an excuse for sitting like this over coffee. Pippen was pushing the idea that the John Thomas death and the accident in which Helen Burke had died represented the same method.

"MO," she said, her lips forming the letters in a way that would have rattled a Trappist. "Isn't that what you call it?"

"Business slow?" he asked.

It was. So how else should she spend her day if not by telling Cy how to do his job?

How many hours a day can you spend reading?

"How is the book club?"

She made a face. "We never get around to the book."

For the next ten minutes, she told him stories of the other women in her book club, all professionals of one sort or another. "All they want to read is best sellers."

"Shame on them."

Cy felt good about getting her off her big theory about John Thomas and Helen Burke, but when they were parting outside the door of the cafeteria, she whispered, "The same MO."

Pippen was getting as bad as Agnes Lamb, with her wide-eyed reproachful look when he joshed away her suggestion that they really had to look into the John Thomas killing. He knew that she knew that he knew what she was suggesting. The Pianones. And she had been in the department long enough to know that they might just as well try to pin a crime on the Four Horsemen of the Apocalypse as expect to get anywhere in the prosecutor's office with a case against the Pianones. It was no accident that John Thomas had ended up in the river, but Helen Burke had met her death by the kind of fluke that never made it out of traffic.

Cy checked out a car. When he pulled up out of the garage, waiting for pedestrians to go past, he looked across the street at the Jury Room. Maybe he should have just gone there. No, he decided, pulling into traffic. There he would have to talk, or listen to others talk, and he wanted to think.

In the privacy of his own mind he could entertain the kind of speculation that Pippen and Agnes insisted on speaking out loud. Of course, it was hard not to think that a guy deciding to open a freelance pizza business in Fox River had better clear it with the Pianones first. They had driven Domino's and other chains out of the city and kept the pizza business confined to dozens of independents. All under the thumb of the Pianones, needless to say. John Thomas might have been one of them, despite the amateurishness of his operation. Maybe he could have struck a deal with the Pianones and been alive today, but a man who held himself to pay off debts of which he had been exonerated didn't sound like a man who would go hat in hand to the Pianones.

John Thomas had been sent on his way into the beyond in a more modest way than Helen Burke. Cy hadn't drawn attention to the obituary in the *Tribune,* but when he showed up at the storefront funeral home, there was Agnes talking with Mrs. Thomas. The other two in evidence seemed to belong to the staff. They did.

"The kids couldn't make it," Mrs. Thomas said, not meeting Cy's eye.

The director, who looked like a retired cop, read from the Bible, having trouble with words. The good news had never sounded sadder. Next to him stood a woman with a long sad face, looking as if they were burying all her hopes. The crematorium was next, and he and Agnes went on with Mrs. Thomas. Where were their kids who hadn't made it to their father's funeral? If you could call it a funeral.

"I'd ask you home . . ."

"No, no," Agnes said. "We're taking you to lunch."

She protested but eventually agreed. "But no pizza, all right? I'll never eat pizza again."

So they went to the Great Wall of China, where Mrs. Thomas ate with gusto and then, prompted by Agnes, talked about her husband, how good he had been, how honest. She looked at them. "But not practical, you know. Not at all practical."

Cy had felt superfluous. All Mrs. Thomas needed was another woman's ear, and she had that in Agnes.

Now, driving aimlessly, he crossed the bridge to the far side of the Fox River, the high side, and followed the river road north to a parking area from which there was an unrivaled view of the city in which he plied his trade. Life has a different look to a police detective, of course. He was often struck by the innocence with which others commented on local happenings. A cop got to know that the public and private faces of people often differ, that the mildest of people turn violent and the nicest kids can spiral into disaster. Where did that put John Thomas?

What did they have but a guy whose wife made pizza in her kitchen that he delivered to those hooked by a pretty primitive flyer? It occurred to Cy that all they knew, or thought they knew of John Thomas, had come from his wife. No need to doubt it, of course, but who knew what lay behind the bankruptcy and the kids who couldn't make it to his funeral? The next time Agnes nagged him about Thomas, he would point this out to her. It might keep her busy for a while.

And Helen Burke? It was ridiculous to liken the way she had been forced into that bridge abutment to John Thomas's going into the river. He thought of Eugene Schmidt, dancing around the accident site, blaming himself for what had happened, a real pain in the colon. Cy had asked about him, but nobody seemed to know much.

"I thought he was another product of Joliet," Nathaniel Green told Cy. "I suppose because he's friendly with Herman."

"You talk with him?"

"Oh, it's largely listening. My family seems to fascinate him."

They sat in silence on the bench, Cy's stretched-out legs extending almost to the opposite side of the walk. He would have liked to ask Nathaniel why he had turned off the oxygen petcock before removing the tubes from his wife.

Nathaniel said, "I can't say I much like the attention he pays Natalie." He was still talking about Eugene Schmidt.

Now, sitting at the wheel of the car, looking out over Fox River, Cy promised himself he would look into Eugene Schmidt if Agnes decided to check out John Thomas.

7

Tetzel kept away from the editorial offices of his paper, and from Menteur, who had developed a fixation about a story exposing the way in which the courthouse had been exempted from the draconian antismoking ordinance that had slipped through the city council on a busy day. It had been Tetzel's own offhand mention of this exemption that had ignited poor gum-chewing Menteur, who like most newsmen his age had been cured like a ham in clouds of tobacco smoke. The puritanical ascendancy of these late years had done little for his disposition. His bite had become as bad as his bark. Perhaps if he had just quit smoking entirely he could have gotten used to abstinence. But Menteur lit up as soon as he was in his car, he smoked four cigarettes on the way home, he would have had a cigarette smoldering next to his dinner if Mrs. Menteur had permitted it, he finished the pack and began another before going to bed, and, the following day, he smoked all the way to the paper, where he had to distract himself with bubble gum until he could flee at noon for a half hour's reprieve from this enforced abstinence. Then to learn that all the crooked politicians, and Tetzel, too, puffed their way about the courthouse with impunity! Wars have been declared with less provocation.

"What good will it do you if they ban

smoking in the courthouse, too?" Tetzel asked.

Menteur's eyes shone. "Justice."

The only way he could escape Menteur's demand for the story was by coming up with something else, something sufficiently big to distract his editor from his longed-for vendetta. But what would it be? In the pressroom, Rebecca was writing a story on the quality of food in the county jail.

"Can they smoke in the jail?" Tetzel asked her.

"Of course."

"Don't mention it in your story."

"Why ever not?"

"Menteur will excise it. The man has become a fanatic."

"I can't believe it."

"He chews bubble gum," Tetzel whispered. Rebecca's brows flew up and were lost behind her bangs.

Across the street in a back booth nursing a scotch and water, Tetzel remembered the success of his story about the return of Nathaniel Green. Unusual as the response to that story had been, Tetzel liked to think that it characterized his work. Like a duffer who makes a lucky shot, he thought he had finally hit his level. In his mind, he reviewed possibilities. Expose local political corruption? A damning portrait of Lubins the coroner? A mean smile twisted his lips. The police department? But that would take him back to the Pianones, and that was a no-no, personal as well as professional. Once only had he dared such a story, and it had meant an ignominious apology to Rocco Pianone and a retraction in the paper. It did not help his mood when Tuttle sauntered in with Peanuts Pianone in tow. The little lawyer might have gladly enlisted with the Pianone forces, but their business went to a Chicago law firm that had opened a branch office in Fox River the better to serve their shady client. A headline moved across the addled surface of Tetzel's mind. LOCAL FAMILY'S MANY CONTRIBUTIONS TO CIVIC LIFE. A paean of praise to the Pianones. Had it come to that?

Tuttle and Peanuts slipped into the booth across from him, and Tetzel scowled.

"I didn't see you at the funeral," Tuttle said, adjusting his tweed hat.

The order Tuttle had called to the bartender as he passed him arrived. Brown ale for Peanuts and a shandy for Tuttle. Wilma called out what she had brought, put it before Tetzel's unwanted companions, and returned to her post.

"Who died?"

"Come on. Nathaniel Green's sister-in-law."

"Did you go?"

"The cream of the city was there. And Rebecca Farmer. Why did she draw the assignment?"

Rebecca! This was news to Tetzel. Was her claim to be writing about the food in the county jail a ruse? He thought of returning to the pressroom and quizzing his colleague, but the thought fizzled away. He could believe that Menteur was exacting revenge by letting Rebecca enjoy the fallout from Tetzel's great story.

"She does the routine things. Tell me about it."

"You've seen one funeral, you've seen them all," Tuttle said. Did the little lawyer suspect he would be pouring salt into the wound?

"How's Hazel?" Tetzel asked.

"She always asks about you."

Tetzel thought of the well-endowed Amazon who dominated Tuttle's office. Peanuts muttered an obscenity. Tetzel knew how the arrival of Hazel had disturbed the even tenor of Peanuts's life.

"Was Nathaniel Green there?" he asked.

"Of course."

"I suppose he'll want you to change his will now."

The tweed hat swung in a negative motion. "No reason for that."

"How can a dead women inherit money?"

"She can't, Gerry. But her son can."

Jason Burke. Tetzel knew the man's reputation. The thought of a drunk and a gambler coming into a fortune was depressing. Or would have been if a dim bulb had not gone on in Tetzel's mind. The heir of Nathaniel Green?

"Tell me about him."

"He's reformed."

"Sure he has." Tetzel had the weakling's skepticism about moral reform.

"He told me he intends to go on with the Foot Doctor."

Tetzel looked blank.

"His business. In the mall. Shoes."

HEIR VOWS TO KEEP TO SIMPLE LIFE?

"Tell me about it."

While Tuttle talked, Wilma arrived with another drink for Tetzel. He almost sent it back. He didn't. "Could you bring me a cup of coffee, Wilma?"

"Coffee?" He had surprised her.

"Black."

Tetzel sat on after Tuttle and Peanuts left.

He finished his second drink and ordered another black coffee. He would have wished that he had not come here except that coming here had brought Tuttle and what Tetzel considered a lead to a story that would get Menteur's mind off all the smoking going on in the courthouse.

He drove to the mall, slowly and carefully, and found the Foot Doctor after cruising around the parking lot. He pulled into a space, turned off the motor, and stared at the storefront. SCION OF PROMINENT LOCAL FAMILY MAKES MODEST FOOTPRINT.

He got out of his car, slammed the door, and inhaled deeply. He nearly passed out. His head cleared, and he took in the normalcy of the mall, eager consumers going from store to store, families, ordinary people. Readers. He made his way to the entrance of the Foot Doctor.

A bell jangled above him when he entered. No one took notice of him. Tetzel took a chair and waited, observing the action about him.

A family of five, all of them in stockinged feet, were being waited on by a gangly young man.

"Be with you in a minute, sir."

"There's no hurry."

One of the kids got up and tried out the tennis shoes that the clerk had just fitted him into. Little lights in the backs of them went on and off as he walked, head turned, appreciating the effect. He walked into Tetzel. The mother rose, grabbed the kid's arm, and hurled him into a seat. Tetzel waved away the collision but was ignored. There was no sign of the proprietor.

The clerk made five sales; the family headed for the door.

"What did you have in mind?" the gangly young clerk asked, coming to Tetzel. He stood, smiling a sunny smile, his Adam's apple riding up and down his throat.

"Something comfortable."

"Loafers?"

"Let me see what you have."

Tetzel had removed one of his shoes and put his foot into a device that measured his size. The clerk adjusted the device. "Ten and a half," he announced and then disappeared into the back room, from which he returned with an armful of boxes. He pulled up his stool, opened a box, and pulled out a loafer, displaying it to Tetzel.

The reporter offered his foot. "You own the place?"

Again the big smile. "Don't I wish."

Did he dream of owning such a store? Tetzel marveled at the ambitions of the simple. At that guy's age he was already on the staff of the *Tribune,* the whole world before him. The loafer slid comfortably onto his foot. Maybe he would buy a pair of shoes.

"Say, this isn't Jason Burke's store, is it?"

The kid nodded.

"He in?"

"There's been a tragedy in his family." He looked up, solemn. "His mother."

Tetzel affected puzzlement, then began to nod. "Oh, that's right. Mrs. Helen Burke. Well, maybe he'll sell you the store now."

"You want to try that out?"

Tetzel rose and took several steps, then sat again.

"Fit all right?"

"Perfect. I'll take them."

Tetzel remained seated while the clerk, having taken his credit card, went to write up the sale. He brought back a slip for Tetzel to sign, then handed him a plastic bag containing his new shoes. Tetzel remained seated. No other customers had come in.

"He came into a lot of money, didn't he?"

The clerk just rolled his eyes.

"Why would he want to keep this store?"

"Because it's been his salvation. Those are his very words."

241

"What do they mean?"

The clerk looked as if he might explain, then apparently thought better of it. All he did was shrug.

After he left the store, Tetzel sat for some minutes in his car before starting the engine. If he wasn't on to a story here, he would eat Tuttle's tweed hat.

8

Madeline Clancy was surprised when Amos Cadbury asked her to come for the reading of Helen's will. When she got there she found the office to be almost crowded. Jason had been given pride of place, directly across the desk from the lawyer. Carmela sat beside him. She had been a constant presence all during these awful days, at the wake, at the funeral, at the cemetery afterward. She and Madeline had hardly exchanged a word, as if Carmela had not wanted to explain the big change to her old friend. It seemed clear that Carmela hoped that the long separation from Jason was over. He looked fresh and healthy and neatly dressed; you could glimpse the young man he had been behind his present puffy exterior. Now his weight seemed almost to lend him gravitas. Well, after all, this was his moment. Jason would finally come into his own.

Nathaniel Green had arrived just before Madeline, with Natalie Armstrong, and Amos's secretary was taking them to their chairs when she came in. Madeline had been wondering what she was doing here, but the same question could be asked about Natalie. Behind his desk, Amos Cadbury looked benignly at the gathering.

"It is seldom that sadness does not bring a little happiness along with it," he began. "These have been difficult days for the family, and you all have borne it well. At such a moment, even pleasant news is not as welcome as it ordinarily would be. Let me just tell you that we are here to learn what Helen wanted for all of you."

The bulk of what Helen had would go, of course, to Jason. He listened impassively to Amos Cadbury, nor did Carmela's expression change. Of course, neither of them could have been surprised to hear what they did. The only surprise was that perhaps neither of them had ever imagined that it would be Helen who brought them together again.

Then there was a surprise.

"Helen's motherly concern continues from beyond the grave," Amos Cadbury went on. "The handling of such a large amount of money is, in its way, a nuisance. It is almost a full-time job. Jason, your mother didn't want to burden you with that. She thought it better that everything be put into the hands of an experienced person who could take the responsibility off your shoulders. I think she expected me to play that role."

Jason nodded. "No one better, Amos."

"I think there is. Carmela has known a good deal of success doing just this sort of thing."

"Carmela would be even better, Amos. I know what my mother would have feared. Who could blame her? Besides, this keeps it in the family."

Delicately, Amos made it clear that Jason would not have control over his new wealth. He could not have acquitted his responsibility if that were unclear in Jason's mind. Even this fuller explanation did not faze Jason. Listening, Madeline wondered if Helen had realized that this arrangement would seal the reunion of Jason and Carmela.

There were further surprises as well, and Madeline understood why she and Natalie Armstrong were there. Helen had not forgotten her distant relatives. Natalie was left a tidy sum. Madeline was left some money but also, incredibly, the house.

"Oh, I couldn't," Madeline cried.

"Why not?" Jason asked, turning to her. "We certainly wouldn't want to live there."

Nathaniel followed the proceedings without visible reaction. Was he perhaps relieved that the money he had bequeathed to Helen, which would now go to Jason, would be in good hands with Carmela?

Amos's secretary came in with coffee and rolls, and the meeting altered its character. Everyone stood and began talking. Amos smiled benevolently at them all as if he had just maneuvered through some very choppy waters without incident. Had he imagined Jason objecting to having money but without control over it? Madeline went to Nathaniel and Natalie.

"I can't believe it," she said. "The house!"

"Blood is thicker than water," Nathaniel said.

Natalie began to explain exactly how she was related to Helen, as if she, too, needed an explanation for her good fortune. Her grandfather Armstrong had been related to Helen's grandfather by marriage. It all sounded very remote to Madeline, but perhaps her own connection was even more tenuous. How very nice it was of Helen to have thought of her. The image of the vindictive old woman at the St. Hilary senior center faded before these developments.

They moved into the outer office, but Carmela and Jason stayed behind with Amos Cadbury. Soon, Jason himself joined them, leaving his wife with the lawyer.

"What will you do with the Foot Doctor?" Madeline asked Jason.

"Keep it. It's the only successful thing I've ever done."

Madeline could not help remembering her visits there, the dinners she and Jason had shared, her silly thought that eventually the two of them would pool resources and live together, two old shirttail relatives heading into the twilight. Jason seemed younger suddenly, no longer the defeated figure he had been.

"I am reforming, Mad," he told her in a whisper. "Laugh if you want, but I mean it."

"Why would I laugh?"

"Is your memory that short?"

"And Carmela, will she go on working?"

"Of course. And I will be her client. You heard the provisions."

More than a client, certainly. How many clients were so thoroughly in Carmela's hands as Jason would be? It was so good to hear Jason's resolution. Madeline had heard others in the past, of course, but now the circumstances were so changed. Helen's death really seemed Jason's chance to grow up at last. What would happen if he didn't change, or if his reunion with Carmela were only temporary?

Carmela came out of the inner office with Amos, and her eyes met Madeline's. She came swiftly to her. "Can you believe this?"

"No. What on earth will I do with that big house?"

"Get a man and move in."

Immediately Carmela seemed to regret the remark, one she might have made years ago when they were girls together.

"Or you could sell it."

"I'll want your advice if I do."

"The first thing is to get your money well invested."

"You've already given me your card!"

"That's right. Let's talk about it."

"Your office is in Schaumburg?"

Carmela hesitated. "I may move my office to Fox River."

She went on to Nathaniel then, embracing the old man. "Oh, I've missed you so much," she said.

In her car, Madeline hesitated, then headed

for St. Hilary's. If Jason meant to continue at the Foot Doctor, she would continue to volunteer at the senior center.

9

News of the disposition of Helen Burke's worldly goods arrived at St. Hilary's rectory. Madeline told Edna Hospers, and Edna told Marie Murkin, and even though the housekeeper was slightly miffed that Edna was her source, she brought the news to the pastor, pardonably skipping one link in the chain. Father Dowling might have thought that Madeline had come directly to Marie. Father Dowling did not further diminish his housekeeper's excitement at the news by telling her he had already received it from Amos Cadbury.

"Natalie Armstrong!" Marie cried. "Who would have thought it? And Madeline Clancy as well. I'm surprised she didn't mention Nathaniel."

"Now, Marie."

"How much did he leave the parish?"

"It will go into your retirement fund."

"Retirement? What do you mean? I'm not going anyplace."

"That is my hope. But one has to look ahead, Marie."

Marie harumped, then grew thoughtful. "I wonder if Madeline will stay on as a volunteer at the center."

"Because of the inheritance?"

"And a house. Do you know what house we're talking about?"

In Marie's description of it, the Burke home was palatial, on two corner lots, back to back, the house built in the center, thus making the alley that led up to it from the far street a cul-de-sac. An arc of a driveway up to the front entrance, sheltered by a great pillared overhang under which cars could park.

"Three stories high, Father. There is actually a ballroom on the second floor."

"Did Helen dance?"

"Her mother did. She was a legend. Oh, what a comedown that family has known. Beginning with Helen, if the truth were told." Marie paused. "The friars loved her, of course."

"Generous?"

"In her fashion. I think they had high hopes. Who knows what she might have done if there hadn't been the shake-up?"

"Shake-up?"

Marie made a face. "When you came."

"Oh, what a comedown the parish has known."

Marie would not be teased. "Do you know what I sometimes hoped? That she would give that house to the parish."

"What on earth would we do with another house?"

"Imagine the parish center there."

"Have you mentioned this to Edna?"

Marie's manner changed. Perhaps the thought of Edna ensconced in the palatial residence she had been gushing over brought her down to earth. "Even so, I can't imagine Madeline living there. She's all alone, you know. Now if Helen had left the house to Natalie . . ."

"Isn't Natalie a widow?"

Marie began humming. "Not all widows remain widows, Father Dowling."

"Is that a threat?"

"You know what I mean."

"I'm not sure I do."

"Eugene Schmidt," Marie whispered. "Don't you have eyes in your head?"

"Isn't he younger than Natalie?"

"Younger! Well, perhaps. Still, you never know."

Marie glided off, as if she were on the floor of the ballroom in the Burke house. Father Dowling, remembering what Amos Cadbury had told him, wondered if he did have eyes in his head. He had felt almost delinquent when he found himself unable to tell Amos anything about Eugene Schmidt.

In midafternoon, when Marie had gone upstairs for what she called forty winks, Father Dowling left the rectory and strolled toward the school. The weather hovered between the just-departed winter and the yet-to-arrive spring, but the promise of spring seemed everywhere. Then he saw a robin! The harbinger of spring. When he was a boy, the sight of the first returned robin had always been occasion for comment. Somewhere ahead, no longer unimaginably distant, lay summer, and with it the days and weeks and months of indolence. He smiled. Indolence indeed. He had caddied from the time he was fourteen. Not that caddying could be thought of as penal servitude. In his memory, caddies seemed to spend most of the day lounging around the caddy shack, awaiting members who stole an afternoon for golf. It occurred to him that he had caddied for Mr. Burke, Florence and Helen's father.

How odd a thing memory is. Why had he never thought of that before? Probably because the disruptive Helen had gathered all attention to herself.

He was distracted by the sight of the

shuttle bus, looking forlorn in a far corner of the parking lot, where it had been placed when the police brought it back to the parish. The image stayed in his mind when he came into Edna's office on the second floor.

"Was there any damage to the shuttle bus, Edna?"

The question surprised her. "I don't know. Of course, there has been no thought of using it since . . ."

"I understand."

"I could have Earl take a look, if you'd like."

"Would you do that?"

"Father, I blame myself for letting Eugene Schmidt drive the bus that day. He insisted. I think he was afraid Natalie would go in Helen's car."

"Thank God she didn't."

"Oh, yes." Edna's eyes were full of thoughts of what might have happened.

"Have you gotten to know Schmidt well?"

Edna laughed. "Father, he'd talk your ear off if you let him. I thought he'd been to see you."

"He wanted to learn about the Church."

Edna was surprised. "Isn't he Catholic?"

"Just because he comes to the center?"

"But he goes off to the noon Mass with Natalie as often as not."

"Where is he from?"

"Where isn't he from? He seems to have been everywhere. I have to say, Herman is skeptical of Eugene's stories. He says Eugene would have to be a hundred to have done half the things he tells of."

"He's not a native of Fox River?"

"Oh, no." She stopped. "Now what makes me so sure? The fact is, Father, I know only what Eugene Schmidt wants me to know about him, and like Herman I take much of it with a grain of salt."

"What is the theme of his stories?"

"Women."

"Women?"

"You wouldn't believe the conquests he claims. Nothing lurid, of course, but he is the hero of all his stories."

"What does Natalie think of him?"

"So you've noticed. Father, he is a totally different man when he is with her. Not subdued, exactly, but deferential. A real gentleman. I can't imagine him telling her what a Don Juan he's been. Or claims to have been."

After he left Edna's office, Father Dowling went downstairs and looked into the former gymnasium. No sign of Schmidt. Outside again, he glanced toward the shuttle bus. Eugene Schmidt was there, walking around the vehicle, as if he were inspecting it. Father Dowling waited until Schmidt noticed his presence and then moved toward him over the asphalt surface.

Schmidt was shaking his head as he came up. "Father, I never had an accident in my life before. A serious accident."

"What could you have done?"

"I could have stayed in my lane, held off the guy who was trying to cut in on me."

That had been Schmidt's account of what had happened from the beginning. He had turned into Helen's path because another driver was turning into his. He had appealed in vain for corroboration from those riding in the bus. Passengers rode facing one another across the aisle and paid little attention to where they were going or where they had been.

"You haven't been to see me lately."

Schmidt seemed to have to remember his interest in the Church. He shook his head. "You're right, Father. I have to get back on track."

"Any time, Eugene."

After he left Schmidt, Father Dowling felt slightly duplicitous. Eugene Schmidt might want to talk theology, but Father Dowling wanted to find out what he could of Eugene Schmidt.

10

To Tetzel's disgust, Rebecca's story — story! Menteur ran it as a three-part serial — on the food provided to inmates of the county jail was the talk of the courthouse if not of the town. On her account, consignment to the jail was tantamount to being sent to Devil's Island, and the food was dished out in a way that rivaled Oliver Twist's orphanage. Tetzel was sure that it was Rebecca's remark that prisoners were allotted only seven cigarettes a day that explained the prominence Menteur gave the story.

"Wait'll readers see that," he gloated to Tetzel. "There'll be floods of indignant letters."

"I think Rebecca's point was that they should be allowed to smoke more than seven cigarettes a day."

Envying the prisoners, Menteur chomped on his gum, studying Tetzel. "How is *your* story going?"

"Maybe I should just write a letter first. To get the ball rolling."

"Get out of here."

Gladly. Rebecca's story was featured on the *Tribune's* Web site, of course. It probably had more readers there than in the print edition. He should have said as much to Menteur. Of course, that sword hung over them all. How long would newspapers grind up the forests of the continent, providing increasingly abbreviated accounts to compete with the kaleidoscopic fare of the Internet? Menteur was like the captain of the *Titanic,* oblivious of disaster ahead. Tetzel had a fleeting image of himself as Leonardo DiCaprio, disporting himself with Kate Winslet on the bow. If he had any sense, he would finish his novel.

The reference was to a file on his computer, largely notes, for the opus of which Tetzel had dreamed for years while tastes in fiction altered into directions he did not comprehend. His hero was a reporter, what else? Write of what you know. It occurred to him that his story should be of a gifted man wasting his sweetness in a doomed profession. *The Last Reporter?* He liked it. He picked up his pace as he returned to the pressroom in the courthouse.

By the time he got there, his novel was forgotten and his mind was once more full of the story he was writing on Jason Burke. He saw it as a prince-and-the-pauper story, from shoe store to golden slippers. Well, something like that.

When he entered the pressroom, Rebecca cried out. She was staring at the screen of her computer, an idiot smile on her face.

"What?" he asked reluctantly.

"My Web site, Gerry. My God, the response."

Tetzel stood beside her. Web site? REBECCA FARMER in a huge font ran along the top of the screen, below it an image of Rebecca that might have been her high school graduation picture. She scrolled down for Tetzel's benefit. Message after message.

"Any complaints about smoking in the jail?"

If Rebecca heard him, she ignored it. Tetzel went to his desk, flicked on his computer, and waited. If he had any principles at all, he would go back to a typewriter. Rebecca's continued squeals grated on his nerves. How could he work here? He took his tape recorder from a drawer, dumped it into his shoulder bag, and rose. Rebecca did not notice him leave.

He took a cab to the mall. He could charge it to the paper. When he got out, he paid, got a receipt, and stood looking at the facade of the Foot Doctor. He walked past it several times, waiting until there were no customers, then went in to the jangling of the bell over the door. The clerk greeted him with a smile that faded. Did he think Tetzel was returning the loafers?

"The boss in?"

"Not yet."

"I'd like to look around." He flashed his ID at the clerk.

"You're from the *Tribune*?"

There was awe and reverence in Eric's voice. Tetzel got out a pad. "Let me get your name down."

Eric Fleischhaecker. With two *h*'s. Tetzel nodded.

"How long have you worked here?"

"Since the store opened."

Almost a year. Tetzel nodded approvingly at such stability of place. "Show me around, would you?"

In the stockroom in back, Eric explained the arrangement of the shoes. "I come back here, I want to be able to grab what I want and get back to the customer. Never keep a customer waiting."

The bell jangled, and Eric looked out. A customer. Tetzel was left alone. Next to the stockroom was a smaller room, a table, some chairs, a little fridge. He opened it. Chock-full of beer. Guinness! Tetzel took a bottle and slipped it into his shoulder bag as he left the room. He stood and smiled sardonically at the sign hanging from the knob of a closed door. DOCTOR IS IN. Not according to Eric. Tetzel pushed open the door, waited, then went inside the office. He stood, taking in the scene, as he described it in his mind. Here, the disinherited son had pursued his honest entrepreneurial labors, little expecting that a tragic accident would propel him into affluence. The clerk had said that Jason intended to go on with the Foot Doctor. Why should he? You work to make money, and if you have money, why work? What would life be like if you never had to work? The bell in the showroom jangled again, but Tetzel was lost in meditation.

"Can I help you?"

Tetzel swung around and faced a man who could only be Jason Burke. He didn't seem angry to find someone in his office.

"Tetzel of the *Tribune*." He flashed his ID.

Jason Burke went past him and was about to sit in the Barcalounger but thought better of it. He took the chair behind the desk instead. "I already have a subscription."

"Ho-ho. Mr. Burke, yours is a fascinating story, and I want to tell it."

Jason shook his head. "No story."

Tetzel smiled. He would write this reluctance into his portrait of Jason. "Your clerk tells me you'll be keeping this store."

"How you fixed for shoes?"

"I bought a pair the other day. I had hoped to talk with you then."

"Okay, sit down. Let's get it over with."

Tetzel took the lounge chair, keeping it at ninety degrees. He got out his tape recorder and without thinking plucked a cigarette from the pack in his shirt pocket. He looked at Jason. "Is it all right if I smoke?"

"Go ahead."

All the odds and ends Tetzel had been picking up since the accident in which Helen Burke died began to fit together. But what he wanted was background, and he got it. All the schools, the rich young kid, and then the navy!

"You were in the navy?"

"I wasn't fat in those days."

"Just an enlisted man?"

"Seaman first class."

"Just give me the high points."

"Well, I served ten days in the brig once." He had been drinking beer with guys from his barracks. "It was the first time I was ever drunk. Just for the hell of it, I smashed a window in the barracks door. Destruction of government property. Ten days in the brig."

It might have been the beginning of the

downward spiral. Jason was happy to talk about all his failed businesses, the lawn service, babysitting pets. He had even been a nurse's aide in St. Mary's Hospital. That hadn't lasted long, either.

"All this was after you were disinherited?"

"Disinherited?"

"Cut off by your family. On your own."

"My mother always set me up in business. I wasn't cut off. Don't say that."

Tetzel's grunt might have been taken for agreement. "Okay. Now, Mrs. Burke."

"My mother was a fine woman."

"I meant your wife."

"I don't want to talk about her."

"Trouble?"

"No. No trouble. That's all over."

Jason pushed back from the desk and stood. He waited until Tetzel got up and packed up his equipment.

It hadn't been much, but with a little imagination Tetzel could work it into a dramatic exchange. Funny how he had clammed up when it came to his wife.

11

Carmela let Augie's calls accumulate on her cell phone without answering them. The past week had turned her life upside down, and through it all she had felt two-faced. She could see that everyone looked on her as the estranged wife returned, especially Jason. Would he have agreed to the provisions of the will if he didn't think that was the price he had to pay to get his wife back?

When Amos Cadbury had explained the provision to her, Carmela had been astounded. "Helen wanted me to look after the money?"

"She didn't specify a name," Amos had said carefully.

Of course, she had come to know this eminent lawyer over the years, thanks to the money he had been given on which she could draw as needed. It was a point of pride not to ask for it, but from time to time Amos had asked her to stop by, and she was happy to let him know how things were going with her.

He had nodded in approbation. "You have enough ambition for two."

She had shaken her head. "Things are better as they are."

So they had been. Amos had resisted at first when she suggested that she take over investing the money Helen had deposited for her with Amos, but eventually he had agreed and been suitably impressed by the results. It occurred to her later that she had been auditioning for the role that Amos proposed.

He had taken her aside after Helen's burial and said he wanted a word with her. They sat in the backseat of his huge car, the window between them and the driver closed, while he laid it out for her. It was pretty clear to Carmela that Helen must have thought that it would be Amos who would have control over Jason's money. Of course, it must have seemed only a remote possibility. Surely she couldn't have imagined that she would die before Amos.

"Are we agreed?" he asked when he had finished explaining.

"Jason will never agree."

"The arrangement is not contingent on his agreement."

It was like taking on another client. That was what she told herself in the car and again when she got out and joined the others. How easy it would be to fall in with what they all assumed. Carmela was back. The great obstacle to her marriage was at last removed. Without Helen's smothering interference, she and Jason could finally make a life for themselves. How proud he had been when he told her of the success of the Foot Doctor.

"I've stopped drinking, Carmela."

"Good." How often had he said that in the past?

"I haven't been in a casino for months. All that is over."

Despite herself, she believed him. It was Madeline's wariness that tipped the scales so that what would have seemed a return to the heartbreak her marriage had been began to alter to a possible future. When Amos responded to her question as to what conditions there were on her if she fell in with his interpretation of Helen's desire that Jason not have control over the money he would inherit, Amos had been careful, but the answer, although oblique, was clear. She could go on just as she was and still fulfill that role. There was no need to bring her separation from Jason to an end. Given Jason's response at the reading of the will, it was clear that he thought that now at last they could begin — but how many times in the past had they begun again? She told herself that she could not risk it, she did not have to go back to him, but surrounded by relatives, confronted by a clearly altered Jason, she wavered. She did not take Augie's calls.

"You and Jason should have the house," Madeline said.

"Madeline, it was left to you."

"What am I going to do with such a house?"

Sell it? Of course, Carmela knew that Madeline had retained her long-term cousin's crush on Jason. Whenever they met, Madeline's talk had been mainly of him. It might have been a not too subtle effort to bring wife and husband together again, but certainly that wasn't the whole of it. Once Madeline had spoken dreamily of how, when they were all old, the three of them could pool resources and live together. The huge Burke mansion could have provided the staging for such an odd trio. Clearly Madeline thought that the usual relationship between male and female was behind them now and they could be brother and sisters together. Madeline had always been a dreamer.

"Tell me about your work at the senior center."

Madeline gave a little wave of her hand. "I won't bore you with that."

It was clear Madeline wasn't bored by it, though. Talking with her, Carmela thought how odd it was that it was she, whose life had crumbled again and again, who felt on top of the world and Madeline, who had taught school for years, retired early, and was now helping out at the St. Hilary senior center, who seemed one of life's casualties.

"Carmela, the first thing you have to do is move Jason out of that dreadful place he lives in."

"I am not his keeper, Mad."

She got a little knowing smile in answer to that.

When she finally had a chance to get back to her office in Schaumburg, Carmela had no idea what she intended to do. She had made no promises, but she had allowed assumptions to be made. The closer she got to the offices of the Avanti Group, the more she thought of the assumptions she had allowed Augie to make.

"Get a divorce," he suggested.

"Augie, I'm Catholic."

"So am I. Sort of. Apply for an annulment."

"I don't want to think about it."

"Okay, we can just live in sin together."

That's what it was, of course. She told herself that no one could blame her, God couldn't blame her, an estranged wife whose marriage had been hell, alone, still young enough, successful, and admired by Augie. More than admired. How could she not think what her life would have been if she had met him long ago? She began to pretend

266

that was what was happening, that she was free and Augie loved her and . . .

After the first time, she went to confession in Barrington. She could hardly form the words. "Father, I committed adultery." She knelt in dread of the scolding she would now receive, but after a pause, the priest said, "Avoid the occasion of sin. For your penance say a decade of Our Lady's rosary."

Afterward she knelt, trying to pray the rosary but feeling that she had received a reprieve, almost permission. After that, it hadn't seemed necessary to confess it when, aglow with wine and a good dinner, enthralled by Augie's chatter, she had let him gather her into his arms. If only he wasn't such a swashbuckler with his clients' money.

Even before she told him what had happened in Fox River, he was giving her his bad news. He had lost half his clients.

"I'll be lucky if they don't sue me." He tried to smile. "Baxter is going back to teaching. He says he finds theory easier than practice."

She had warned them. Well, not warned them exactly, but showed her disapproval. She took chances, every financial advisor took chances, but there were chances and chances. It occurred to her that she was the only successful partner in the Avanti Group.

The circumstances weren't ideal, but she had to tell him of her own great turn of fortune.

"You're going back to your drinking husband?"

Later she would realize that was the moment when she could have done unequivocally what she had thought of doing while in Fox River, what everyone there assumed she would do. She could have told Augie that, yes, she was going back to her husband. Everything was changed now. Everything was different. Instead, what she said was "I think we should move our offices to Fox River. You'll find new clients there."

She did not resist when he took her in his arms.

12

Cy Horvath kept running into Maxwell, and when he wasn't running into him he was made aware that the investigator seemed to have been everywhere he was. Maxwell had talked with Herman at St. Hilary's; he had talked with Edna Hospers; he had examined the accident report that involved the shuttle bus. Cy came upon Maxwell lolling on a bench along one of the parish walks. He sat down beside him, upwind from Maxwell's cigar.

"Long time no see."

"Ah, Horvath."

"You thinking of spending time here at the senior center?"

Maxwell looked like the insurance man he had been until he became fascinated by the investigators who looked into questionable claims. He took a paralegal course, got a license, and then landed Amos Cadbury's firm as a client, a first fish that led to many more. If he was prospering, though, it was not evident in the neat but nondescript clothing he wore. A sport coat off the rack, open shirt, tan slacks, shoes with soles several inches thick. The cigar seemed a prop.

"What are we working on, Maxwell?"

"We?"

"I keep tripping over you."

"What are you working on?"

"Eugene Schmidt."

Maxwell extended a little finger, and Cy locked it in his.

"He just went by with his lady love to church," Maxwell said.

"Want to have lunch?"

At a nice little place several blocks away, Maxwell ordered a Greek salad and iced tea. Cy asked for a cheeseburger and Coke. Maxwell told Cy what he had learned of Schmidt, some of it news to Cy.

"I wonder if that's his real name, Cy. He came here by Amtrak three months ago and at first took a room in the Pelican Motel." Maxwell's brows danced. "Then he moved into the parish."

"Why do you say that?"

"He asked around about where people his age hung out and was told about the center here. You know he's a ladies' man."

"In Detroit?"

"He lived off a widow there for a year, until the family ran him out, probably dashing his plans. Funny thing. He apparently has babbled to Herman about all his conquests."

"You figure he's on the prowl again?"

"Natalie Armstrong."

"Even before she came into big money?"

Maxwell nodded. "Herman says Schmidt is taking instructions from the priest."

"Is he eligible?"

"Isn't everyone?"

"I meant for marriage."

"I've found no marriages involving Eugene Schmidt. Of course, marriage records are a mess. Not many states have centralized them. County by county." Maxwell sighed.

"He gave Herman the impression that he has been married several times."

"I suppose Amos Cadbury will warn Natalie Armstrong."

"By the look on her face when they went by, I don't think she'll believe him."

Cy wondered whether Amos would act on what Maxwell could give him. A widow in Detroit hardly looked like a federal case.

Maxwell wanted to talk about the accident when Schmidt had been driving the shuttle bus that had forced Helen Burke into the bridge abutment.

"He said he was forced into her lane," Cy said.

"Anyone else see that?"

Cy shook his head.

"I suppose the bus was examined."

"Earl Hospers, Edna's husband, looked it over. The parish bought it secondhand from a car rental agency. It was pretty battered at the time. There's a dent on the left front fender that may be recent, but Earl wouldn't swear to it. Schmidt kept insisting it was all his fault."

"Hmm."

"Everybody was pretty excited, of course."

They sat there and thought of the vehicle that supposedly had forced Schmidt into Helen Burke's lane, thus forcing her into the bridge abutment. Even if true, how could there be anything premeditated about it?

Maxwell said, "I'm still awaiting word on Schmidt's Detroit address before he moved in with the widow."

"Keep me posted."

"You got anything for me?"

"Marie Murkin likes him."

"Who's she?"

"The parish housekeeper."

"Tell her to be careful."

Dr. Pippen was fascinated by the story of Helen's will that was embedded in the story Tetzel had written about Jason Burke.

"The son, of course. But all those distant cousins."

"And there'll be more."

"How so?"

"Nathaniel Green's will, when he goes."

"Oh, Cy, that poor old man."

Pippen had responded to the story of Florence Green's death and Nathaniel's trial and conviction with unfeigned sympathy. His release from prison had been the subject of another Tetzel tearjerker and enlisted Pippen's sympathy even more. Nathaniel's decision to leave most of his money to his vindictive sister-in-law won her permanent allegiance.

"Is it true that the case will be reopened, Cy?"

"No."

"But that story in the paper . . ."

"Was a story in the paper. Tell me what you know of oxygen."

"We'd be dead without it."

"Exactly."

He told Pippen about the oddity of Florence Green's life support system. "Nathaniel said he had removed the mask from her face and thus killed her. How soon that was noticed at the nurses' station is hard to say. In any case, the oxygen petcock on the wall had been turned off."

"Before or after?"

"By whom is the question. Until I talked to him, Nathaniel never mentioned turning it off, only removing the mask."

"I suppose a nurse would have turned it off when she saw what he had done."

"But turning it off could have alerted the nurses' station."

"You must have looked into this at the time."

She might have kicked him in the shins. Cy had been kicking himself ever since he remembered the oxygen tap. Nearly a decade later. His only consolation was that memories of such long-ago events were untrustworthy.

"What will the one who got the house do with it?"

"Madeline Clancy? Who knows? She's unmarried."

"If she wants to sell, Dr. Kildare and I might be interested." Kildare was her name for the ob-gyn she had married.

"I'm told it has a ballroom."

"Shall we dance?"

Cy said nothing. His expression did not change. But his stomach turned slowly over at the thought of gliding across the floor with Pippen in his arms.

13

Eugene Schmidt came back to tell Father Dowling that his difficulties with the doctrine of the Trinity were all cleared up.

"How did that happen?"

"Natalie explained it by means of the three-leaf clover."

"Many have found that helpful," Father Dowling said carefully.

"So what's next?"

"How far have you gotten with the catechism?"

"Natalie gave me this." He pulled out an

old Baltimore Catechism. "She says this is much simpler. I like the way it begins."

" 'Why did God make me?' "

Schmidt nodded. "That gets you right into it, doesn't it?"

Father Dowling's interest in this unusual catechumen had been quickened by Amos Cadbury's intention to have the man's past looked into. Someone named Maxwell had been asking around, arousing Marie's indignation.

"What's the world coming to, Father Dowling? We're surrounded by spies."

"What did he want to know?"

"The family's put him up to this, you know."

"Did he say that?"

"He didn't have to! Who else would it be?"

"You told him all you know?"

"I gave him an earful, certainly."

"Marie, why would you think the family hired him?"

Marie made an impatient sound. "Natalie. Especially now that she's inherited all that money."

"Eugene was interested in her before that happened, wasn't he?"

"Of course. Not that Natalie didn't already have plenty."

"Really?"

Marie's expression was a knowing one, but her lips were sealed. Who knew what plenty meant for Marie Murkin? Or Eugene Schmidt, for that matter. "Did you tell the investigator that?"

"If he needs me to tell him, he's not much of an investigator."

"Does he know your net worth, Marie?"

"Ha."

"For all we know his coming around to see you was just a ruse."

"A ruse?"

"Maybe Eugene Schmidt isn't the only one attracted to handsome widows."

"He can eat his heart out for all I care."

And off she went to her kitchen.

It was Phil Keegan who told Father Dowling what had been learned thus far about Eugene Schmidt.

"A broken-hearted widow in Detroit?"

"Un-uh. She married someone else." Phil contemplated the ash of his cigar as if it were a symbol of lost hopes.

"Before he left?"

Phil didn't know. He would put the question to Cy. Meanwhile he had come to watch the Cubs on television. During a lull, he said that someone was loading up Jason Burke with liquor. First there had been a refrigerator full of beer at his shoe store, and then a case of scotch showed up in a back room. Jason had thought his clerk, Eric, was trying to lead him astray so that his own importance to the business would be clear.

"And?"

"The kid laughed when he was told the cost of a case of scotch. He has a base salary and gets a cut on each pair of shoes he sells. Buying beer and liquor for the boss just doesn't figure in his budget."

Amos Cadbury came by the next day and wondered if the Detroit widow wasn't reason enough to warn Natalie that she was being pursued by a fortune hunter.

"His interest dates from before the inheritance, Amos."

"She had money then."

"Her own?"

Amos nodded.

"But how could Schmidt know that? Most of the seniors were surprised to learn that Helen Burke was so well off. If she told Schmidt herself, she wouldn't need any warning, would she?"

Amos wasn't sure. "You couldn't have a conversation with her, could you, Father Dowling?"

"About that? Good Lord, no."

Amos nodded. "I couldn't do it myself."

Two days later, Natalie and Eugene came to the rectory to announce that they intended to marry. They had decided not to wait until Eugene became a Catholic.

"Is that your intention, Eugene?"

"There are one or two difficulties still, Father."

"I see."

"Original sin, for one."

Natalie smiled tolerantly. "I told him all he has to do is believe it, not explain it."

Father Dowling wondered how long Natalie would have had to wait if Schmidt's conversion was a condition of their marrying. He got down to business, explaining that he would want Eugene's baptismal certificate. The little mustache twitched.

"I don't think I ever was baptized."

"Oh, Eugene. You must have been."

"I don't remember."

"Of course you don't remember. You were a babe in arms." The description was fraught with tenderness.

"Sure I would." Eugene seemed to be thinking. "We were Baptists."

"No infant baptism," Father Dowling remarked. "Were you ever married before?"

The couple exchanged a look. Natalie said, "We've talked about that, Father. It wasn't what you would call a marriage anyway."

"A wedding chapel in Las Vegas," Schmidt said sheepishly. "I had met her the night before in one of the clubs. I was very young."

"You divorced?"

"She divorced me."

"Ah."

Eugene Schmidt's past became more mysterious as the interview continued. What had he done for a living?

"What I haven't done would be a better question, Father. I've been a rolling stone." He took Natalie's hand. "Now I've come to rest at last."

Natalie wanted a May wedding, and Father Dowling booked them for the first Saturday in May. Weddings were now a rare event at St. Hilary's. Perhaps Schmidt's past would become less mysterious before then.

At least Eugene Schmidt's Nevada marriage seemed cleared up. Father Dowling mentioned it to Amos Cadbury, who passed on the information to Maxwell.

Two days later, the lawyer called. "There is no record of a divorce in Nevada, Father."

Father Dowling looked at the appointment book, open on his desk. Would he have to X out that entry for the first Saturday in May?

"There is no record of a marriage, either," Amos said.

"It all sounded very vague, Amos."

"Vagueness seems to characterize the man's past."

Father Dowling talked to Eugene alone. The dapper little man seemed surprised. "You checked up on it?"

"Amos Cadbury is the family lawyer, Eugene. He thought it best to look into it."

Schmidt laughed. "Do you know, Father, I'm really not surprised. I'm afraid neither of us was completely sober at the time."

"What was the woman's name?"

After some moments, Schmidt said, "Holly. Yes, I'm pretty sure that's what it was. Holly."

"A last name?"

"She was more interested in acquiring mine."

"There seems to be no record of the marriage."

Schmidt threw up his hand. "Now I wish I hadn't mentioned it."

"Are there other things I should know, Eugene?"

"As I told you, Father, I've been a rolling stone, but there's nothing else that could prevent my marrying Natalie."

Father Dowling wished he could believe the man. Did Natalie realize what she was getting into? He had seldom seen a young bride more enthralled with her prospective husband than Natalie Armstrong was with Eugene Schmidt.

He decided he would ask Madeline Clancy's advice on how to deal with this sensitive subject.

14

Tuttle heard about Maxwell from Peanuts, who had seen the investigator with Cy Horvath.

"What's he looking into?"

Peanuts didn't know. His was a limited curiosity, but Tuttle was glad that the slow-witted Pianone had at least taken notice of Maxwell and brought the information to him. Now the question was, what could he do with it? A little scouting around told Tuttle that Cy Horvath was now on the same quest as Maxwell. What that quest was emerged from a chat with Herman the German in his basement apartment at St. Hilary's school.

"Geez," Herman said, accepting the six-pack Tuttle had brought to smooth the waters. "What's the guy wanted for, anyway?"

"You'd probably know better than anyone else."

"Me!" Herman was alarmed. Ratting on Schmidt or anyone else was not in his repertoire. "You want one of these?" He pulled a can loose from the plastic rings from which six cans swung like toneless chimes.

"Thank you."

Herman reluctantly handed over one of the beers, took another for himself, and put the four remaining in his fridge. It looked empty to Tuttle.

"You fix your own meals or what?"

"I eat at the rectory."

Tuttle was surprised, so Herman went on to explain his early dinners in the rectory kitchen. "But it's what she prepares for him."

"Him" would be Father Dowling. "Herman, people would kill to get a job like yours."

The only fly in the ointment was Marie Murkin, who seemed to think she was Herman's boss. "I got a boss other than the Father it would be Edna Hospers."

"A wonderful woman," Tuttle said unctuously. "I suppose you knew her husband . . . before."

Herman shrugged. "It all depends on what you mean by 'knew.'"

"You ever think of running for president?"

Herman didn't get it. Well, maybe he hadn't followed the news closely when he was in Joliet. "He was out here the other day," Herman said.

That did not seem a special event to Tuttle, until Herman mentioned Earl had been checking out the center's shuttle bus.

"Was there damage to it?"

"Ask him." Herman tipped back his can and drank thirstily.

Tuttle nodded, as if making a note of the suggestion. "Did Maxwell talk to Eugene Schmidt?"

"Ask him."

Tuttle nodded at this sage advice. "Wasn't Schmidt driving the bus when the accident happened?"

"Accident! He says it was all his fault. For days he talked about nothing else. Swerved right into the path of her car without looking into the rearview mirror. All the old people were whooping it up behind him, and then some guy cut in front of him and he swerved into the right lane to avoid getting hit. The bus went bumping onto the shoulder and nearly turned over. When Schmidt got out, he looked back and saw the car crumpled into the bridge abutment."

"You sound like you were there."

"I got it, blow by blow. He couldn't shut up about it. He practically begged the police to run him in."

Herman finished his beer and crunched the can. "Another?" he asked as if he were willing Tuttle to say no.

"I'm fine. I brought the beer for you."

Herman got a fresh can from the fridge and popped the tab. He settled back in his chair now. He was still three cans to the good, and he was ready to shoot the bull with Tuttle.

"You were Nathaniel Green's lawyer, weren't you?" Herman asked.

"Was? I still am."

This was a delicate point. Nathaniel had yet to come to him since the reading of Helen Burke's will. Not that he was a beneficiary or anything, but as Tuttle saw it his client had been absolved of the will Tuttle had drawn up for him, leaving the lion's share to his sister-in-law.

"Call him," Hazel had urged. Reading about all that money changing hands had her salivating. Surely some portion of it

284

should come to Tuttle & Tuttle. Tuttle liked the thought so much he didn't tell her how unlikely it was. Of course, Nathaniel had promptly paid the bill Hazel sent him after Tuttle drew up his new will.

He had been as surprised as anyone that Helen hadn't left the whole bundle to her son, Jason. Jason was a loser, but blood is thicker than water. Unless Nathaniel changed his will, Madeline Clancy and Natalie Armstrong were in for another bonanza when the old man died.

"He around?"

"Who?"

"Nathaniel Green."

"They don't check in with me, Tuttle."

"You two have more in common than anyone else here, Herman."

"Nathaniel didn't kill his wife," Herman said.

"Why do you say that?"

"Because he confessed."

"That doesn't make a lot of sense."

"To a priest. He told me. Look, it's like Schmidt claiming he's responsible for that accident. If he was, he would have shut up about it."

"Interesting."

"Now he's getting married."

"Nathaniel?" Tuttle sat forward in alarm

as if prey he had been stalking had been jumped by another predator.

Herman gurgled. "Ha. No, Schmidt."

"Come on. Who's the lucky lady, Marie Murkin?"

Beer improved Herman's sense of humor. His laughter made Tuttle feel like a wit. "Natalie Armstrong."

Tuttle fell back. "She's loaded."

"I know what you're thinking," Herman said.

"What am I thinking?"

"The lady comes into money and right away Schmidt goes for her."

"It would be a powerful incentive."

"He was sweet-talking her long before the accident." Herman made it sound like proof of true love.

"They're really getting married?"

"They've talked to the priest. Schmidt doesn't even have to turn Catholic first."

Herman crunched his empty can and took another beer from the fridge, not offering Tuttle one this time.

Here was food for thought. No wonder Amos Cadbury had put Maxwell on the trail of Eugene Schmidt. The man had been a frequent presence at the St. Hilary senior center for months, but where had he come from? Who was he? Tuttle could understand that Amos Cadbury did not like the thought of a stranger coming to town and marrying a woman whose lawyer he was. Particularly when that woman had some money of her own, had just come into a packet from Helen Burke's will, and stood to add to all that when Nathaniel Green bit the dust. Whatever secrets there might be in Schmidt's past would not be secret long.

Tuttle went off to the courthouse and looked into the pressroom. Only Rebecca was there.

"Where's the ace reporter, sweetheart?"

"The two of clubs is across the street."

"I have half a mind to give the scoop to you."

"Half a mind is all you've got, Tuttle."

Why couldn't he josh with Hazel like this? He could propose to Rebecca and she would go right on hitting her keyboard.

"Too bad about the smoke-free ordinance."

Rebecca tossed her head. "We're protected."

"Then you haven't heard?"

"Heard what!" She swung from her computer and looked openmouthed at Tuttle.

"Of course, it's just a rumor."

"For God's sake, tell me." She was nervously lighting a cigarette although a half-smoked one still tilted from her ashtray.

"Whatever I know I learned from Tetzel."

"That son of a bitch."

"Any other message for him?"

Tetzel had confided in him Menteur's insistence that his reporter write a piece blasting the hypocrisy of the city council for exempting the courthouse from the smoke-free ordinance.

"What'll you do?"

Tetzel had looked sly. "I'm interviewing the man in the street. One gripe after another about the ordinance. We should have done this when it was before the council. It's the beginning of my campaign to have it repealed, Tuttle. That ought to please Menteur."

He found Tetzel in a booth in the bar across the street, a scotch and water before him, a pleased smile on his face. Tuttle slid in across from him, having placed an order for a shandy when he passed the bar. Passed the bar. Unpleasant memories of the number of attempts it had taken him to be admitted to the local bar came and went.

"Rebecca says you're a son of a bitch."

"I didn't know you were taking maternity cases, Tuttle."

Tuttle squinted. "There is a resemblance."

Tetzel dismissed this. His pleased expression had not gone away. "My story on Jason Burke is featured on the paper's Web site."

Tuttle's shandy arrived, and he toasted Tetzel. "Let me be the first to congratulate you."

"What do you mean, first? Menteur actually gushed about the story."

"I suppose you've heard about Maxwell?"

Tetzel's smile faded, but there was wariness in his eye. "The coffee?"

"Are they still in business?"

"Who the hell is Maxwell, Tuttle?"

"I thought you'd never ask."

He hunched over the table, and Tetzel followed suit. Tuttle pushed his tweed hat to the back of his head, then took it off and put it on the seat beside him.

Tetzel didn't know who Eugene Schmidt was until Tuttle reminded him of the accident that had killed Helen Burke. "Schmidt was driving the shuttle bus."

Tetzel remembered.

"Okay. I don't have to tell you who Natalie Armstrong is. She's going to marry Eugene Schmidt."

Tetzel sat back in disgust. "I don't do the society page, Tuttle."

Tuttle waited. Tetzel was no idiot, no matter what people said. Thoughts came and went. He sipped his drink. Finally he said, "It's like a series, Tuttle. All involving the same family, more or less. First the return of Nathaniel Green and his new will. Then Jason Burke, son and heir who is determined to go on with his shoe store. And now . . ."

"Now one of Helen Burke's heirs is about to marry a man that Maxwell has been hired to check out. Cy Horvath is on it, too."

"What do we know of the man, Tuttle?"

"I wouldn't presume to do your work for you. I suppose you'll talk to Maxwell."

Tetzel offered another shandy to Tuttle, but the little lawyer held up a staying hand. "I have miles to go before I sleep, Gerry."

"Who doesn't?"

15

Warn Natalie about the mysterious Eugene Schmidt? Madeline had begun to shake her head even while Amos Cadbury was formulating the question.

"Madeline, the man's life can be traced back less than a year, to Detroit. Before that is a total blank."

"Have you been investigating him?"

"Not personally, of course. Madeline, would I be a worthy lawyer to the family if I just shut my eyes to this development?"

Madeline thought about Eugene Schmidt, the heartthrob of the widows at the senior center until his interest had focused on Natalie. Such a harmless little fellow, with his twinkling eyes and neat little mustache. He looked like fun, and Madeline felt she understood why Natalie had responded to him. Was he as old as Natalie? Not that a little age difference made a particle of difference at their time of life. Working at the center had restored Madeline's sense that she was still young, that life lay ahead of her, not just behind. She imagined that Natalie and Eugene would live together as she had once dreamt she and Jason might.

"We don't need another sensational story about the family, Amos."

He closed his eyes as if in pain. Tetzel's story about Jason and the Foot Doctor had made Jason seem a minor hero. Come into piles of money, he intended to just go on as he had before. Winners of the lottery often made similar claims. What Madeline had feared was that Jason's turn of fortune would reawaken his vices, but he seemed genuinely through with drink and gambling.

Amos said, "Thank God the story didn't mention Carmela's control of his money. Think of what the reporter would have made of that."

Madeline said nothing. When at the reading of Helen's will Amos mentioned this proviso, adding that he and Jason had already discussed it, Madeline had assumed that Amos was taking Jason under his wing. But Carmela! Jason's estranged wife had established herself in Schaumburg; she was by all accounts successful, which no doubt was the reason she had been chosen as custodian of Jason's money. Madeline couldn't believe that Carmela would accept such a role. All her experience with Jason had been unhappy; why should she think he would be different now?

Madeline knew immediately that this arrangement would bring Jason and Carmela together again. She wouldn't be surprised if that had been Amos Cadbury's intention. No one could ever convince Madeline that Aunt Helen would have wanted such a reunion. Now Carmela had moved the Avanti Group to Fox River.

"Is it still a group?" Madeline asked.

"One of the partners is moving with her. A man she calls Augie Liberati."

"Calls?"

"I assume Augie is short for August. Maybe even Augustine."

■ ■ ■ ■

It was short for August. He was there when Madeline stopped by the new offices of the Avanti Group.

"How would you like to have been named after a month?" he asked her.

"I was named after a repentant sinner."

"Mary Magdalene?" Carmela said. "I never thought of that. It seems so inappropriate."

Why should she have been annoyed at the suggestion that she was not a repentant sinner? Oh, everyone was some kind of sinner, of course; Madeline made no great claims for herself. She had led an uneventful life. Temptation had never come her way.

Augie said, "Look who's talking. You were named after a candy."

"I was not. The allusion is to Our Lady of Mount Carmel."

"That's a high school football team."

Other women seemed so at ease with men, joking with them, able not to take them seriously, an easy and comfortable equality. Madeline envied her old friend's ability to banter with her partner. Not that she wasn't all seriousness when Madeline explained why she had come. They were in Carmela's office then.

"Madeline, I am flattered." She paused. "I do have some misgivings, however. As you know, I now have responsibility for Jason's assets. Which are considerable. And I manage a little account for Natalie."

"Really?"

"If you didn't know, consider it a confidence. You can see what I am getting at. I would feel uncomfortable with even more family money in my hands."

Madeline was disappointed and must have shown it.

"Not that I would want your money to get away from the group." Carmela smiled.

She meant Augie. That did seem a solution. Madeline felt less rejected. Carmela called Augie in. He listened, all seriousness now. He nodded his head. In a minute, Madeline was in his office, trying to explain that she hadn't the least idea how to handle the money that was suddenly hers.

"That's what we're here for, Madeline. You want it in professional hands."

"It was Amos Cadbury's suggestion." Hadn't he more or less intimated such a thing? In any case, it seemed a pardonable stretch of the truth. Amos had cautioned her to proceed carefully in selecting someone to manage her money.

"It's a considerable sum, as you know, Madeline," the old lawyer had purred.

"That is a considerable sum," Augie said as she sat in his office. "What we need is a plan. I will work it out and submit it for your approval."

"I suppose it was silly asking Carmela to do this."

"This is the best solution. But we have no secrets in the Avanti Group. Carmela and I pool our expertise."

Of course, there would be a fee for all this, but Augie smiled when he said it. "That will be absorbed in the money you will be earning. Your principal can only grow."

"Wise move," Jason said when she went by the Foot Doctor to tell him what she had done. "The thing about money is to be able to forget it."

It seemed to be his way of indicating his acceptance of Carmela's role in managing his assets. She couldn't resist trying to find out what else the arrangement meant.

"And now Carmela has come back."

"Well, her business has. She still has her condo in Schaumburg."

"Jason, you should get out of that dreadful place in which you're living."

"So we can set up housekeeping again?"

Her breath caught until she realized he meant Carmela. "Will you?"

He tipped back in his Barcalounger. "In good time, perhaps. We're both out of practice." He righted his chair. "Say, do you remember that pizza man who was found in the river?"

Madeline needed a reminder of John Thomas.

"He was on his way to make a delivery here. Eric ordered it. The poor widow is destitute. I decided to do something about that. Carmela approved, of course. I have settled a little annuity on Mrs. Thomas."

"Oh, Jason! What a wonderful thing to do."

"Carmela's partner wasn't wild about the idea."

"Augie?"

"Yes." Jason's eyes went away from Madeline as he said it. Which is when Madeline had a dreadful thought, only it wasn't really so dreadful when she thought about it.

She and Jason went to the Great Wall for dinner. When he asked for hot tea, she could have kissed him. This was indeed a new Jason. Would he really care if Carmela did not come back to him as everyone seemed to assume he would?

The fact that Carmela had kept her condo in Schaumburg and there were no immediate plans for a reunion with Jason filled Madeline with a hope she would not have wanted to analyze. She remembered the bantering couple at the Avanti Group. She could imagine that Carmela in her loneliness had found her partner attractive. Augie's reaction when she had told him she was unmarried came back to her.

"You may find it difficult to keep it that way now."

"Is that an offer?" She couldn't believe she had said that.

"Well, I am eligible."

That was that. Madeline wondered if she was getting the hang of banter between the genders.

Augie was unmarried. Carmela had known him during her years of loneliness. Was it unthinkable that theirs had been more than a business arrangement? And wasn't it odd that he had agreed to move to Fox River with Carmela?

Then Jason told her that a man named Maxwell had come to him to talk about Eugene Schmidt. "What in God's name would I know about him?"

"He is going to marry Natalie, Jason."

Clearly this was the first Jason had heard

of it. He seemed to be searching for a way to react to this. Finally he just shook his head.

"I'm surprised he didn't go after you, Madeline."

16

Madeline, Natalie, and Nathaniel had asked Father Dowling to say a special Mass for the repose of the soul of Helen Burke. Jason was there as well, but not Carmela. Amos Cadbury, kneeling erect, in black as usual, was in a pew just behind the family. The Mass took place on the Thursday of the fourth week of Lent, and when Marie Murkin hurried over from the rectory, she found the church much fuller than usual. A tribute to Helen? Perhaps. As likely as not, just being nice to all these well-to-do people among them.

Shame on me, Marie said to herself, trying to mean it.

Father Dowling came out of the sacristy then; members of the congregation got to their feet, some with relative ease, others by grabbing the back of the pew ahead and pulling themselves upright, others with the aid of canes. It did Marie's heart good to feel spry and comparatively young among these regulars at the senior center.

People grow old in different ways, Marie knew that. It's all a matter of genes. Why else did doctors always ask how old your mother and father were when they died? So let people jog themselves into cadavers, pursue one crazy diet after another, quit smoking. Did that add one cubit to their stature?

"How biblical you've become, Marie," Father Dowling had said when Marie developed this thought for him.

Was that why the phrase had come so easily? Catholics get the Bible in the readings at Mass, selections, bits and pieces, and it just sticks to the mind like phrases from the liturgy. Priests are different, of course. Father Dowling was going through the Bible for the second time since Marie had known him. She had opened it once and been surprised.

"Latin?"

"The Vulgate."

"It's been translated, you know."

"So has Dante."

That seemed to be an answer. The pastor seldom went on about anything he didn't want to talk about. Not that he wasn't communicative. Marie was certain that she knew more about parish affairs now than she ever had under the friars. Her great regret was his unwillingness to seek her advice in matters on which, let's be frank, she knew a lot more than he did.

So they'd had a pretty good talk about Nathaniel Green when all that came up, but where would they be if Marie had not taken action in Helen Burke's campaign against her brother-in-law? And now Helen's will and the way it had changed the lives of so many people. Marie was mystified by the way Father Dowling wasted hours with Eugene Schmidt.

Oh, he was a charmer, no doubt about that. He had tried to sweet-talk Marie a time or two, but she had all the experience she needed of that type. The Don Juan of the senior center. Breaking hearts right and left and then coming to the rectory saying he wanted to take instructions.

Ha. What he wanted was to marry Natalie Armstrong, and if the only way he could do that was by becoming a Hindu, he would. Marie had happened to overhear some of those exchanges. What is worse than an amateur theologian? Of course, Father Dowling would go that extra mile in the line of duty. And he should, Marie conceded. She herself would have bounced Schmidt out the back door on his second visit.

"It's Natalie Armstrong, you know."

Father Dowling looked at her.

"He's interested in her."

"Is there some impediment, Marie?" His eyebrows rose, and she got out of there.

But after Natalie and Eugene came to say they wanted to get married, Marie sensed that curiosity about the little fellow had begun. Father Dowling had meetings with Amos Cadbury, and then that man Maxwell had come around asking questions about Eugene Schmidt. Even then, Father Dowling wouldn't open up. So Marie had gone to talk to Edna Hospers.

Such visits were always a matter of high diplomacy, only possible if they were conducted as between sovereign nations. Marie had given up trying to treat Edna as an underling, and Edna was a lot less huffy now when Marie showed up.

Marie sat across from Edna, looked at her in silence for a moment, then said, "Eugene Schmidt." Just the name. She waited. Everything depended on Edna's response.

"I can't believe that Natalie is such an idiot," Edna said.

Marie relaxed. They were off on the right foot. "Someone should talk with her."

"Would you want to, Marie?"

It was a problem, no doubt about that. Who had ever had any luck convincing a woman that she was about to pick a lemon in the garden of love? Marie shook her head.

"Father Dowling?"

"He's going to marry them!"

Edna shook her head. "That sort of thing happens from time to time here. Crushes, little flurries of emotional attachment. A little twinge of arthritis and it's gone. I knew he was trouble from the beginning."

"How so?"

"He's like a salesman, always giving a pitch. But what he's selling is Eugene Schmidt."

"And Natalie is buying."

"She can afford it."

That put it on the table. Was Eugene Schmidt a fortune hunter or not?

"He did start showing interest in Natalie before Helen left her all that money."

"But she had money of her own before."

"I didn't know that."

Marie did not say that there were many things about St. Hilary's that she knew and Edna Hospers did not.

"Where is he from exactly, Edna?"

"Did that man Maxwell talk with you?"

"Of course."

"That's what he wanted to know."

"Where does he live?"

Edna displayed her palms. "I should have asked Maxwell that."

"Can't you ask Schmidt?"

"Would you like to?"

"Well, Edna, if I was seated behind that desk I would think I had the right to such routine information as that."

"They don't register, Marie. They just come. It's very informal."

"But that means that just anyone can come and prey upon those poor women."

"Not the poor ones, Marie."

Now, in church, distracted by all this, Marie shook herself back into attention to what was going on on the altar. But how could she concentrate on the Mass when the little cottony head of Eugene Schmidt, seated in the front pew when all around him knelt, was in her direct line of vision?

17

When Amos Cadbury came to the new offices of the Avanti Group, he met Augie Liberati for the first time. A more susceptible man than Amos might have been flattered by the deference shown him by Carmela's partner.

"Welcome to Fox River," Amos said.

"I have a sister who lives here," Augie said.

Carmela swept out of her office then and hurried up to Amos, embracing him. This form of greeting had, of course, become widespread. Amos did not approve, though nothing in his manner of expression revealed this.

"You've met Augie? Good. Come in, I want to tell you what I've been doing."

Amos was suitably impressed by the new offices — he had never seen the old, however — and even more impressed by the investment plans Carmela had drawn up. It was clear that Jason was in good hands. If only they had hit upon this arrangement years ago, how pleasant the lives of Carmela and Jason would have been.

"So, you're all settled in," he said, when she closed the folder.

"As you see."

"I meant personally."

"I am keeping the condo in Schaumburg for the present."

Amos went smoothly on. "You will find housing in Fox River much less expensive."

"Isn't it wonderful that Madeline has that wonderful house?"

"It is a wonderful house. Whether it is wonderful for Madeline remains to be seen."

Carmela thought about that, as if it had

just occurred to her that the Burke house was far more than any unmarried woman could need, or use.

"She'll manage, Amos. Madeline always has."

Amos found this surprising. Of all those so tenuously related people, Amos had always thought of Madeline as a somewhat lost and bewildered woman. Well, doubtless Carmela knew her better than he did.

"And how is Jason?" he asked.

"Do you want me to clear this plan with him?"

Amos considered the question. The pattern for the arrangement would be set now. There was no use pretending that Jason had veto power over what Carmela did with his money. Not that she had utter carte blanche. Amos considered himself the general overseer of her activities. Hence this visit.

"That is up to you, of course."

"But you approve the plan?"

"Certainly. I can understand the success you have had."

As he was leaving, Augie came out of his office to say good-bye to the distinguished visitor.

"I wonder if I know your sister," Amos said.

"Amos," Carmela cried, laughing. "Even I

don't know her."

Through the door the two of them went to Amos's waiting car. She actually helped him in and then stood waving as the car pulled away.

"Downtown, sir?"

"No, Marvin. Let's go to the mall."

"The mall?"

"I want to see a store called the Foot Doctor."

Marvin nodded, and Amos settled back. He and Marvin had worked out a modus vivendi over the years. Amos was as democratic as the next man, but in the car he preferred silence and a chance to think. The visit to the Avanti Group provided much food for thought.

There certainly had been no announcement to that effect, but Amos had assumed that his interpretation of Helen Burke's will, giving control of Jason's assets to Carmela, had brought the two together again — or would — but Carmela had given little credence to that view just now. Retaining her condo in Schaumburg. Doubtless it was unrealistic to expect that a couple that had gone through what Carmela and Jason had would find it easy to reconcile immediately. All in good time. Still, the smiling, too diffident Augie gave Amos pause. It was odd, too, that Carmela had shut off all inquiries into the man's Fox River sister.

The satisfaction he had felt when Carmela outlined her investment plan for Jason's assets was somewhat diminished by his disappointment that she seemed in no hurry to return to her husband. Well, who could blame her? Jason's apparent reform was reassuring, but he had made such resolutions many times before. Now, in the absence of the suffocating presence of Helen, there seemed a chance that the resolution would stick.

Amos sighed. How difficult it could be to acquit oneself of one's duty to clients. Such a family. The tragic Nathaniel, who had insisted on his guilt when Florence died, who had been tried and sent to prison and now, released, seemed a mere shadow of himself. One did not have to be a lawyer to wonder at Nathaniel's decision to frequent the senior center at St. Hilary's, where Helen, his nemesis, was a constant presence. Surely he had not been surprised at her reaction to his coming there? And then the new will, drawn up by the ineffable Tuttle, and with dubious ethics announced to the world. Nathaniel's subdued and distant air made it difficult to interpret this as a vindictive move, but surely it had that effect on Helen.

Armed with what Cy Horvath had learned, however ambiguous, Amos had undertaken to relieve Nathaniel's mind.

"You didn't do it, Nathaniel. You couldn't have. The oxygen supply was cut off when the wall tap was turned. You know you didn't do that."

"But I did. Can one intend to do what he did not do?" Nathaniel asked.

Amos advised him to discuss that with Father Dowling. He was as certain as he could be that Nathaniel had confessed to a crime he had not committed and spent long years in jail unjustly. Nathaniel's indifferent reception of this enabled Amos to see how infuriating Helen Burke had found her brother-in-law.

And Natalie! All efforts to piece together the past of the man she was determined to marry had failed. The very fact that his past was a vast unknown should have been sufficient reason for Natalie to have second thoughts, but she was as excited as a girl at her impending nuptials, scheduled for the second week after Easter.

Now, going on to the Foot Doctor, where he hoped to talk to Jason, Amos was oppressed by the seeming futility of his efforts.

But how far did the writ of his responsibility run? It was no part of his task to make certain that everyone lived happily ever after. No, it wasn't. Of course it wasn't. Still, wouldn't it be pleasant if at least someone emerged from all this happy?

Marvin crept along the mall road when they got there and found the Foot Doctor. Amos asked him to park, but then he sat on in the back, wondering what the point of all this was. Well, now that he was here, he would go in. When Amos sat forward, Marvin got out, glided around the car, and opened the door.

Before going in, Amos saw that there were half a dozen customers in the store. Doubtless they would be replaced by others when they left. He pushed at the door and a bell went off. No one looked at him. Amos glanced toward the back of the store, then went to an empty chair and sat, watching the clerk help people try on shoes, going back and forth to the stockroom.

"I'll be with you in a minute, sir," he said as he went by Amos.

Amos lifted a hand from the armrest. How long had it been since he had been in a shoe store?

A woman who could not make up her

mind was contemplating two different styles of shoe, one of each in either hand, her face a mask of indecision.

"Maybe you should take both," the clerk said, in a half-serious voice.

Her face lit up. Of course. He had hit upon the solution. When the clerk finally came to him, Amos congratulated him on his Solomonian suggestion. The clerk — Eric by his name tag — smiled radiantly, but there was no comprehension in his eyes.

Amos got out his wallet and gave a card to Eric. While waiting, he had been wondering if Jason would emerge from his office, thus shortening his time in the showroom. He had thought of just marching to the back and looking for Jason's office, but, of course, he could not do that.

"Would you tell Jason Burke I am here?"

Eric threw up his hands. "You've been waiting all this time to see him?"

Amos smiled and nodded.

"But he isn't here." The clerk was whispering. "This is the second day he hasn't come in."

Doubtless this confidence was inspired by Eric's connection of Amos Cadbury with his employer. Unstated in the whispered confidence was that Jason had fallen back into his old habits.

"You've called his home, of course."

"He doesn't answer."

"Hmmm."

Amos asked for and got Jason's address and telephone number, then rose. Eric came with him to the door, and Amos exited to the jingling of the bell.

Madeline had said something to him about the way Jason lived, but as Marvin drove slowly among the decrepit buildings, searching for the address Eric had given, Amos felt his spirit sink. The development looked like the objective correlative of Jason's years of irresponsibility.

Marvin had come to a stop. His eyes in the rearview mirror were on Amos. "Would you like me to come with you, sir?"

"That might be best."

They approached the doorway together, and as they did Amos saw that the door was not completely shut. He pushed it slightly more open and called, "Jason."

There was no sound from within. Amos went inside with Marvin beside him.

The smell of alcohol was overpowering, as if it had been splashed around the room rather than drunk. The room, visible in the light from the open door, was a shambles. Marvin turned on a light, but that only made the scene more sordid.

"Jason?" Amos called again. "It's Amos Cadbury."

He went toward the bedroom, reaching in to turn on the light.

A crumpled and bloody Jason lay on the floor beside the bed.

■ ■ ■ ■

PART FOUR

■ ■ ■ ■

1

Marvin called 911, and, while they waited for the arrival of the paramedics, Amos called Phil Keegan. He gave the captain of detectives a dispassionate description of the scene he and Marvin had come upon.

"Is he dead?"

"I don't know."

In the doorway of the bedroom, Marvin shook his head.

"Apparently not, Captain."

"I'll send Cy Horvath immediately. I don't have to tell you not to touch anything."

Marvin kept vigil by the body, but Amos waited in the car for the arrival of officialdom. Birth and death and everything in between are private events that must concern the public — and where would the legal profession be if that were not the case? Soon the wail of a siren was heard, then another. People in the neighboring units had been showing curiosity about Amos's car, but at the sound of sirens they withdrew behind closed doors. Amos got out of the car when the ambulance arrived; almost immediately, Cy Horvath was there. He nodded to Amos and followed the paramedics into the house.

Agnes Lamb stayed with Amos. "You found a body."

"Jason Burke. My driver thinks he is still alive. He was brutally beaten. The place is a mess."

"I think it always is."

Amos was surprised.

"We've been here before, in the line of duty. What brought you here today?"

"I called at his store. He hadn't been in for two days." He looked at Agnes. "I wanted to make certain he was all right."

"As his lawyer?"

Amos might have resented being reduced to a cipher in an investigation if he had not heard so many good things of this young officer.

"There was no need for him to live like this."

Agnes looked around. "Some of the places have been fixed up."

She was right. Would Amos have noticed if she hadn't pointed it out?

"Yuppie slumming," she said, an edge to

her voice.

She might have lapsed into a foreign language, or some jargon unknown to Amos. He said nothing.

Jason was alive, but in serious condition. He seemed to have been beaten mercilessly and left to die by himself. Only that hadn't happened, at least not yet. The imperative now was to get him to the hospital, and soon the paramedics, having done what they could on the spot, were carrying Jason to the waiting ambulance.

Cy Horvath appeared in the doorway of Jason's unit. "Where the hell are the lab people?"

When the medical examiner and his team arrived, Cy gave the instructions as to what he wanted.

"Yes, master," said the butterball leader of the team, saluting sharply. Cy ignored this.

He came to Amos then, and they sat in the car while Agnes was talking with Marvin.

"A drunken brawl?" Amos said, but it was a question.

"Booze has to be taken internally if you want to get drunk."

"But the smell of liquor, Cy."

"We'll see."

"The poor fellow."

"God knows how long he's been lying there. Well, Agnes and I will check out what the neighbors might have seen." Cy then asked Amos exactly when he had arrived.

Amos told him of the open door, of going in with Marvin, being appalled at the way Jason lived, and then finding the body on the floor beside the bed. "I talked with the clerk, Eric, at the store. When he said this was the second day Jason hadn't been in, I thought the worst."

"We'll see," Cy said again.

Agnes had finished with Marvin, and he returned imperturbably to the car and got behind the wheel.

Cy got out. "Let's talk to the neighbors, Agnes."

"I think we can go, Marvin," Amos said.

A nod, and then the engine started and the car moved slowly away from the scene of the crime.

It was the following evening, dining with Father Dowling at the University Club, that Amos was made privy to what had happened to Jason. The man was in serious condition, a concussion inducing a coma from which he had yet to emerge.

"There was no alcohol in the blood,

Amos. So it wasn't a relapse."

"The place reeked of liquor."

Father Dowling was silent for a moment. "Have you heard of the beer and liquor that had appeared at the Foot Doctor, Amos? Someone seems to have been anxious for Jason to have a relapse."

Someone. Almost immediately Amos thought of Carmela, but, of course, he said nothing. If he had, he would have gone on to express his reaction to Carmela's partner, Augie Liberati. Partner in how many senses? That would have been sheer speculation and, moral considerations of calumny aside, the prudence of his profession kept Amos silent on that matter.

"The squalor in which he lives, Father. Unbelievable."

"I would have thought Helen Burke would want him with her in that huge house."

"She might have wanted that, yes."

"But not Jason?"

"His mother was already too constant a presence in his life."

"Ah."

"Who knows if Jason's marriage would not have survived without her constant interference in his life?"

"What kind of interference?"

"She always came to his aid when he

failed at one thing or another."

2

Tetzel was intent on making what had happened to Jason a sequel to his recent story on the son and heir of Helen Burke. Menteur had just glared at him when he turned in the story on public reactions to the smoking ban. Saloons — Tetzel mentioned no particular places — were ignoring it. "I'm a bartender, not a cop," one had growled to Tetzel. The man and woman in the street were equally opposed. If they weren't, they didn't make it into Tetzel's story. His only stab in the direction of balance was to point out the *Tribune's* adamant support of the prohibition.

"That was dictated by you-know-who," Menteur said.

You-know-who was the absent proprietor, a billionaire who had bought up newspapers as if they had a future and from time to time spoke ex cathedra on the editorial pages of his many papers. Somehow he had heard of the proposal of a no-smoking ordinance in little Fox River and demanded that the full moral authority of the *Tribune* be placed in support of the ban. Moreover, he cast it into words that, with suitable editing and respect for the English language, duly appeared.

"I'm told the SOB goes through two packs a day," Menteur said.

"Of gum?"

"Get out of here, Tetzel. I'm thinking of reassigning you."

Tetzel got out of there, glancing at the poor devils who spent their day in the smoke-free city room. If it came to that, he would expose the hypocrisy of exempting the courthouse from the ban. That, though, could lead to the pressroom in the court-house becoming as oppressive as the city room. Such a story might win him fame, but afterward he would die of fresh air. It was a true dilemma. He could postpone that evil day, but it was folly to think that Men-teur did not long to have the injustice he suffered under shared by Tetzel. If he would not forget, at least he could be distracted. Therein lay the promise of the dreadful beating Jason Burke had taken.

"What do we know?" he asked Tuttle.

"Have you become a skeptic? Do you doubt your mental powers?"

"What do we know about Jason Burke?" Tetzel emended patiently.

"I can only tell you what I know."

Tuttle smacked his dry mouth and sighed. They went across the street, where, in a booth, Tuttle sipped his shandy while Tetzel got a grip on his bourbon and water.

"He was beaten with a baseball bat," Tuttle began. "His own. Apparently a memento of his healthy boyhood."

A lead sentence formed in Tetzel's mind. "Go on."

"He was found bloody and beaten by Amos Cadbury. Found by, not beaten by."

"Is Cadbury his lawyer?"

"Only indirectly, I believe."

"What does that mean?"

"He was Helen Burke's lawyer."

"Any leads on his assailant?"

"Just some unidentified prints on one of the liquor bottles."

"So he'd gone back to drinking."

"He might have dabbed a little behind his ears. There was no alcohol in the bloodstream. Whoever beat him went to a lot of trouble making it look like a relapse. Three bottles of booze were splashed around; Jason's clothes were soaked with it."

"Splashed around?" Tetzel was shocked.

"Of course they're wondering if there is any connection with the case of scotch and month's supply of beer someone left in the lunchroom at the Foot Doctor."

"Tell me about that."

Tuttle told him. A conspiracy formed itself

in Tetzel's mind. "Who would do such a thing?"

"Not a friend," Tuttle said.

"So who were his enemies?"

"I thought you were the reporter, Tetzel."

"Why do you think I'm talking with you? Tuttle, this could be big." As he had so often in the past, Tetzel saw a possible story eclipsing all the actual ones he had ever written. "How is Jason now, by the way?"

"He's come out of the coma. I haven't been able to see him yet."

"You?"

"As his lawyer. This experience should bring home to him the wisdom of having a will."

"What an ambulance chaser you are, Tuttle."

"And you chase the ambulance chaser."

That seemed to make it a draw. Whatever old animosity existed between the two men evanesced. Tetzel pushed away his drink. "You got any gum, Tuttle?"

"Gum?"

"I'm going down to the hospital."

"For treatment?"

Turn himself in, get issued a patient's gown, roam the halls of the hospital, sit at Jason's bedside, and get the whole story from the lips of the victim? Tetzel shuddered away the thought. Besides, who would ever believe he had a problem with drink?

Tetzel went first to the detective division in the hope of finding Cy Horvath. With what he had learned from Tuttle he thought he could begin a conversation in medias res. But Horvath was not there.

"Can I help you?" Agnes Lamb asked.

"Did you happen to read the story I did for the *Tribune* on Jason Burke?"

"Very touching."

"Thank you. You can imagine my reaction to what has happened to him."

Agnes said nothing, perhaps imagining.

"Could we talk about your investigation off the record?"

"Press relations is in another office."

Hedwig! She was about five feet tall and another five around the middle and knew less of what was going on than the janitor.

"You've briefed her?"

"Lieutenant Horvath is in charge of the investigation."

"He seems to be out."

"Is that what you were told?"

"Isn't he?"

"I report to him, not the other way around."

"You're good," Tetzel said grudgingly.

"Would I be a cop if I weren't?"

This little lady could write legends for fortune cookies.

"You've been a great help."

Then, just to show that the universe was favorable to Tetzel, in walked Cy Horvath.

"Horvath! I've been waiting for you."

Horvath continued to his inner office, and Tetzel went along after him.

"What can you tell me about the investigation into the break-in at Jason Burke's?"

"Nothing."

"Aw, come on, Cy."

"There wasn't a break-in." Cy sat and looked at Tetzel with his all-purpose expression.

"He let the assailant in?"

"Have you talked with Hedwig?"

"When can I talk with you? Look, Horvath, what I have in mind is a feature story, a follow-up on the one I already wrote about Jason Burke. Did you read it?"

Cy just looked at him.

"Please, Horvath, give me a break. Do you know what my editor wants me to write about? The exemption of the courthouse from the no-smoking ordinance. What leads do you have?"

The ashtray on Horvath's desk was piled high with cigarette ends. The whole detective bureau reeked with the heavenly aroma of stale tobacco smoke. Horvath glanced at the ashtray.

"We have some fingerprints. None of the neighbors admits to knowing who Jason Burke was, let alone what happened to him. You might have better luck than we had."

"Sure. Oh, I'll talk to them. I'll leave no stone unturned. Who are your suspects?"

"It's too early to say."

Then, twice in one day, providence smiled on Tetzel. Phil Keegan came in, puffing on a cigar, and said to Cy, "We have a clear footprint." Then he noticed Tetzel. "Print that and I'll break your neck."

"I told Cy. I'm writing a feature, not doing daily reports. Of course I'll hold it. Have you talked to all the relatives?"

"Get out of here, Tetzel."

Tetzel got out of there, hugging the information he had just accidentally obtained. FOOTPRINT UNDOES ASSAILANT OF THE FOOT DOCTOR.

3

Marie Murkin watched with dread and foreboding as Holy Week loomed, and beyond it the planned marriage of Natalie Armstrong and Eugene Schmidt. Honestly,

326

how a woman that age could be taken in by the fast-talking little man with his cottony hair and trim little mustache was more than Marie could understand. Isn't there a statute of limitations on female frailty? Father Dowling seemed to grant Eugene Schmidt the benefit of every doubt. Even when the man confided that he had not been born Eugene Schmidt but had legally adopted that name seven years before, Father Dowling reacted as if this were the most ordinary admission in the world.

"Has he told Natalie, Father Dowling?" Marie demanded when Schmidt was gone.

"Told her what?"

"That he changed his name!"

Father Dowling looked at her sadly. "My, what large ears you have."

"He wasn't exactly whispering, Father Dowling."

"It was a confidence, Marie."

"But who in the world is he?"

"Eugene Schmidt, legally."

"Legally!"

"Did you hear the reason he gave for changing his name?"

"What was it?"

"So you didn't hear that. Of course, I would not break a confidence."

Back in her kitchen, Marie did not regret

that she had overheard Schmidt tell Father Dowling of his change of name, nor did she regret letting the pastor know she had overheard him say it. Her only regret was that she had not stayed at her post and learned the reason Schmidt or whoever he was had given for the change. Heaven only knew what would happen to St. Hilary's if she did not keep on the alert.

Natalie should know, but Marie could not be the bearer of the news. Father Dowling would never forgive her if she told Natalie what Eugene Schmidt had confided to the pastor. She tried various ways in which she might pass on the information, but none of them was plausible. Until Rebecca Farmer came calling, identifying herself as a writer for the *Tribune.*

"You want to see Father Dowling?"

"Would I have come to the kitchen door if I did?"

Aha. Marie invited her in, sat her at the kitchen table, closed the door to the hallway, and asked her guest if she liked tea.

"I am a coffee drinker."

"Then coffee it will be."

She made coffee, put a plate of oatmeal cookies on the table, and sat across from Rebecca Farmer, certain that word of the impending post-Easter nuptials had gotten to the reporter.

"A story I've been planning for a long time has to do with women abandoned by men."

Marie could have cheered. She nodded receptively.

"Some women are reluctant to talk about the experience, and I respect that. I'll take every precaution to avoid embarrassing my sources."

Marie nodded at this sound policy, wishing the woman would get on with it.

"So anything you can tell me about what happened to you . . ."

"To me! What are you talking about?"

"Several people told me that your husband deserted you."

Marie was speechless. Who would have passed on such gossip, and to a reporter? She slumped in her chair and managed to say, "And I thought you were interested in Eugene Schmidt."

Rebecca took a sip of her coffee, studying Marie. "Perhaps I am."

Marie straightened and leaned toward her guest. "This is a story you won't believe."

"Try me."

Speaking softly but distinctly, Marie told Rebecca Farmer everything she knew about Eugene Schmidt. His sudden appearance at the parish senior center, quickly becoming the darling of the widows there, and finally setting his cap for Natalie Armstrong.

"Natalie Armstrong. Isn't she one of the beneficiaries of Helen Burke's will?"

"Exactly!"

"Eugene Schmidt. Wasn't he driving the bus that forced Helen Burke's car into the bridge abutment?"

"The same Eugene Schmidt." Marie paused. "If that is his name."

"You don't think it is."

Marie put her fingers to her pursed lips, twisted an imaginary key, and threw it away. She did say, "I suppose that is the sort of thing a reporter could find out."

Rebecca nodded, as if few mysteries could withstand the scrutiny of the press. "Marie, can I regard this as an exclusive interview?"

"You mustn't mention my name."

"Agreed. But I have to talk to Natalie Armstrong."

"Nothing easier. You will find her at the senior center. No doubt in the company of Eugene Schmidt."

"All the better. Will you promise not to pass this on to any other reporter?"

"I am not in the habit of chatting with reporters."

"Is that a yes?"

Marie nodded. "More coffee?"

"I will. This is delicious. You should taste the mud we drink in the pressroom at the courthouse."

Rebecca wanted to know how long Marie had been at St. Hilary's, what the job entailed. She began to take notes as Marie talked. "This could make a nice little feature by itself. How many people understand the role of a rectory housekeeper?"

"But no mention of . . ."

"Of course not."

"He's dead, you know. He came back and then he died."

"We'll just forget all about him," Rebecca said.

Marie went out on the porch with Rebecca, showing her the walkway to the senior center. As she watched the reporter march off, briefcase slung over her shoulder, her beige beret set at a resolute angle on her head, her sensible shoes an index of seriousness, Marie inhaled deeply. It might have been a prayer of thanksgiving. Whatever happened now happened, and that was all there was to it. She hadn't told the reporter anything she couldn't have learned from any number of people. She particularly liked the way she had finessed the matter of Eugene

331

Schmidt's name. Surely not even Father Dowling could find fault with her on that score.

4

Madeline hated hospitals, hated to see people weakened by illness and pain, hated the smells and oddly echoing sounds of the place, but of course she could not keep away when she heard what had happened to Jason. How long had it been since she had been here? Not so long that she had forgotten that one never stopped at the great circular desk and asked to see a patient. Inevitably there would be delay. The volunteers who served at the desk preferred doing something rather than nothing. Who could blame them? Madeline thought of those few months when, inspired by Jason, she had volunteered to help at the hospital several nights of the week. She hurried toward the elevators at the far end of a long hallway whose walls were hung with photographs of long ago.

Intensive care was on seven, at least it had been. When she emerged from the elevator, it was clear she could not bypass the nurses' station. Where was Jason? She put the question to a nurse in blue.

"Mrs. Burke? Follow me."

Madeline followed. Did the nurse's question mean that Carmela was not yet here?

She wasn't. Jason lay on his back, a mountain of a man on a white bed, under a white coverlet, liquids dripping slowly down plastic tubing to his wrist, a great swami-like bandage on his head. Madeline was left alone with Jason.

"Madeline," he said, his eyes rolling toward her.

She took his hand. She tried to say his name, but only a sob came forth.

His eye was still on her. "I'll be all right."

"Of course you'll be all right."

Bedside exchanges in hospitals will never make it into any collection of great conversations, but when the patient is in intensive care, semiconscious, teetering on the edge of the abyss, language becomes merely therapeutic, music rather than meaning, just the sound of another human voice that can reach into the pain and darkness and serve as a lifeline back to normalcy. Jason had recognized her, and that was good — not that she made too much of that, any more than she had of the nurse's thinking she was Mrs. Burke.

Madeline stayed with Jason for hours, and Carmela did not come. Agnes Lamb and

Cy Horvath did, wanting to talk to Jason about what had happened to him, but he was not yet ready for that and didn't look like he would be for some time. Madeline took a break and went down to the cafeteria and had coffee with them.

"Any ideas?" Agnes said.

"About what happened? No."

"No enemies?"

"Jason? Of course not."

"Isn't he married?" Agnes smiled slyly and her eyes opened wide as she said this.

"Sort of. They've been separated for years."

"I wondered why she wasn't here."

A terrible thought occurred to Madeline. "Has she been told?"

Agnes looked at Cy. It was clear they didn't know.

Agnes said, "I'll call the office in Schaumburg."

Madeline was surprised Agnes Lamb knew of that. "Oh, they've moved their offices to Fox River. Amos will know where."

Carmela was told — she hadn't known; she had been off on a quick business trip to New York and hadn't kept up with the *Fox River Tribune* — and rushed to the hospital. Madeline rose when she came in. Carmela hardly noticed her but went and stood beside Jason, looking in stunned wonderment at her battered husband. She reached a hand toward him, then drew it back. He had opened his eyes. He mumbled something, and Carmela leaned over him. He spoke again, and she stepped back, glancing at Madeline. Madeline had grown used to Jason's slurred speech. What he had said was "Ah, my caretaker."

"What in God's name happened?" Carmela said when she and Madeline stepped into the hall.

"Apparently someone attacked him, in his apartment, and tried to make it look as if he had been drinking."

"Had he been?"

"The police say there was no alcohol in his blood."

"A historic first."

"Carmela," Madeline began, then stopped.

"What is happening to this family?"

Carmela, having been treated like an interloper by Helen, could be forgiven for thinking now that she had married into a very strange family indeed.

"Your partner should have called you, Carmela."

"My partner?" Carmela stared at Mad-

eline. Then she understood. "Oh, Augie."
Another pause. "Yes, he should have. Well,
now I'm here."

She might have been dismissing Madeline,
but that wasn't it.

"Not that I can be of the least bit of help
to him."

She wanted to go. She wanted to flee this
scene. Madeline understood.

"I'll stay for a few more minutes."

Carmela touched her arm and then
walked away, slim, her heels sounding in a
businesslike way, her large purse on her
shoulder, hand gripping its strap. Madeline
went back to Jason.

Madeline kept intermittent vigil for days.
From time to time, Carmela stopped by,
stayed for a few minutes, patting Jason's
hand, then left. On one occasion, Agnes
Lamb went off with Carmela, to have a little
chat in the cafeteria.

Carmela consulted her watch. "It'll have
to be short."

At the bedside again, Madeline asked, "Jason, who was it?"

"Carmela."

"No, no. Who attacked you?"

He didn't know. He seemed not to care.

Eventually he was removed from ICU to a

room where there could be flowers and other visitors. There was a television set perched high on the wall, but it was always turned off. Agnes Lamb and Cy Horvath came, and Father Dowling accompanied by Father Pringle, the hospital chaplain. Madeline withdrew discreetly on these occasions.

She began to fear that her constant presence would be misinterpreted. How? She didn't know how, but it was clear that whenever Carmela looked in and saw Madeline there she didn't like it. Not that she ever said so. Indeed, quite the opposite.

"Madeline, you're an angel."

"There are good and bad angels."

"You're one of the good ones. Sometimes I think you should have married Jason."

"Oh, I thought of it."

"You did!"

"I also thought of marrying Cary Grant."

She told the reporter, Tetzel, all she knew, but he had the facts already.

"I want interpretation," he said urgently. "The human side. Who would do this to that big gentle man?"

"Did you know him?"

Tetzel looked offended. "I have written about him." He spoke as if his prose had taken Jason out of nothingness and conferred reality on him. Still, it was nice to have someone she could just babble to.

"You're cousins," Tetzel said.

"Of a sort."

Tetzel had an epiphany. "You're one of the heirs."

Madeline nodded.

"Cousin and co-heir," Tetzel murmured.

"That sounds like St. Paul."

"I'm from Minneapolis." It was a joke.

She told him that she and Jason had grown up together. She and Jason and Carmela.

"The wife?"

"Yes."

"Of sorts."

He was fascinated by the way she had fixed Carmela up with Jason for a school dance.

"Little old Cupid, that's me."

"You never married?"

"Not yet."

Where did that remark come from?

When the time came for Jason to be released, Madeline had him taken to her new big house.

5

Amos, having met Agnes Lamb at the hospital, where he had looked in on Jason, asked the officer if he could give her lunch. She was dressed in civilian clothes, a lovely, intelligent young person, and one whose persistency he had come to admire. Twice she had quizzed him about the will, and he had been evasive. It occurred to him now that he should be more cooperative.

"McDonald's?"

"I was thinking of the University Club."

When they were in his car, she said, "I've never ridden in one of these."

How easy it was to forget that the way one lived, which after all was simply the way one lived, could look extraordinary to others.

"I'm not a very good driver."

She smiled.

Their entrance caused a subdued sensation, and Amos walked slowly behind his guest to their table, rather liking the image of himself as an aging roué.

They had shrimp cocktails and a white wine, and Agnes surprised him by talking of John Thomas, the bankrupt who had gone into the pizza business and then into the Fox River, in that order.

"Of course, that's roped off from us."

"A cordon sanitaire?"

"Maybe. What's it mean?"

He told her. "You're suggesting that there might be a connection with one of our more prominent families?"

"*The* family. Who else controls the restaurants?"

"This is just speculation," Amos Cadbury said.

"We always begin with speculation. Then we see if it can be sustained. But not in this case, or others like it. Oh, we could investigate, even make the case, but nothing would come of it."

"That is unfortunate. The world is a most imperfect place, Agnes."

She sipped her wine, her eyes never leaving him. "Tell me about Jason and his wife," she said.

"It's all a matter of public record," Amos said. He might have been reminding himself. He told her what there was to tell, not sparing Helen Burke.

"Gambling and drink both?"

"Mainly drink. And now he has stopped."

"He told us there had been deliveries of liquor and beer at his shoe store. From whom he didn't know, or even when it had come."

"Any signs of a break-in?"

She shook her head.

"And who had keys?"

"The clerk. Eric."

"Yes, I met him."

"He denies any knowledge of it. He was the one who ordered pizza from John Thomas, the pizza that never arrived."

"Very mysterious."

"Who would want him to fall off the wagon, other than liquor stores?"

"I can't imagine. There was general relief when his mother's death turned him around."

Agnes said, "Is it true that his wife has control of Jason's money?"

"It was his mother's wish." He paused. He did not want to mislead this young woman. "No, that's not quite true. She didn't want him controlling his money, but she didn't specify who should control it."

"Who decided?"

"I did."

"Why?"

"It seemed a way to bring them back together."

Agnes made a face. "It's not working, is it?"

"Not yet."

"Not ever, I would say. Do you know her

partner, Augie Liberati?"

"I have met the man."

"Carmela is the star of the Avanti Group. I think she has been carrying Augie. And of course they're lovers."

"They are!"

"No doubt about it. I checked it out."

"Why?"

Agnes paused. "Both Cy Horvath and Phil Keegan tell me never to go by hunches. Of course, they do it all the time themselves."

"And you had a hunch?"

"Which proved to be true. And that raised another question. If something happened to Jason, who would get the money?"

"Surely you don't think that Carmela . . ."

"My hunch is Augie."

"Good Lord."

Agnes leaned across the table and whispered, "His sister is married to a Pianone."

Amos remembered the way Carmela had seemed to divert attention from Augie's remark that he had a sister in Fox River. He sat back, absorbing what Agnes had told him. And he had thought that she would be seeking information from him. He told her this.

"I *would* like to ask a favor of you."

"What is it?"

"We came upon some unidentified fingerprints in Jason's apartment. On one of the liquor bottles, on the handle of the bat that was used to beat him. There's a footprint, too."

She waited. No need to spell it out. Amos's admiration for this young police officer was now greater than it had been. Of course, it helped that suspicions were not directed at any of his clients.

"I'll see what I can do."

Agnes's smile was almost reward enough. "This is very good wine."

"Another glass?"

"That would be one way you could do it."

He nodded. Indeed it would.

Back at his office, he telephoned Carmela and asked when she would be free to see him.

"Oh, Amos, today is awful."

"I was thinking of a preprandial drink in my office."

"I could come at six."

"Could you bring your partner?"

"Augie?"

"It wouldn't be just right if I asked you to manage a little money for me."

"We'll be there, Amos."

"Good. Good."

■ ■ ■ ■

He felt devious, of course, but that feeling was dimmed by the thought that he was doing a favor for Agnes Lamb. Carmela came, with Augie, Amos poured their drinks, and then they chatted about what could be done with a small amount, fifty thousand, say, managed not too safely but not too cavalierly, either. Carmela let Augie respond.

Amos took notes. He looked thoughtful. "Give me a day or two."

"Of course," Augie said, lifting his glass in a toast.

When they were gone, he called Agnes and told her what he had for her.

6

Agnes Lamb brought the plastic sack containing the glass Amos Cadbury had given her to Cy Horvath's office, and together they went off to the lab with it. Agnes had played a hunch. Now it would be tested. Would Agnes drop her suspicion of Augie Liberati if the tests proved negative?

Lester Coe's white lab coat looked like a dinner jacket, maybe because of the shirt and necktie he wore beneath it.

Agnes placed the plastic bag on the counter between them. "Prints," she said.

He waited.

"Check them against those found at the scene of the assault on Jason Burke."

Lester took the bag by a corner and held it up as if were a rabbit. "How soon?"

Cy said, "How about now?"

"That urgent?"

"It's important."

"You want to wait, is that it?"

"Not for long."

Lester lifted his chin, turned, and retreated to his lab.

Agnes was trying to be nonchalant, but Cy knew how much this meant to her. To himself, too, of course. For weeks they had been chasing down one dead end after another. First, the revival of the death of Florence Green because of Nathaniel's release from prison. Nathaniel's claim to have killed his wife had seemed odd at the time — killing a dying person? — and rechecking on the basis of his notes after all the time that had passed did not make it any less odd. But why would he say he killed his wife if he hadn't? Maybe Dr. Gleason was right. Maybe it was a mercy killing in a sense other than Tuttle's. His wife was shriven; while she lived there was the danger that her despair would return, so Nathaniel prevented that happening by cutting off her life support and letting her die. For that he had wasted years in Joliet, welcoming the punishment.

The great flaw in Nathaniel's account was that by the time the mask was removed from Florence's face, the oxygen tap on the wall had been turned off. Nothing was flowing through the plastic tubing. Removing the mask deprived Florence of nothing. Weird.

Nathaniel had just listened when Cy explained to him about the oxygen tap. "It was closed. Shut off." He waited for a response.

Nathaniel said, "Yes, I did that. I shut it off."

Convicted for a crime he didn't commit. Should whoever shut off that oxygen tap get the same treatment? Discovering who that had been, after all these years, seemed a definition of the impossible. The nurses were out; Cy had talked to every nurse who had worked on the floor at that time. There was no way any of them would have deprived even a dying patient of life support. Had it been turned off by accident? The monitors at the nurses' station would alert them to such a shutoff. But how soon had that been noticed? Apart from the possibility that some visitor had popped into Florence's room and shut off the oxygen while Nathaniel was down the hallway, the only explanation of what had happened was Nathaniel. His including turning off the tap in his confession seemed only a way to keep himself guilty.

Agnes said to Cy, "I should have asked Lester how long it would take."

"Want to go for coffee?"

Agnes looked into the lab and then at Cy. "I'm not nervous."

"I know."

"Either they match or they don't."

"That's right. Let's go for coffee."

They went for coffee. Dr. Pippen joined them.

"Work, work, work," she said. She placed her coffee on the table, unbuttoned her lab coat and sat.

"We're waiting for the outcome of a test," Cy told her.

"Mine were positive."

Agnes widened her eyes and sat back. "What test?" Cy asked.

"Oh, Cy," said Agnes.

Pippen was pregnant. She was radiant. Cy felt ambivalent. Would this exorcize his fascination with the assistant coroner?

"When?" Agnes asked.

The date she mentioned was nearly to Christmas.

"Will you go on working?" Cy asked.

"Of course. Why not? Oh, I'll take maternity leave."

Pippen as mother. Cy decided he liked the idea. Lester appeared in the doorway, looking around. Cy raised his hand, and Lester joined them.

"I thought you were in a rush."

"Boy or girl?" Cy asked.

"They match, if that's what you mean."

Agnes let out a little whoop and pushed away from the table. Cy stood.

"What's going on?" Pippen asked. She was a little peeved, as if she had been upstaged.

"I'll tell you later," Cy said.

"Tell me now."

"Lester can explain."

They brought the news to Phil Keegan. The fingerprints on the glass Amos Cadbury had supplied, the glass Augie Liberati had used, matched the few prints that had been found in Jason's apartment.

"Bring him in," Phil said.

On the way to the offices of the Avanti Group, Agnes babbled joyfully. How would she have taken it if the prints hadn't matched? A moot question now.

"You know what I would like, Cy? I'd like to tie him to John Thomas, too."

"The pizza man?" Cy frowned. "Don't get carried away."

"Did you know that Augie's sister is married to a Pianone?"

"Let's settle for the assault on Jason. That we can get an indictment on."

The receptionist told them Mr. Liberati was not in yet. Was Carmela there? As if in answer, Carmela emerged from her office. Her welcoming smile faded slightly when she saw Cy and Agnes. Then it was altogether gone.

"Has something happened to Jason?"

It seemed an odd question. Jason was out of the hospital and ensconced in the house in which he had been raised, occupying the room he'd had as a boy. Only Amos Cadbury had raised a question about the propriety of this.

"Amos," Madeline said, "there is a nurse on duty all day."

"And at night?"

Madeline, according to Edna Hospers, had been almost pleased at this suspicion. Amos's question might have suggested that Jason was no safer in the Burke house than he had been in his slovenly apartment.

"When do you expect Augie Liberati?" Agnes said.

"Come into my office." Carmela stepped aside, and in they went. She closed the door before going to her desk. "Please be seated." Then, "Why do you want to see Augie?"

Cy detected apprehension in her voice. Did Carmela guess why they were here?

"Some routine questions," Agnes said.

"About what?"

Cy said, "The attack on Jason."

The handsome competent professional financial advisor morphed into a frightened woman. "What have you found?"

"What you think we have," Cy said. Agnes looked at him in surprise.

"Oh my God," Carmela murmured. She reached for the bottle of water on her desk, then let her hand drop.

"You've been expecting this, haven't you?" Cy asked, telling himself it wasn't a hunch, he was merely reading the significance of Carmela's reaction.

There was the sound of conversation in the outer office, followed by a tap on the door.

It opened, and a grinning Augie looked in. "I'm interrupting," he said, backing away.

Cy had risen and went to the door, opening it wide. "Come on in. We were just talking about you."

"Me?" Several expressions flitted across his face. Cy took his arm and led him into the office. Augie shook Cy's hand free and looked at Carmela. "What's going on?"

"We want to talk with you about the attack on Jason Burke," Agnes said, rising. Cy had remained standing, between Augie and the door. He pushed the door shut.

"Talk away."

"You should have a lawyer present."

"A lawyer!" Augie tried to laugh. He looked an appeal at Carmela; he glared at Cy. "I don't have a lawyer."

"Amos Cadbury," Carmela said. "I'll call him."

She made the call; she was put through to Amos. She explained the reason for the call and then listened. And listened.

"I understand, Amos." She put down the phone.

"Try Tuttle," Agnes said.

7

Tetzel seemed to have been the last one to learn that Augie Liberati's prints matched those found in Jason Burke's apartment, on a liquor bottle and on the bat that had been used in the assault. Tuttle, fresh from a

351

conference with his client, seemed unperturbed by all this.

"I doubt that it will come to trial." He collapsed into Rebecca's chair in the pressroom, the picture of unruffled confidence.

"Because of the incompetence of the defense counsel?"

Tuttle laughed indulgently. When Peanuts Pianone came in, the reason for Tuttle's insouciance became clear.

"How is Augie related to you, Peanuts?" Tuttle asked, watching Tetzel for his reaction.

"His sister is married to my cousin. Let's go eat."

"A splendid suggestion," Tuttle said, scrambling to his feet. "Will you join us, Gerry?"

"I'm fasting."

Tuttle looked puzzled only for a moment. "Ah. Holy Week. Good man."

Out the door the two went, the most modest representatives of law and order. Tetzel felt sick. He looked at Rebecca's desk, at the gray eye of her computer. It was there that she had sat, tapping out the story that was all over the front page of the *Tribune.* What a sly witch she was; never a murmur about what she was writing. The way she had hummed as she worked should have warned him. He glanced at the paper, winced, and turned it over. All the while he had been devoting himself to a story on Jason Burke, a follow-up on the assault without a single new fact, a story Menteur had hardly glanced at before consigning it to the circular file.

"Old news, old boy. Old news."

He should have read more into Menteur's attitude than he had. The bastard had obviously been conspiring with Rebecca, keeping her big story a secret until it burst upon the reading public of Fox River and on all those, near and far, who consulted the paper's Web page. Tetzel was not fasting, Holy Week or not, but it was like a Lenten penance when he turned over the paper and looked at the odious headline. VAGABOND LOVER STRIKES IN FOX RIVER.

A more magnanimous colleague would have admired Rebecca's story on Eugene Schmidt. The name was always in quotation marks in the story, and no wonder. Rebecca had scared up court records in Charleston, where one Marcus Matthews had legally changed his name to Eugene Schmidt. And why would Marcus Matthews change his name? Because Marcus Matthews was not his name. The little man who had been a frequent presence at the St. Hilary senior center had been born in Durham, North Carolina, the son of Mr. and Mrs. Patrick Collins. Their son had been baptized Thomas. Photocopies of the relevant documents accompanied the story. Allusion was made to Tom Collins's lucrative if brief career as an evangelist on the margins of the Bible Belt. The swath that "Eugene Schmidt" had cut at the senior center was described at length. Tetzel noted that Natalie Armstrong was not named, and an unnamed widow in Detroit had refused to be interviewed. A sequel was promised for tomorrow, "the first in a series of follow-ups to this remarkable story."

Tetzel flung the paper away, aiming at the wastebasket, missing, and it lay scattered on the floor. Rebecca — Rebecca! — had eclipsed him. Menteur had called him "old boy," as if he were over the hill, but Rebecca was at least as old as he was. Now Tuttle was patronizing him. Where would it all end?

Across the street, as it happened, in his favorite booth in a back corner, a triple bourbon and water before him on the scarred surface. The oblivion alcohol promised beckoned. Any self-respecting man would go on a weeklong toot in circumstances like these. Where had sobriety ever gotten him? Tetzel drank, he brooded, and then down the dark tunnel of his mind a weak light went on. It grew brighter and brighter. My God! Out of the nettle of despair he plucked the flower of hope. The ineffable Tuttle had dropped the means of redemption in his lap, and he had not recognized it. He straightened in the booth; he strove for consecutive thought. The idea that had come to him, while dangerous, was a natural, a smasharoo.

Augie Liberati had been indicted for assault and battery committed on Jason Burke, but the the motive for this action had so far been left vague. Why would Augie beat Jason Burke to a pulp and take the trouble to make it seem that Jason had been drunk as a lord at the time? What was Jason Burke to him or he to Jason Burke? Think, Gerry, think. Jason had just come into a bundle of money, money controlled, however, by his estranged wife. Augie Liberati was Carmela's business partner. Business partner? Tetzel had listened while Maxine Flood, a gofer in the detective division, had said in a carrying whisper to those at her table in the cafeteria that there had been something going on between Augie and Carmela. But Carmela was still married to Jason. Jason was thus an obstacle to Augie's uniting himself with the custodian and doubtless rightful heir of all Jason's money.

All that was true. The facts could be shaped into a story that would rival Rebecca's. But it was not that alone that had turned on the light that illumined the hitherto dark tunnel of Tetzel's mind. Augie was related to the Pianones. Tuttle clearly saw that as an obstacle to his client's being found guilty of what he had done. Here, as so often in the past, the forces of justice confronted the force of the Pianone family. Judges were in their pocket; juries could be bought. Even Tuttle could get Augie off, and nothing would be said about why such an assailant had been set free.

Back in the pressroom, at his computer, Tetzel composed a memo to Menteur. The time had come for the *Tribune* to stand up to the Pianones and cleanse the city of their nefarious influence. He faxed it over to the editor after he had e-mailed it to him. He waited. His phone rang.

It was Menteur. "You're out of your mind, Gerry."

"Perhaps."

"We run a story like that and they'd feed you to the fish."

Tetzel chuckled. "May I point out what you are overlooking, old boy?"

"Tell me. Quick. I'm busy."

"We have a new owner. You-know-who. A distant plutocrat who from time to time remembers that one of the papers he owns is in Fox River, Illinois. Need I remind you of the no-smoking ordinance?"

"I want that story on the courthouse exemption, Gerry!"

"Later. Have you grasped my point?"

Menteur grasped the point. With the backing of their distant owner, who could nationalize the story and put pressure on corruption in Fox River it had never known, it would no longer be simply the *Tribune* versus the Pianones.

"You could fly me out to have a talk with him," Tetzel suggested.

Menteur began to laugh but killed it. "I can't spare you. I'll go."

"But how can you be spared?"

Menteur hummed. "I'll have Rebecca sit in for me."

8

Even without the deterrent of Helen Burke, Nathaniel Green kept aloof from the others at the St. Hilary senior center. He did spend more time inside now, but he continued to be more of a spectator than a participant. He always carried a book. It was one of

Father Dowling's regrets that he had not grown closer to the man, a regret that increased when Barney O'Connell, the chaplain at Joliet, asked how Nathaniel was doing.

"I read about the death of his sister-in-law," O'Connell said.

"Did he talk about her?"

"What was significant was that he didn't. But I knew how she had treated him."

"Are all families unhappy, Barney?"

"Who asked that, Tolstoy?"

"Not quite."

"That was quite a riposte, leaving his money to her."

Who could blame O'Connell for seeing in that a kind of response to his vengeful sister-in-law? What a chain of events that had set in motion. After Helen's death in that tragic accident, many people had come into large amounts of money. Poor Natalie Armstrong. She had come fleeing to the rectory when the exposé of her intended husband filled the pages of the local paper.

"Father, I feel like a fool."

"There's no need for that, Natalie. Trusting people is not a fault."

"Of course, the wedding is off."

"Of course."

When Natalie left the study, Marie took

over. Father Dowling felt that Marie would be far better than himself at soothing Natalie's wounded sensibilities. Thomas Aquinas argued that we should always judge people for the better, a rule that could, of course, lead to the kind of sad situation in which Natalie found herself. Meanwhile, Eugene Schmidt, as Father Dowling still thought of him, was nowhere to be seen. Father Dowling felt a little foolish himself when he thought of the explanation Schmidt had given him for his last change of name.

"I was once a sort of rival of yours," the little man said, his eyes twinkling.

"How so?"

"I ran a revival tabernacle for a number of years. The day came when I saw I was making a mockery of religion. I decided to cease to exist as the man so many had known. I suppose that was cowardly."

"You said you had never been baptized," Father Dowling said.

"The problem is that I had been baptized so many times. Before I set up my own tabernacle, I went to many others, getting the hang of it. I came forward to be baptized in at least four of them. I told myself it was part of my apprenticeship. Can God forgive me, Father?"

"God can forgive anything. If we're truly

repentant."

"I have turned over a new leaf, Father. Being here at St. Hilary has transformed my life."

Well, it had certainly transformed poor Natalie's. Eugene Schmidt's housekeeper said that her lodger had disappeared.

The news that Jason Burke's assailant had been identified was not likely to make Jason heal any quicker. Father Dowling visited him at the Burke home, where he was still bedridden. His misfortune had rendered him philosophical.

"What a life I have led, Father Dowling."

"How does it go with you and Carmela?"

"I never see her. She came by the hospital once or twice, but not here. I suppose this house has too many sad associations for her."

"Has Nathaniel been to see you?"

Jason was silent for a moment. "I don't expect him to."

"Oh?"

Jason rolled onto his side, a major undertaking, and looked directly into Father Dowling's eyes. "I don't think he wanted to hear what I told him."

"What was that?"

"I thought it would enable him to close the books on Aunt Florence's death. He had to know that he had not done what he accused himself of. He couldn't have." Jason paused. "My mother turned off the oxygen when he was out of the room."

"How do you know that?"

"She told me."

"Good Lord."

"Oh, she felt fully justified. Florence was dying, everyone knew that. Yet there she lay, day after day. It was the sight of Nathaniel that infuriated my mother. She thought he was dramatizing his own role. So she decided to cut it short."

"And let him confess and stand trial?"

"She didn't think anything would come of it. Even if he had done what he thought he had done, it was what she herself had really done and she had no regret or remorse."

"And you told Nathaniel."

"I sometimes wished I hadn't. He certainly didn't react as I thought he would."

"How long ago was it that you told him?"

"Shortly after his release."

Madeline came in then, and that marked the end of the conversation. After a time, a very preoccupied Father Dowling drove back to his rectory.

9

Thanks to a decree of Benedict XVI, Father Dowling followed the old rite during Holy Week. Kevin Brown was ecstatic. Monica Garvey seemed not to be in church. Kevin wondered if perhaps next year they couldn't have Tenebrae. On Easter Sunday, both Masses were in English, and Monica Garvey was very much in evidence. Her Easter bonnet was a marvel, broad brim, ribbons, flowers.

"I could write a sonnet," Father Dowling said when, still vested, he was chatting with Monica and others outside the church.

"Upon my Easter bonnet?" She actually broke into song.

"Alleluia," grumbled Kevin Brown.

Even Marie Murkin looked almost festive for the occasion. A lacy black mantilla, a white silk scarf at her throat. Natalie Armstrong hesitantly joined the group, and the others made way for her.

"Happy Easter, Natalie."

"Happy Easter, Father."

That was all it took to remove the uneasiness of the others. When the little group dispersed, Madeline took Natalie's arm and led her to her car.

Father Dowling entered the church and

had started down the aisle toward the sacristy, to take off his vestments, when he noticed a solitary figure in the back row, eyes shut, lips moving. Father Dowling went on to the sacristy.

Phil Keegan was the only guest at the Easter feast Marie prepared — a great ham prickled with cloves, mashed potatoes as well as sweet potatoes, several vegetables, cranberry sauce, relish, pickles, olives. Thus did Marie say good-bye to Lent. She joined them and kept Phil's wineglass, and her own, brimming. She might have been priming the pump.

"Why on earth did Augie Liberati choose Tuttle for his lawyer?" she asked.

"Agnes recommended him."

"What a sly one she is."

"He may get help." Phil told them of Augie Liberati's odd connection to the Pianones.

"Will they want to rescue him, Phil?" Father Dowling asked.

"We're waiting for the other shoe to drop." One of Augie's shoes matched the footprint found at the scene of the crime.

Outside the church, Madeline had told Father Dowling that Jason was so recovered he had wanted to come to Mass, but she had vetoed it. One might have thought that she was reluctant to let the Foot Doctor out of her house.

Herman the German, at his own insistence, was enjoying his meal in the kitchen, but he came into the dining room to have mince pie and coffee with them.

"I suppose you miss Eugene Schmidt," Marie said to him. There seemed to be quotation marks around the name.

"It's the ladies that'll miss him."

"Ha."

Father Dowling thought of the lonely figure he had seen sitting in a back pew, apparently praying. If so, it would have been for his wife, Florence. Where was he having his Easter dinner?

"I should have invited Nathaniel to join us," he said.

"He and his niece are going to eat together in Schaumburg," Herman said.

"Carmela?" Marie asked.

"Is that her name?"

Marie harumphed and began clearing the table. Herman took his leave, and Phil and Father Dowling repaired to the study.

"Bring your wine, Phil."

"I'd rather have a beer."

A beer was brought to him by Marie. "After I do the dishes, I'm going upstairs for my nap."

"Sleep tight," Phil said.

"I only had two and a half glasses." Off she went.

"Tetzel is spreading the rumor that the absent owner of the *Tribune* will allow the paper to mount a crusade against the Pianones." Phil spoke in a monotone.

"Surely the Pianones won't protect Augie Liberati then."

"We'll see," Phil said. "What time does the game come on?"

During the coming week, no crusade began in the *Tribune.* Tetzel had gone AWOL, doubtless drinking away his disappointment. Tuttle, by contrast, was jubilant. This proved premature. There was no sign of any intervention by the Pianones as the indicted Augie Liberati faced a jury of his peers and a bright young judge who was substituting for one of those in the Pianone pocket. She was scarcely thirty, wore her hair in a crew cut, and ran the trial as if she were in moot court in law school. Despite Tuttle's efforts, his client was convicted and sentenced to eighteen months in Joliet.

"It wasn't a murder trial, Marie," Father Dowling said when the housekeeper grumbled at this light sentence.

"And Eugene Schmidt is still running around free."

"Breaking hearts is not a crime, Marie."

There was no pursuit of Eugene Schmidt; no charges had been brought against him.

"Breaking hearts? Do you really think it was an accident when he forced Helen Burke's car into that bridge abutment?"

"You don't?"

"Think of it, Father. Get rid of Helen, Natalie becomes rich, Schmidt leads her down the aisle."

Father Dowling did not comment on the logical leaps in this theory. Nor did he mention the long thoughts he himself had been having about the accident. He called Earl Hospers one weekday and asked him for a favor. The results took some days to verify, but they were what Father Dowling had feared.

That afternoon, he strolled down the walk toward the school. Nathaniel was sitting on a bench, in the sun, reading. Father Dowling sat beside him.

"What are you reading, Nathaniel?"

"*Crime and Punishment.*"

"There is also sin and forgiveness." Father Dowling remembered hearing Nathaniel's confession weeks ago, a confession that had ended with the surprising remark that it was Florence who had disengaged herself from the life support system. Since then, Nathaniel had learned that, even if she had, it would have been no more lethal than if Nathaniel had removed that oxygen mask from her face. And Jason had told his uncle who had turned off the oxygen tap.

Nathaniel seemed to be waiting for the priest to say more.

"Paint from your car matches some found on our shuttle bus."

Nathaniel looked at him. "I thought of having my car repainted."

"Why didn't you?"

"I left it in the hands of God." He might have been remembering words from the wedding ceremony. *The rest is in the hands of God.* "What are you going to do?"

"Hear your confession, I hope."

"And then?"

"Give you absolution."

"That's all?"

"That's everything, Nathaniel."

What Nathaniel had done would be trivialized in any court of law, the evidence tenuous, susceptible of any number of imaginative explanations by a shrewd attorney. If any charge were brought against Nathaniel, and that was not likely, the deed would be reduced to the dialectics of a trial. Nathaniel would be cleared of the charge.

Nathaniel closed his book and set it aside. "Sin and forgiveness," he murmured.

"Here or in the rectory?"

Nathaniel stood. "How about in church."

So it was in the church, in a confessional, that Nathaniel whispered through the grille that he had brought about the death of his nemesis.

"I hated that woman, Father. She killed Florence."

"Let's concentrate on your sins."

A sigh on the other side of the grille. "That made everything seem ridiculous."

His insistence that he had killed his wife, the long years in Joliet, the shunning when he had come to the senior center.

"Say an act of contrition, and I will give you absolution."

Blessing the penitent, saying the words of absolution, Father Dowling, acting for their common Lord, absolved the sins of Nathaniel Green.

10

The following week Father Dowling drove north to talk once more with Willy Nilly. It was a gorgeous late spring day, and through the leafy trees he caught glimpses of the Fox River moving with the incessant movement of every river. The Fox River valley did not seem a good metaphor of the Vale of Tears, but of course it was. The evil we do often has a lovely setting.

Father Nolan sat on his patio, glasses on the end of his nose, reading a manuscript.

"My memoirs," he explained.

"Are you finished?"

"Am I finished or are my memoirs finished?"

"May that day be far distant."

"I do have several more chapters to write."

Father Dowling lit his pipe and then brought his lighter to the tip of Willy Nilly's cigarette. He told the old priest of the exemption from the no-smoking ban in the courthouse that had recently been lifted, thanks to an exposé by Rebecca Farmer.

"We can't have people enjoying themselves, can we?"

"Do you remember the case I brought to you a month or so ago?"

"Remind me."

Father Dowling brought his old professor up to date on the death of Florence Green and its sequel. He was breaking no confidence in telling Willy Nilly that Nathaniel Green's car had been involved in the accident that killed Helen Burke. That he had learned from Earl Hospers.

"Will charges be brought against him?"

"The tests were not made by the police."

Willy Nilly frowned at Father Dowling. "And you are wondering if you have an obligation to bring those perhaps inconclusive results to the attention of the police?"

"No."

"Good."

"The husband confessed to the crime because he thought his wife had ended her own life."

"Did he think that would have prevented it from being suicide?"

"He thought it would prevent people knowing it was suicide."

"And it wasn't."

"She would have been no more guilty than he if she had done it."

"Surely you don't mean that."

"The oxygen tap had been turned off."

"But neither of them would have known that. The question would be what either intended to do."

They sat on for an hour on the sunny patio, letting what they both had said drift away. Father Nolan spoke of his memoirs.

"What will you call them?"

"Willy Nilly."

A squinting look at his old student.

"I like it," Father Dowling said.

On the drive home, Father Dowling thought of the mystery of human action. We can intend to do what in fact we do not do, and do what we do not intend. It reminded him of the death several years ago of Sylvia Lowry. Earl Hospers had spent years in prison for something he had in some sense done although not intending to do it. Odd that it had been Earl who had compared the paint of Nathaniel's car with that found on the fender of the senior center shuttle bus. But life is often odd.

Meanwhile, he shook his mind free of thought and enjoyed the pleasant drive back to his rectory at St. Hilary's.

ABOUT THE AUTHOR

Ralph McInerny has written more than forty books, including his popular mystery series set at the University of Notre Dame, where he has taught for more than fifty years and where he is the director of the Jacques Maritain Center. The recipient of the Bouchercon Lifetime Achievement Award, he has also been appointed to the President's Committee on the Arts and the Humanities. He lives in South Bend, Indiana.

The employees of Thorndike Press hope you have enjoyed this Large Print book. All our Thorndike and Wheeler Large Print titles are designed for easy reading, and all our books are made to last. Other Thorndike Press Large Print books are available at your library, through selected bookstores, or directly from us.

For information about titles, please call:
(800) 223-1244

or visit our Web site at:
http://gale.cengage.com/thorndike

To share your comments, please write:
Publisher
Thorndike Press
295 Kennedy Memorial Drive
Waterville, ME 04901

4/23/18 - 1/23/19